# Mysterium IV

## Judea

MITCHEL FIDEL

Paper back ISBN-13: 978-1-946469-64-9
Hardcover ISBN-13: 978-1-946469-65-6


ShelteringTree.Earth, LLC Publishing
PO Box 973, Eagle Lake, FL 33839

### Did you enjoy this book?
We love to hear from our readers.
Please visit the author at
ShelteringTreeMedia.com

**About the Back Cover:**
The backcover displays a third century Christian floor mosaic depicting a
dove, which was becoming a symbol of the Holy Spirit in that era. This
mosaic is in the Basilica of Santa Maria Assunta, in the Udine region of
Italy.

# DEDICATION

To all those who sing life's psalm.

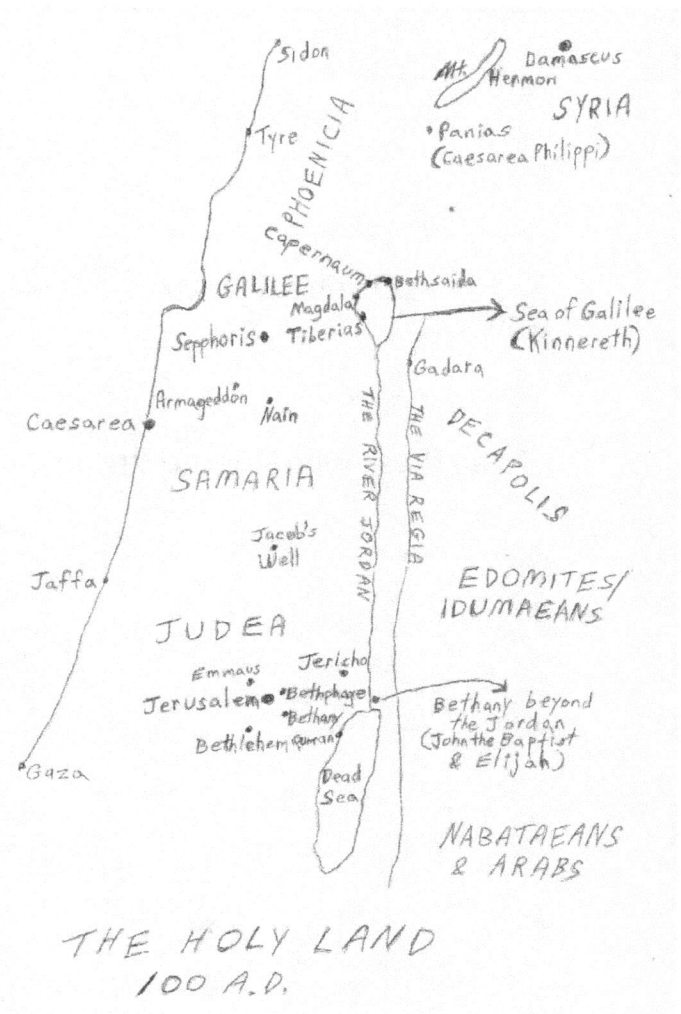

THE HOLY LAND
100 A.D.

# MYSTERIUM IV JUDEA

# CONTENTS

# FOREWORD

The premise of the **MYSTERIUM** series of novels has aroused a great deal of interest. That premise is the decision of a young Roman scholar in the year 100 AD to seek out the last surviving eyewitnesses to the life of Jesus, in order to ascertain the truth behind that life of unparalleled significance. **MYSTERIUM I ROME** was the first in a pentalogy of novels that led our hero, Theophilus, to four other **MYSTERIUM** settings: Greece, Asia, Judea and Egypt. Within this sequence there awaited for Theophilus ever more mysterious lands and ever deeper aspects of the Grand Secret that exceeds all other secrets, known in ancient times as the **MYSTERIUM.**

Theophilus' quest brings him into the presence of some of the most fascinating greats and near-greats of ancient times: Tacitus, Pliny, Clement of Rome (alias Pope Clement), and even Emperor Trajan and Emperor Hadrian, the last character being, it so happens, the most powerful human being on earth until the Industrial Revolution. Moreover, there rang out the distant voices of Paul (Theophilus has the opportunity to meet this saint's attorney) and the voices of the authors of the gospels, as part of the evidentiary trail in this nonpareil detective novel. And despite this epic's insistence, on the first cover, that important ancient wisdom resides in ancient scrolls, Theophilus's adventures are not all scholarly ones. He is driven not only by youthful vigorous curiosity, but also by youthful vigorous lust. These two drives converge in such unusual and uproarious scenarios as Theophilus's torrid affair with an actual daughter of the man who was regarded as the *Beast* of the Bible.

Our protagonist's peregrinations are highly picaresque, in an age that was far more picaresque than the later age in which that word was coined. Ancient Rome was raw, raw, raw. And it was raucous. And it was colorful to a rather mad degree. Theophilus, a thoroughgoing Roman, carries that particular setting into settings that become ever more exotic as he trudges down Roman road after Roman road. Such is his ever stranger, yet ever more fruitful, hunt for the genuine Jesus. And one is justified in saying that that matters, because Jesus stands out as the single most important personage at the base of our western culture.

Theophilus explores the raw and raucous side of "the eternal city" which was also very much "the capital of the world" in 100 AD, but his passion is to delve into such mysteries as are to be found in such venues as ancient archives, the catacombs, and the Vatican whose name reverberates with the meaning "Witches' Hill."

Theophilus's spirituality-yearning wanderlust stemmed from a matter that first struck him like a bolt from Mount Olympus, one day in the great reading hall of the Library of Augustus. Perusing a deluxe double volume of scrolls called the Gospel of Luke and the Acts of the Apostles, he is immediately gripped by the fact that both works began with dedications to an unknown figure named Theophilus, meaning "lover of God." Something about the saga of Jesus that he reads for the first time, all at once, that day touches him deeply, while the "coincidence" of the two dedications to an unknown Theophilus touches him personally.

Immediately Theophilus looks further into Rome's relatively recent and little-known *superstitio* called Christianity. And he becomes engrossed in other papyri, each of which presents the Jesus tale quite differently, such as the very early and poignantly simple Gospel of Mark and the very late and astoundingly sophisticated Gospel of John. Who was Jesus, really? What did he accomplish and proclaim, really? Surrounded by a gritty and troubled world sorely in need of deliverance, Theophilus cannot take his mind off the promise of the one *superstitio* among Rome's many that conspicuously stood out in its grandeur.

Theophilus feels impelled to discover the truth about

Christianity, and he realizes that he is uniquely placed to do so, and even has a duty to do so. He needs to travel to Judea and find the last few eyewitnesses to the life of Jesus before it is too late. And so, his unique and vital Odyssey is fated to encompass **MYSTERIUM II GREECE, MYSTERIUM III ASIA, MYSTERIUM IV JUDEA** and **MYSTERIUM V EGYPT AND BEYOND**. He could never have imagined the scope of the adventures that he would experience in the oriental half of a Roman Empire that was saturated with ancient **MYSTERIUM**.

> The mighty, the tall, the grand Pillars of Hercules
> The locked gate that blocks the horizons of man
> Arise, soul of man, at the Pillars of Hercules!
> And fly, as one limitless, wherever you can!
> Gateways are meaningless, for one who knows Daedalus
> This craftsman forged wings, so a human could fly
> More temperate than Icarus, use wings forged by
>     Daedalus!
> Your fate is to be like the gods who soar high!

Theophilus is a devoted and talented poet, both in Latin, the language of the western half of the Roman Empire, and in Greek, the language of the eastern half of the Roman Empire. All of the New Testament of the Bible is in Greek, a language in which Theophilus excels. And in Theophilus's time no country is more saturated with Christians than is Greece. The tie between Greece and early Christianity is a very tight bond indeed. Thus, after Rome Theophilus's next destination in his multi-realm investigation is the country described in **MYSTERIUM II GREECE**.

In Greece, Theophilus visits the most sacred site in the classical pagan world, Delphi. There he consults the most famous of ancient oracles, the Oracle of Delphi, about the essence of his investigative journey. His question to the Oracle, "Was Jesus as wise as Socrates?" receives the staggering reply, "Socrates in his wisdom said, 'Know yourself.' But Jesus Christ is the wisdom. He is the self. He is the knowing." And in Delphi Theophilus has lengthy discussions with Plutarch, world-famous Plutarch whose writings set the stage for the more arcane elements of Christology.

In Greece Theophilus is hot on the trail of Jesus' primary proselytizer, Paul, who carried out his zealous missionary work all up and down that highly philosophy-oriented peninsula, some five decades earlier. Paul is, in every respect from the linguistic to the theological to the personal, notoriously difficult to pin down, even in the city of Corinth where he spent so much time that his two Letters to the Corinthians were to become two of the main pillars of the Christian faith.

Steeped in Greek philosophy, Theophilus is well equipped to make progress in understanding the philosophical elements in the teachings of Paul and Jesus. Paul was something of a Stoic philosopher, histrionically debating with himself about rather opaque matters in the Stoics' question-and-answer style. Jesus was notably different. He resonated with the tones of a genuine old-fashioned Cynic philosopher, like Corinth's own celebrity philosopher Diogenes. Luke, especially, portrayed Jesus as uttering many statements indicative of man who was living in nature, *physis*, but was woefully surrounded by a society governed by self-satisfied ignorant convention, *nomos*. Jesus always had, at the ready, retorts for people that he encountered who lived a blinded conventional lifestyle, and who huffily objected to his independent lifestyle which could be considered antinomian.

"Go out as lambs in the midst of wolves." "Ask each day for the bread of the day." "Judge not lest you be judged." "Bless those who curse you." "Be as the sparrows and the lilies of the field."

In 100 AD Corinth is the very crux of both Greek philosophy and Christianity, as the largest city in Greece and as the world's largest concentration of Christians by far. Theophilus sees this city, founded by the goddess Kore or Kardia ("The Goddess" and "The

Heartbeat of the World"), as engaged in his era's battle over the soul of mankind. Puritanical Paul faced off against Kore or Kardia, whose Temple of a Hundred Temple Prostitutes had loomed high over the city for a thousand years.

In Greece, Theophilus begins his acquaintance with the elusive Gnostics, mystics who claim to possess a secret "Gnosis," a highly personalized wisdom which is beyond all usual understanding (as in the Delphic Oracle's message to Theophilus), and which is too powerful to be offered to the uninitiated. Accordingly, Paul at one point sounded very much like a Gnostic, when he told his Corinthian followers, "I fed you with milk, not with meat, for you were not able to bear it." Paul also sounded like a Gnostic when he described an out-of-body experience in which he was caught up into heaven and "heard things which cannot be told, which man may not utter."

Theophilus looks into, one after another, books of Chrisitan scripture that are thoroughly wrapped up in matters Greek: Corinthians, Acts, Thessalonians, Philippians, Timothy, Titus. But above all he dives headlong into the supreme mystery that is everything concerning the man, or men, named John.

Theophilus hopes that he will get to the nub of "the mystery of John" on his way from his adventures in **MYSTERIUM II GREECE** to his adventures in **MYSTERIUM III ASIA**. On the way there, lies the tiny but dramatic volcanic island of Patmos (meaning "the Fall"), where the Apostle John, the very "apostle whom Jesus loved," wrote the phantasmagorical ending chapter to the Bible called Revelation or the Apocalypse. Theophilus undergoes his own phantasmagorical experience on this highly magical island, one which leads him to his own conclusions about the actual author of Revelation and that book's actual meaning. However he is more interested in a spellbinding rumor that he keeps hearing. John, "the apostle whom Jesus loved" is still alive! Though surely near death at the age of something like 100, John, the youngest apostle and the author of the most enigmatic eyewitness gospel, is still alive and living, just a short distance across the Aegean, in one of the most important cities in the Roman Empire and in the Bible: the capital of the Roman province called Asia, Ephesus!

So, **MYSTERIUM III ASIA** opens in perhaps the most dramatic possible way. On his way to Judea to supposedly conclusively settle the matter of the true identity of Jesus, Theophilus believes that in Asia's capital Ephesus he will meet the 100-year-old man who is genuinely Jesus' youngest apostle, "the apostle whom Jesus loved," John.

**MYSTERIUM III ASIA** does not shortchange the reader. During Theophilus's sojourn in magnificent Ephesus, the fourth largest city in the Roman Empire, matters Johannine, matters Pauline, and all kinds of other matters pertinent to the reality of early Christianity do indeed come to light.

To wide-eyed Theophilus, Ephesus oozes significance and message. Its Temple of Diana was so sumptuous that it prompted an ancient traveler to invent a list of the Seven Wonders of the World, while insisting that that temple put all of the other six Wonders in the shade. And Paul did battle with that particular Diana, in many senses. This, Diana's city, was where one could observe the first sparks of the notion of devotion to Mary. In Ephesus, Theophilus gazes upon a famous globe, really a bronze hemisphere, with sacred Delphi as its *umbilicus mundi,* its "navel of the world," at its center. This globe neatly divided the known world into three equal parts: Europe, so-called "Libya," and Asia. The continent threesome was surrounded by a quite-unknown "Oceanus." As Theophilus strikes out over "Asia" (whose definition is destined to expand relentlessly far, far ever eastward) he is struck by the vastness of a land that can in no way be compared to his previous puny destinations. He writes in wonderment about Asia:

Hail to broad Asia! Whose coasts glow with violet.
Whose mountain snows loom over fields of red poppies.
Sing of broad Asia! Where Troy's heir is *knowledge*!
Pythagoras, Logos, Miletus, and Thales.
O, Seven Wonders! Diana the proudest!
Her pillars to heaven must rank with Olympus!
River Meander. And caverns of splendor.
A Black Sea of Amazons, zephyrs and tempests.
Hail to broad Asia! The wealth of King Midas!
The Eros of Phrygia! Primeval Galatia!
Sing of a country that bridges all nations!
That pleases all spirits! Superlative Asia!

Theophilus's Asian adventures are multitudinous. He befriends the governor of Asia, who is privy to many fascinating secrets and insights, such as how the matter of Barabbas could not possibly have been a matter of Roman jurisprudence but was surely a matter of Jewish Day of Atonement scapegoat folklore. He meets men who would later become famous as important Christian Church Fathers, Polycarp and Ignatius, men who virtually remove the blinders from his eyes as to how Christianity has been developing and will develop. He visits many a *katalyma,* or domestic animal shelter, equipped with a *phatne,* or highly symbolic sustenance-providing manger, which provide him with a full understanding of what Luke was essaying to express with his story of the Nativity. Theophilus tours a country that is swimming with history, and with multiple gods, and with multiple histories of multiple gods. And one recent god stands out. More than anywhere else in the Roman Empire, in highly spiritual Asia the Emperor is fervently worshipped as a god. A typical inscription honoring this deity would read:

AUGUSTUS WAS SENT TO US AS A SAVIOR, AND THE BIRTHDAY OF THIS GOD HAS BEEN FOR THE WHOLE WORLD THE BEGINNING OF THE EVANGELION (Formally Proclaimed Great News) CONCERNING HIM

And, oh, what a climacteric Theophilus experiences in mid-Asia, a frightful surprise in the remote and windswept hilly plains. He witnesses a crucifixion. He witnesses it among the pretty fields of poppy, which can, for some at least, alleviate the pain of experiencing or even witnessing that horror. At the price of terrible revulsion, Theophilus gains precious comprehension of the nature of Christ's Passion.

Especially intriguing to Theophilus is the province of Galatia, obscure and remote but for some reason a province crisscrossed by Paul three times or more. Moreover, Paul's Letter to the Galatians turns out to be the oldest known Christian scripture of them all. And there is still more: in that earliest known Christian scripture Paul described Christ as a mystic One Spirit that he carried within him. The deep mysticism of Galatia is matched by many other regions of this peerless ancient peninsula known as Asia or Asia Minor. Theophilus explores antecedents to Christianity in a holy Mithraeum cave permeated with the scent of cannabis and the like. And he explores antecedents to the Christ Passion among the many "hanged gods" of Asia, and antecedents to the traditions of Mary in Asia's innumerable sacred caverns devoted to the Mother Goddess of many names.

Paul was commonly called Paul of Tarsus, and Theophilus visits this Tarsus, a surprisingly sophisticated and beautiful community located between mountains and sea. Theophilus learns all about this community's annual Festival of Attis, which Paul surely knew about down to the last detail. In Tarsus on every 25th of March, the Spring Equinox, a donkey carried an effigy of the resurrected god Attis, son of Myrrha, into town while the townspeople cheered and waved branches. After a communal meal came the ceremony of the carrying of the evergreen tree under which Attis would die. This tree was then laid in a sepulcher. Last came the high point of the festival, a joyful celebration of Attis' rising from the underworld on the third day, a Sunday.

**MYSTERIUM III ASIA** takes Theophilus to Syria for the last of his adventures in this volume. He is overwhelmed by the wonders that fill the great wide world, particularly when he beholds Baalbek, which, like the Temple of Diana in Ephesus, is far grander than the Parthenon which is far better known to Romans like him. And natural wonders like the vast Cedars of Lebanon also amaze. But Theophilus is repelled by Syria's capital Antioch, the third largest city in the Roman Empire, but a city which Roman writers have derided as "the sewer on the Orontes."

Antioch was a relatively new city, one without spiritual lore, without hoary traditions, and even without much economic justification. Antioch had bludgeoned itself into existence through pure military necessity and might. Antioch had an evil reputation, and it lives up to Theophilus's negative expectations. He discovers that here, where the terms "Christianity" and "Catholic" (Greek for "universal") were coined, the Jesus philosophy developed into the Jesus dogma.

Theophilus discovers that in 70 AD, with the destruction of the Jerusalem Temple and the devastation of the Holy Land, refugees flooded in two directions: Antioch and Egypt, carrying with them few possessions, but a weighty longing for a Savior. Those who flooded into Egypt established a Christianity based on *mysticism*, while those who flooded into Antioch established a Christianity based on *dogma*. Theophilus endures a frightening interview with the Church Father Ignatius, who named himself for his fiery fervor, and who is the most horrifying person that Theophilus has ever met, a hellish co-inventor of hell. Here in Antioch is founded a form of Christianity whose zealotry and whose certainty of universality enable it to flourish far more than the other forms. This "Catholicism" favors the gospel of Matthew, a gospel writer who seems to have made Antioch his home. Theophilus ascertains that Matthew wrote for the refugees of 70 AD, for the downtrodden, for the despairing, for the Torah-studious, and for those who yearned for a Messiah and for a replacement for a

Judaism that had just been shattered.

Preparatory to entry into the Holy Land, Theophilus is transfixed by the site of Jesus' Transfiguration, Jesus' appearance to a select trio of apostles as a being both human and divine. This site is long and mighty Mount Hermon in Lebanon and Syria. To Theophilus' mind, this mountain is the equal of wondrous Mount Olympus, the supposed home to the Greek gods which he has beheld in Greece. These sites are imbued with the aura of portals to heaven. Hence, the Transfiguration. At the foot of Mount Hermon lay a site whose ancient pagan portent was hidden in the Bible by it being called Caesarea Philippi. Since time immemorial this place had been called Pania, meaning "the Realm of the God of Nature known as Pan" or "the Realm of Everything."

The event known to all the world that occurred at Caesarea Philippi was Jesus proclaiming, "You are Peter, and upon this Rock I will build my Church." The god Pan was Father Nature. Theophilus comes to suspect that Jesus' chief apostle Peter was actually an adaptation of the notion of Father Nature. More precisely, Peter the Rock, being a rock, was symbolic of the Material World, the Material World being the obvious, indeed the only possible, place where Cosmic Spirit would build his Church. Thus was explained Peter, stumblebum, Jesus-denying, uncomprehending, non-water-walking Peter who was headed for glory despite himself.

At glorious Pania, Theophilus is prepared for imminent entry into the Holy Land with a sort of Transfiguration all his own. He is aided and confronted by the Gemini brothers, one of whom represents the mortal aspect of man, and the other of whom represents the divine aspect of man. And in a flash Theophilus understands the next two most important apostles after Peter, the two who joined Peter to view Jesus' Transfiguration. These two were the brothers John and James, who asked Jesus if they could flank him on both sides in heaven, just as the brothers Gemini flanked statues of gods all over the Roman Empire. James was the first apostle to be martyred, symbolizing the mortal. John, the most mystic of the apostles, was said to be the apostle who would never die, symbolizing the divine.

At long last, after a blistering and freezing slog on the longest journey of his life, all through vast Asia, Theophilus comes to the Sea of Galilee, and gazes over that blue mirror to the Holy Land. **MYSTERIUM III ASIA** is about to give way to **MYSTERIUM IV JUDEA.** Surely all mystery would open up now. Surely all questions and uncertainty would give way. Theophilus glimpses fishermen, and wonders if such folk will provide him with tales of the original "fishers of men." He glimpses Magdala and wonders if there will be tales of Mary Magdalene. He glimpses Capernaum and wonders if there will be tales of Jesus. His heart bounds with hopefulness. After all, he is a scholar, and he knows that the name Sea of Galilee is purely an invention of gospel writers. The true deep and ancient name of this lake is Kinnereth, intoning awesome harmonic vibration of the universal.

# I MALAKH... THE ANGEL

"Eureka!"

This esteemed word, old Archimedes' joyous proclamation of discovery that meant "I've found it!" was inevitably Theophilus's exclamation the moment he came upon the Sea of Galilee, and then rushed into it to splash about like a child.

Reaching the Sea of Galilee meant that Theophilus had finally reached Judea, the so-called Holy Land. And the Holy Land was the object of his life's quest.

The Sea of Galilee was known locally as Kinnereth, "The Harp." However this lake reminded Theophilus not of a harp, but of a mirror, a gigantic mirror for the blue sky amidst all the brown of a semi-parched land. He played with the warm water of Kinnereth, offering it in splatters and bunches up to the sky. Theophilus was ebullient and playful, as well as very thankful. For this country was Jesus-country; and Theophilus was on a quest after Jesus.

Wide-eyed, Theophilus watched fishermen casting their nets from boats in Kinnereth. After so many disappointments chasing after the man who was known as the Christ, now at last the gospels seemed likely to come alive before his eyes. Jesus' disciples had been fishermen exactly like these fishermen. On these shores Jesus had preached his sermons. On these very waters, literally *on* these very waters, or at least so it had been reported, Jesus had walked.

Stepping out of the water, Theophilus walked past fields that seemed bountiful although they were strewn with black volcanic boulders. And presently he was in a lakeside town that was constructed mainly of the same black volcanic stone. This town was Capernaum. This was a famous name. This was reputed to be one of the main sites of Jesus' ministry. One black stone building in this town was somewhat bigger than the others. It was a combined Roman military garrison and provincial customs post. Theophilus paid a visit to this establishment to inquire about something unsettling that he had heard in Damascus.

Theophilus introduced himself to the officer on duty, who, for his part, informed Theophilus that he was the garrison's surveyor, and that locally he liked to go by the local-sounding name Michael. This officer was not like anything Theophilus had expected to encounter in Judea. This man had chosen to wear a tunic of calming white rather than the Roman army's customary blood-themed red; and this white-clad, golden-haired young fellow looked charming, and somehow quite special, when set against the black volcanic stone of Capernaum. After having heard the nature of Theophilus's quest in Judea, this officer spread his maps out in front of Theophilus and indicated that he would be glad to explain the sticky matter of "Nazareth" that Theophilus had just asked him about. The officer indicated that he had explained the matter to curious travelers quite a few times before.

"What you tell me that you heard-tell in Damascus was correct," asserted Michael the officer and surveyor. "Though it surprises many people to hear this, it's true nonetheless. The fact is, there is no such place as Nazareth."

"I can't believe it." Theophilus scanned the maps on the broad table, the maps that lacked a Nazareth, and ruefully shook his head.

"Still, it's a fact," declared Michael. "Here we absolutely have to know such things. For taxes, for the census, for military contingency plans. Lots of people who come through this area are surprised to hear that there is no such place as Nazareth. By now most people have heard of 'Jesus of Nazareth.' But see for yourself!" The surveyor waved his hand over his maps. "No Nazareth! And, by the way, there's another place mentioned in the Jesus tales that you won't be finding anywhere either. That place is Bethsaida. 'Bethsaida' means 'place of fishing,' and it has been used for many a little village as a nickname. The name doesn't carry much significance, because locales nicknamed 'Bethsaida' are all over the place. Sometimes 'Bethsaida' just refers to a temporary fishing camp."

Theophilus shook his head, a head which was accommodating his hand as he rubbed his chin. "Still, Judea has been through such incredible upheaval since Jesus' time! That means that a place called Nazareth could well have existed in Jesus' time!"

"No. No. We have plenty of old maps and records, plenty of the Jews' own. Plenty from Augustan times, and from Herodian times, and from all other times as well. Doubtless you're familiar with the Jews' revered writer Josephus. Though people have strong opinions about Josephus, one can't deny that he was a pretty thorough writer. He wrote about 45 towns in Galilee. That's a lot of towns! But in so doing, he made no mention of a place called Nazareth. There is no Nazareth and there never was one. Still, if you really hanker after a Nazareth just be patient and wait for one to appear! If interest in Nazareth keeps up the way it has been, then I wager that there *will* be a Nazareth someday!"

Theophilus sighed out the words, "I still can't believe it."

The friendly officer tried to be helpful. "I think I know exactly what caused all the confusion about this elusive town called Nazareth. You know, the Jews haven't got any Nazareth but they do have something called 'Nazarenes' or 'Nazarites.' A Nazarene is a sort of Jewish holy hermit. They're said to be recognizable by their trait of never cutting their hair. One famous Nazarene was Samson. Samson: you know, that Hebrew Hercules whose strength was in his hair. I've talked to various learned Jews about this Nazareth matter and here's what they told me. They said that it went this way in the holy books. After Samson's birth a prophet declared that Samson's hair should never be cut. That was because from birth Samson was sanctified to God as a Nazarite who would save the nation of Israel.

Then centuries later, along came this Matthew the tax collector who wrote about Jesus. And, duplicating the Samson story, Matthew stated that Jesus was born in Bethlehem but went to live in Nazareth *in order to fulfill the Samson prophecy about the one who would save the nation of Israel: 'He shall be called a Nazarene.'* It has been explained to me that that's the way that Jewish writings generally operate. Generally they're all about the fulfillment of old prophecies."

Theophilus slapped his forehead in an attitude of "Eureka!" and felt ready to contribute to the discussion. "You know, when I was in Damascus some people tried to explain the Nazareth matter to me in the way that you just did. They claimed that Nazareth is a fiction that was concocted to fulfill a prophecy about the prophet who is born to save Israel. First came Samson, about whom it was written, 'No razor shall come upon his head, for the boy shall be a Nazirite to God from birth. And he shall begin to deliver Israel from the hand of the Philistines.' Then centuries later Matthew took a bit of the Samson tale, and did what he did all throughout his gospel: he cooked up one more aspect of Jesus' life that was purely a fulfillment of Torah prophecy. Thus, Matthew wrote about Jesus, 'And he went and dwelt in a city called Nazareth that what was spoken by the prophets might be fulfilled, 'He shall be called a Nazarene!'"

Michael the surveyor nodded. "That about sizes up the situation. Anybody who insists that there existed an actual Nazareth should carefully weigh exactly that obviously-mythmaking sentence from *Matthew:* 'And he went and dwelt in a city called Nazareth, that what was spoken by the prophets might be fulfilled, 'He shall be called a Nazarene!'' Matthew said pretty plainly that he was summoning up a myth-town called Nazareth in order to easily and instantly make Jesus into a Nazarene! There's no Nazareth, but there probably will be someday because people like the Jesus tales so much. People will always be telling tales, and they'll always be telling tales that lead to other tale-telling. As for Nazarenes, you won't really find any Nazarenes, *per se.* My understanding is that over the centuries 'Nazarene' has become a totally diluted term, similar to the way in which the holiest Jewish men are sometimes called Hasid or Sadducee, which are nowadays just generalizations that connote holiness. I've heard that all through the centuries this land of Judea has been full of Nazarenes, Nazarites, Noserim, Nasoreans, Nasara, Notzri, and on and on and on. They're all people endowed with a very generalized sense of hoary holiness.. At one point the *Book of Acts* mentioned that Paul led a band of Nazoreans. I've been told that this 'Nazarene' word, in all its variations, refers to a 'keeper,' and hints at something a little more specific: 'a keeper of secrets.' Anyone can form a holy group and designate its members as keepers of things that are holy, in just that way. The terms are totally fluid. So there will always exist vague Hasids, vague Sadducees, vague Nazarenes. But Jesus is becoming ever more popular these days, so other Nazarenes tend to be forgotten, and people tend to think that only Jesus was *the Nazarene!* And there came a time when that situation was just begging for the invention of a Nazareth.

"By the way, there are those that try to plead that maybe Nazareth did exist but was simply too small to be noticed. But according to Luke, Jesus began his ministry by reading from the Torah about the coming of the year of Jubilee, the time of liberation, and stating that today that prophecy had been fulfilled. He supposedly read that passage in the supposed synagogue of Nazareth. But if Nazareth was large enough to have a synagogue, it had to be more than just a forgettable flyspeck that couldn't be found on any map."

Theophilus determined that later during his sojourn in Judea he would plot ways to hunt down Nazarenes. For now, he was spellbound by his sudden discovery that there was no Nazareth, and, more importantly, he was spellbound by his discovery as to *why* there was no Nazareth. "Jesus the Nazarene" was exactly what Jesus was called in Greek, and that epithet did not necessarily presuppose the existence of any place called Nazareth. Actually, in Greek "Nazarene" would not be the proper term for someone from a place called Nazareth; the proper term would be "Nazaraios." That orthographic fact, all by itself, was a strong indication that there existed no Nazareth. Another orthographic fact that militated against the existence of Nazareth was the fact that Matthew gave the town three different spellings: Nazareth, Nazaret, Nazara.

Reasoned Theophilus: Under scrutiny the town of Nazareth shriveled to nothingness like a water-drop in the sun. After all, Paul made no mention of Nazareth whatsoever. Meanwhile, the other earliest biographer of Jesus besides Paul, Mark, mentioned Nazareth only once; and, very importantly, that lone "Mark-mention of Nazareth" occurred only in corrupted editions of his gospel. Basically, that meant that the Mark-mention of Nazareth did not really count at all. It had probably not existed in the original Mark gospel. Mark stated: "In those days Jesus came from Nazareth of Galilee (*apo Nazaret tes Galilaias*) and was baptized by John in the Jordan." This particular Greek construction was extremely clumsy, and seemed to have been an alteration of an original passage which lacked a Nazareth and which read, "In those days Jesus came from Galilee (*apo tes Galilaias)* and was baptized by John in the Jordan." So it was evident that Mark's minuscule and grammatically odd mention of Nazareth was actually a later interpolation. By the process of elimination, then, the first real mention of Nazareth was Matthew's mention, and Theophilus had just heard that mention explained away, quite convincingly, as a fictionalization.

In sum, the oldest sources on Jesus were fully in accord with the opinion of a local surveyor, who was a man who really should know: there was no Nazareth.

With "Nazareth" explained away and discarded, Theophilus turned his attention to this surprising Roman military surveyor who displayed an interest in Jewish lore, a man who had proved most helpful. It certainly was curious that he was calling himself Michael. Theophilus asked about that in a roundabout way.

He asked the man, "Have you taken an interest in Jewish antiquities as a way to make your stay in this land more profitable and interesting?"

The reply came accompanied by a winning smile, a smile that seemed to come in reaction to a rare opportunity to spend some time at this humdrum desk job in intelligent conversation.

"Ya, obviously I'm from quite far away." The officer ran his fingers through his light blond hair by way of demonstration. "I'm from Germany. I'm from the Rhine. This is an interesting exotic country in many ways, this Judea, but I miss so many things about my homeland: the bracing coolness, the snow, the forests of deepest green. And the wonderful sausages and ale. I do like the wine here in Judea, though. We've come to like wine up there along the Rhine. Wine was introduced there not so many generations ago. We've got the world's northernmost vineyards, you know. I think that above all else I miss the Rhine itself. Such a big meandering beauty of a river that plays among gorgeous green hills. You know, the Rhine is a far mightier river than anything you'll find in Italy or Greece or Asia. And there's no river worthy of the name 'river' around these parts. The Jordan is just a brook."

"I'd love to see the Rhine. The fact is," admitted Theophilus," even though I've traveled extensively I've never even set eyes on a large river."

"Ya, the Rhine is a real beauty. I wonder if it ever occurs to the Romans to thank their gods for the existence of that river. Why do I say that? Well, the Rhine provides the Roman Empire with a natural boundary against the wild tribes of the northernmost lands. It's part of the natural boundary that the Roman Empire has against the wild tribes. It forms part of the *limes,* the imperial boundary, along with the Alps and the Danube River, a river which I hear is even longer than the Rhine. But the Rhine is not only important as part of the *limes,* it's also the Roman Empire's outstanding commercial river. A river is much easier to use for commerce than Roman roads, good though those roads may be."

"I can vouch that the Roman roads very good indeed. I've already walked and ridden a lifetime's worth of them." That statement seemed a good signal for Theophilus to take out a cloth and wipe from his brow the sweat that had been produced by the formidable summer heat of Judea.

The Romanized German continued. "I'm from Colonia Agrippina, the biggest city on the Rhine. That's a city to watch, mark my words. It's growing so very fast. It's the center for the Empire's trade with the larger part of Germany, the huge unconquered eastern part of Germany. That's the part that we call Germania Libera, 'Free Germany.' That part is where, you might say, the real Germans abide, the Germans who live the same as they have for thousands of years. They live in small clans in small collections of waddle huts. And if they can see another clan's chimney smoke in the distance they start to feel crowded and start to feel violent. They assemble into large groups only for the occasional ennobling purpose of warfare. Well you must know all about this already. You must have read Tacitus' *Germania.*"

"Yes, of course. And I've even met Tacitus in person, and discussed the book with him. So tell me, in Germania Libera do they still wear animal skins and enormous beards, and charge into battle naked and shrieking like madmen?"

"Mmm, no, not so much any more. Now then, you asked me if I'm interested in Jewish antiquities. The fact is, I developed that interest because so many Jews have been pouring into the new Romanized cities along the Rhine. They've been doing so over a period of several generations now. Emperor Vespasian's expulsion of most of the Jews from Judea was one impetus for that migration. But the fact is that Jews are people who just can't resist the lure of new commercial opportunities, and there's no place that's growing faster economically than the Rhine. I really like the Jews. Such a multi-faceted people, and so dynamic. So, yes, I've read up a lot on their history, and I've made a lot of oral inquiries too."

Theophilus smiled at the thought that his own life had recently become nothing but a series of exactly such inquiries. He inquired, "So what is the situation with *Christians* up there in Colonia Agrippina?"

"That situation is much like here, it seems to me. Christians are just a type of Jew that likes to tell stories about Jesus the healer, or Jesus the parable-teller, or Jesus the ascended ghost, or Jesus of Nazareth, if you'll pardon the silly misnomer. People will always love to tell tales. They love to tell tales to make a point, or to get attention, or to make a bid for power, or whatever. As a matter of fact, I have a little tale to tell you about Colonia Agrippina that you'll probably like, since it has everything to do with the matter that brought you to Judea."

"Indeed, do tell."

Michael told.

"Well, first of all, we on the Rhine like to refer to our city as just 'Colonia.' That's partly because 'Colonia' is so much prettier and easier to say than 'Colonia Agrippina,' and partly because we all detest the name 'Agrippina.' We detest the name 'Agrippina' because of who Agrippina was. The original Agrippina was the wife of the imperial prince Germanicus, who was honored with the title Germanicus because he conquered much of Germany. The problem began when Agrippina gave birth to that despicable human being Caligula, and raised him in various army camps in Germany, where he received that odd name of his, meaning 'little army boots.' So this woman Agrippina was certainly bad enough, being the mother of Caligula. But then there was a *second* Agrippina who befouled the name even more. Because she was the mother of Nero! So you see, this name Agrippina was double-cursed!

"Was anybody on earth ever worse than that detestable Nero? No, certainly not. One way to explain the foul character of detestable Nero was the foul character of his mother. *She* was this second Agrippina, the insufferable Agrippina. She married silly old Emperor Claudius, then inveigled him into naming her son Nero as the imperial heir. Once that matter of the heir was taken care of, it didn't take long for Agrippina to kill Claudius with poisoned mushrooms, and for Nero to quip that mushrooms must be the food of the gods since Claudius became a god by eating them! All right then, surely you already know these stories. And surely you know all the stories about how this vile imperial mother and vile imperial son were suspected of having sex because of the sounds that sometimes emitted from their closed litter, and the stories about how, far from loving this mother who put him in power Nero tried to murder her in various ways."

"Of course I've heard about all that," stated Theophilus, and then asked, "but what does it all have to do with my researches in Judea?"

"I'm getting to that," assured the officer. "Vile Nero became *damnatio memoriae,* 'damned to all memory,' but we in Colonia Agrippina were still stuck with a city-name that was reminiscent of the mother of vile Nero, and reminiscent of the mother of vile Caligula as well. A double ill omen like that can really damn a city! A city named for horrible imperial mothers who were both named Agrippina, twice over! Well, as I've said, people are always making up colorful tales for all kinds of reasons. So in order to alleviate the 'curse of Agrippina' and to endow Colonia with some charisma besides its commercial worth, people made up the story that the Three Magi who are revered by the Christians were buried in Colonia."

"The Three Magi from Matthew's gospel? The ones who supposedly came to the newborn Jesus to venerate him and give him gifts?"

Michael nodded. "The very same. The Three Magi, which is to say the Three Magicians. They've sometimes been falsely called the Three Kings because that name sounds so nice to add to a tale, but they were basically three oriental astrologers. Matthew actually never specified that there were *three* of these astrologers, but everyone infers that because of the three gifts that they gave to the baby Jesus: gold, frankincense and myrrh. They gave to the baby Jesus the three most expensive substances known. That was the point of the gold, frankincense and myrrh. Out of love for my city, I've looked into this matter of the 'Three Magi' quite thoroughly. So then... I've read that all over the world there have always been innumerable stories about astrologers who recorded fantastic omens at the birth of a hero who is destined to crush a nation's great villain. Great villains like Nimrod, Balak and Moab. In baby Jesus' time and place the great national villain was *Herod.*

"I've concluded that two old tales inspired Matthew to create the tale of the Three Magi. Upon the birth of Octavius an astrologer announced, 'The ruler of the earth is now born,' and of course this young fellow Octavius was destined to become the great Augustus. Matthew seemingly invented three astrologers, his Three Magi, whose purpose was to announce that with the birth of Jesus the *real* ruler of the earth was born, a ruler who was destined to be greater than Augustus. After all, the birth of Augustus was announced by only *one* astrologer! So then, the astrologer's prognostication at the birth of Octavius or Augustus was the first tale that influenced Matthew. As for the second such tale, it involved a certain King Tiradates of Armenia, whom Pliny specifically called a magus. Note that: a magus. This tale used the same term as in 'The Three Magi.' When Tiradates came to Rome to pay homage to Nero he brought with him several genuine magi. All of those magi knelt in homage to vile Nero, amid great fanfare and blaring of trumpets. Therefore I can well imagine how eager Matthew was to erase and supersede that foul image of Nero-worship by creating magi who *instead* knelt in homage to Jesus! And I think that all of this imagery might also give you, my scholarly friend, a pretty good idea of *when* Matthew made up his little tale about the three *kneeling* magi!

"And there's so much more. In the Jews' Torah, when heroes arise to save Israel their coming is sometimes presaged by a rising star. Such a rising star is *anatalei astron,* 'rising star,' in the Greek Torah. Then, customarily, the star is seen by stargazers 'from the east,' in other words *ap anatolon.* Matthew used *exactly* those same two Greek phrases in his story about the Three Magi! As always, Matthew was just piecing together bits of Jesus biography from phrases or predictions that he found in the Greek version of the Torah."

Theophilus's eyebrows had been going up, and his jaw had been going down. He had unexpectedly run into an amateur scholar who had neatly wrapped up an explanation for an important element in the biography of Jesus, and who had done so for the second time in an hour. At this point Theophilus decided to cut to the heart of the matter, and ask who, then, was this Jesus who was making such a stir around the world, but whose biography so easily fell to tatters at every inquiry. He asked this, and, once again, in reply the amateur scholar came forth with gems.

"I do believe that if you strip away all of the many

biographical embellishments this Jesus was a charismatic magician who made quite an impression when he wandered around Judea, or, more poetically stated, wandered around the Holy Land called Israel. The stir that he caused invited all kinds of fanciful tale-telling about him, fanciful tale-telling that will probably erase forever the truth about who he really was. You hear about such people all over the world, these charismatic itinerant magicians, I mean. And Jesus' stripped-down life-story basically parallels the life-stories of the other itinerant magicians. He started with a long period of fasting in the desert, where he wrestled with the temptations of the devil. Such behavior is standard for a magician. The 'spirit of heaven' descended upon his head in the form of a bird. That's also standard for a magician. Then once he had undergone his initiation and his spirit-descent, he was able to do healings and exorcisms that left people awestruck. His tricks included some sort of levitation, and the ability to make things appear out of thin air, and to revive people who seemed to be dead. His disciples were a mesmerized bunch who hadn't a clue about understanding him. He made cryptic predictions about his end, and, sure enough, his end was mysterious, to such an extent that no one can made any sense out of his end to this day. In some way, shape or form he still hangs about as a spirit that can be contacted. Such was Jesus! He had, all in all, a perfectly typical life for a charismatic soothsayer!"

"What you've said is all probably all true, and very well told," complimented Theophilus. "But here I am now, at last, in the land where Jesus actually walked. Surely if I talk to enough people

I'll get to the truth about the life that Jesus actually lived here!"

The officer burst that bubble. "You won't be getting any solid information of that sort around here. Lots of us in the garrison have talked to the locals about the Jesus superstition. Around here Jesus is just one more hazy figure about whom people tell tall tales. As a matter of fact, more numerous than tales told about Jesus are tales told about the prophet after whom Capernaum was named. He was a certain Nahum. You see, Capernaum is, in the local language, Kefar Nahum, 'the village of Nahum.' The Jews rank Nahum among their minor prophets. Around here, you'll hear various versions of a few familiar fantastic stories about Jesus, that's about all. Jesus walked on the water. He caught a thousand fish. Or a million fish. He healed all the beggars. Or just some of the beggars. Or certain really special beggars. But none of that stuff is credible. And none of it is even set in Capernaum, not definitively."

Theophilus recalled, "Mark and Matthew mentioned that a prophet is without honor in his own country, and therefore Jesus did not do many great works in his own country, because of the people's lack of belief. Maybe that explains the lack of memories about Jesus in Capernaum."

"No. That's all rather beside the point. The real reason for a lack of memories here is that this whole area was swept clean during the Jewish Revolt of thirty years ago. Most of the Jews in this region didn't revolt against the Empire, but Vespasian crucified or enslaved and deported nearly everybody anyway. This was the very first area that Vespasian entered that was part of the most dangerous rebellion against the Empire that ever arose, so he didn't treat the area kindly. How many died? We'll never know. When a few stragglers later came in to settle this nearly-emptied area, hardly any of them were originally from around here, and most of them weren't even Jews. It's still a pretty underpopulated region, and a tense one."

Theophilus asked, "Have you heard that right here in Capernaum Jesus encountered a centurion whom he declared to be more full of faith that any Israelite? Jesus cured the centurion's beloved slave at a distance, and because the centurion was a man accustomed to orders being fulfilled unquestioningly he believed in Jesus' remote cure straight away, without needing proof?"

Michael nodded. "Yes, I've seen that tale in the scriptures. But there's no folk memory of it here. There are no centurions here any more. There's no one of that high a rank around here any more. There would have been centurions here in the old days, during all the troubles. And perhaps during Jesus' time. And maybe Jesus really did impress a centurion right here in Capernaum, and that would have been quite a notable thing, the first gentile to go over to Jesus. But, anyway, that centurion tale is just one more example of no memories at all having been passed down that concern Jesus' activities here in Capernaum."

"Surely some of the older people have some plausible recollections about Jesus' time."

"No, there's nobody around here who goes back to Jesus' time, which would be Emperor Tiberius' time. That's for certain."

Theophilus asked, "But if the people here are not Christians why do they tell stories about Jesus, stories none of which are set in Capernaum?"

"Yes, a lot of them do that, both the Greeks and the Jews. They relate little stories about Jesus, but they don't worship him. What they accord Jesus is little mentions, certainly not anything like veneration. Mostly he seems to be a figure worth quoting, just like many other figures who are worth quoting. And above all else he is *a name to invoke*, a name that has powerful magic, and that is handy for using in epithets. 'Jesus, this!' And 'Jesus that!' His name is a name to be used in making a point, or in casting spells. The women especially seem to like Jesus. But for the love of Jupiter don't you go trying to talk to this town's women! We've got enough potential causes for trouble around here! Talk to the men in the town all you want, and you'll quickly enough find out that what I say about the lack of Jesus-lore here in Capernaum is true."

Theophilus sighed. "It's all somewhat disappointing. Capernaum is so very, very intimately linked with the life of Jesus, yet I arrive here and find that there's not much trace of Jesus here. I have to begin to wonder if the tales told about Jesus being here were just that: tales. Matthew placed Jesus here, in the first place, to fulfill one of his Torah prophecies. As usual. He said that Jesus 'dwelt in Capernaum by the sea, in the territory of Zebulon and Naphtali, that what was spoken by the prophet Isaiah might be fulfilled.' Then he went on to quote a long passage from Isaiah about the people of the land of Zebulon and Naphtali seeing a great light. It was a pivotal matter, this matter of Jesus moving to Capernaum. Because it was exactly at that point that Matthew said, 'From that time Jesus began to preach.'"

"Yes, well said. But I wonder if you know about the other factor that made the gospel writers plunk Jesus down in Capernaum. Remember how I mentioned that 'Capernaum' means 'town of Nahum'? I propose to you that *the gospel writers placed Jesus in Capernaum because of one simple statement that that obscure prophet Nahum made.* Nahum was the only prophet in the Torah to mention the *evangelion,* which is also known as the 'gospel' and the 'good tidings.' Nahum said, 'Behold on the mountains the feet of him who brings *good tidings,* who proclaims peace!'"

Theophilus nodded. "Truly interesting, that. In fact, quite possibly extremely revelatory! And enlightening, as with the great light seen by the people of this land of Zebulon and Naphtali, as mentioned in Isaiah. It's conceivable that the gospel writers placed Jesus in Capernaum purely because of one strong *"evangelion"* quotation from this fellow Nahum after whom Capernaum was named."

The man in white offered, "It is revelatory, isn't it? Capernaum. The town of Nahum, the only prophet who mentioned the *evangelion.* Proclaiming peace. All tied to this humble little Capernaum. As was that seeing of a great light!

At that moment when he heard the words "seeing of a great light" it seemed to Theophilus as though the sun reached an angle that allowed it to pour through the windows and doors of the rather dark public office that he was in. Michael, already so bright-white and golden in appearance, seemed to merge with this light and thus cease to be visible. Theophilus was temporarily blinded by this intrusion of light, and shielded his eyes with one hand, and closed them. When the intensity of light returned to normal and Theophilus looked around, he saw that he was alone. He found it odd that his polite and engaging partner in conversation would depart without saying a word, but he reasoned that he had been in conversation with a busy man, after all. Still, this was a slow-moving little town, and he figured that he would have plenty of time to continue the talk the next day.

## II KINNERETH… THE HARP

On his second day in Capernaum Theophilus awoke bright and early to make contact with the town's little military contingent, which was perpetually obliged to start its day bright and early. To his surprise, all of the few members of this contingent insisted that they had no idea who Theophilus had been talking to the day before. They knew of no blond surveyor from Germany who liked to dress in white. Of course, the man probably usually went by a name other than Michael, but that point turned out not to matter; no one knew of anyone who fit the description. As Theophilus pursued the matter with the military contingent, the replies began to become a little brusque, and Theophilus felt he had better simply put the matter aside.

This was a most curious town, he said to himself.

Indeed, Capernaum was like nothing he had ever experienced before. And it was all the more so as he looked around this hamlet, which, as one could see from any direction, provided habitation to only a few hundred inhabitants.

Theophilus had known communities that were smelly, but this community was the smelliest, largely because the place's staff-of-life was fish. There were people eating fish, transporting fish, gutting fish, hanging fish, and mending boats and nets for the sake of fish. Middens, which were always an odiferous sector of a town, were especially full of stink here, because of the overpowering presence of fish. To add to the general smell, there were plenty of livestock, just as there were in almost any little town in the Roman Empire. Goats and cattle chewed their food and bellowed while wandering free or stomping around in courtyards. Chickens claimed most of the town as their own. Capernaum consisted of little dwellings made of black volcanic rock, which were all partially covered to some degree with casually applied stucco of tan or brown. Roofs were thin affairs of mud and straw. That allowed for Mark's gospel account of friends of a paralytic digging through a roof to lower that paralytic to a room where he could attend a talk by Jesus and be healed. There were to be seen a few attempts at building shoddy second stories, but almost all buildings were of one story. Everywhere there prevailed vibrant family life, which was pretty much identical with vibrant work life. People did not spend much time indoors, but worked, ate, played and gossiped in courtyards, in alleys, or on flat rooftops. The marketplace and the lake-shore were one and the same, with fish being the primary object of trade, of course.

Theophilus prepared to make his list of inquiries around town by drawing up a list of the miracles which were ascribed to

Jesus while he was in Capernaum.

**I** Healed a paralytic who was lowered through a hole in a roof.

**II** Healed a servant of a centurion.

**III** Healed Peter's mother-in-law.

**IV** Healed two blind men.

**V** Healed a mute.

**VI** Raised Jairus' daughter from the dead.

**VII** Told Peter to find money inside a fish's mouth to pay the Temple tax.

**VIII** Secured an amazing haul of fish.

**IX** Healed a demoniac.

**X** Healed a man with a withered hand.

**XI** Healed a nobleman's son from a distance.

**XII** Healed "many who were diseased."

Theophilus' research had shown him that Jesus' miracles bore strong resemblance to miracles presented in the Torah's books of *Isaiah* and *Kings*. In those books, the blind received sight, the lame walked, lepers became clean, the deaf could hear, the poor received good news, and the dead were raised. So a literary basis for Jesus' miracles in Capernaum was clear. Theophilus set out to see if he could find a folk-memory basis for those miracles as well as a literary basis.

Capernaum was small, and his inquiries did not take long.

The men of the town were friendly enough, but he soon found out that that was the case only if he did not press his inquiries very hard. It turned out that no one in town had memories that went back to the time of Emperor Tiberius. Many folk mentioned that that situation was a result of the town being cleared of its populace during the horrible Jewish Revolt of thirty years ago. Not a single soul had anything to say about Theophilus' list of Jesus' activities in Capernaum. Some people had heard of Jesus the wandering preacher, and that was about all. Theophilus felt that it was time to take to heart the hackneyed phrase, "Back to the calculating tablet."

He gathered his materials and reviewed what he had ascertained about the earliest days of the preaching career of Jesus.

The earliest known geographical detail about Jesus' career was Mark's simple sentence, "In those days Jesus came from Nazareth of Galilee and was baptized by John in the Jordan." But from previous textual analysis Theophilus had ascertained that those words "came from Nazareth of Galilee and" were interpolations. They were bogus insertions that were to be found only in later, corrupted, versions of *Mark*. Here was textual evidence to back up the vital matter that he had just learned: Nazareth was entirely fictional. Unfortunately, Capernaum was turning out to be not much better. Capernaum was proving to be very problematic.

Much of the widely-accepted geographical material on Jesus was turning out to be counterfeit at its very beginnings. And things did not get much better from there. A few lines after supposedly placing Jesus initially in Galilee, Mark pronounced his infamous line about Jesus, "And passing along by the Sea of Galilee, he saw Simon and Andrew." The trouble was that in Greek the words "passing along by the Sea of Galilee" were topographically confusing and stylistically odd. To someone well-versed in Greek, these words looked like part of an older tale to which someone had clumsily added the locale of Galilee, just as someone had added the words "came from Nazareth of Galilee and" that came slightly before. This "passing along" line of Mark's was reminiscent of Luke's line about Jesus' meanderings: "On the way to Jerusalem he was passing along between Samaria and Galilee." For an expert in Greek this statement of Luke's was, once again, topographical and stylistic nonsense. The more one looked at the gospel writers' portrayal of Jesus' actual whereabouts, the less any of it made any sense.

And this incomprehensibility applied not only to the geography of Jesus' ministry, but to its timeframe as well. Once again, the earliest gospel writer mattered the most, so Theophilus reviewed Mark's time-phrases pertinent to the chronology of Jesus' ministry. "In those days"... "When after some days"... "One Sabbath"... "On another occasion"... "That day"... "He left that place"... "On one of his teaching journeys"... "As he was starting out on a journey"... "On leaving those parts." Mark's time-and-place expressions tended to be the vaguest of expressions. Later gospel writers tried to clean up Mark's prose and make it seem less as though Jesus were an aimless wanderer among the clouds. But the damage was done. Anyone who looked at the work of the earliest gospel writer, Mark, could see that he was just stringing together previously-established tall-tale episodes, which were perhaps an oral heritage. He did not seem to be writing a genuine biography at all.

Theophilus thought back to the surprisingly cogent theorizing of Michael, the military surveyor from Germany. That man claimed that Jesus was little more than a name to invoke, for the purpose of quotations and incantations. It was indeed looking ever more likely that Jesus was an itinerant magician who made a tremendous impression in his time, but whose story had been sanitized and reorganized by various people for various purposes. Theophilus reckoned that it was perfectly understandable for Jesus' career as a sorcerer to have been minimized, in order to make him into something much greater than a sorcerer: a messiah, a king, a martyr, an inspiration, a god, or whatever. Sorcerers were very suspect people. Exotic people like the Three Magi could be wondered at and admired, but that was only because they *departed* from Judea as quickly as they came. Magi were everywhere, but they were also everywhere *suspect*. If Jesus had been one among the world's magi, in the context of Judea he would have been called not a magus but a *pharmakos*. Yet nowhere in Christian writings was any *pharmakos* mentioned with admiration. Jesus' career as a healer and exorcist and charismatic persona left little doubt that he was in some sense a *pharmakos*. The question was: to what degree did he proceed beyond that vocation, or to what degree did he *become dragged beyond* that vocation by sheer embellishment?

Theophilus realized that his sojourn in Judea would not put him in the simple position of "interviewer of eyewitnesses to the life of Jesus" as he had once envisioned. He was stymied. He was as though marooned. That being the case, it now felt right to hire a boat and spend a day paddling alone in the Sea of Galilee.

Theophilus sat in his boat and stared at the surrounding Sea of Galilee, crestfallen that his first days in Jesus' homeland were so full of disappointment. The lake was quiet and empty, and did not even offer any fish to his casually thrown hook and line. He paddled absently in the rather overly-warm water. He felt as though he were in a theater scene. The play had built up an exciting plot, then suddenly had gone flat and dead. Now here he sat paddling alone.

The common understanding was that on one of the hills overlooking this lake Jesus had articulated the essence of Christianity, in by far his most extensive offering of preaching: his Sermon on the Mount, which was quoted only by Matthew. But no local knew anything about that sermon. And the dead-end nature of the trail leading to the Sermon on the Mount caused Theophilus to recall more about the dead-end nature of his trail leading to Jesus. He looked around at the various low hills fraught with lovely orchards and asked himself, "Which mount might it have been?", but quickly answered himself that that was completely idle speculation. He recalled that he had read that the inspiring Sermon on the Mount might never really have been spoken. It appeared to have been cobbled together from well-known fragments from several sources. Those sources were: the Psalms, the *Book of Isaiah*,

*Ecclesiastes, The Secrets of Enoch,* and *The Eighteen Benedictions.* As soon as he recited to himself this list he felt amazed that he had been able to do so. His scholarly erudition concerning Christianity certainly had come a long way. But where had all of that led? He was paddling alone in warm water, feeling flat and dead.

The Sermon on the Mount assured that all those who suffer will be comforted. Theophilus recalled as many as he could of those so-called "beatitudes," those lovely assurances that: "Blessed are the... because..." True, his own suffering was of the most petty nature, but he nonetheless recited some of the familiar lines from the Sermon on the Mount to see if they were of any assistance to his discomfiture. They were not. Spontaneously, another quite unrelated line concerning Jesus came to him, and he shouted it out over the lake.

"And Jesus rebuked the winds on the sea and there was a great calm!"

This line, too, failed to relieve his inner torment. The disappointment he felt welling within him was devastating. He could think of nothing to do, and knew that if he did nothing his little theater scene would become even more aptly symbolic, and off he would float down Jesus' lake, called the Sea of Galilee, and down Jesus' river, called the Jordan, and straight down into the waiting flat nothingness of the Dead Sea.

Then he recalled that Jesus instructed the crowd that listened to his Sermon on the Mount crowd on something quite important. Jesus instructed the crowd on how to pray. This prayer offered by

Jesus to the multitude was often called the Lord's Prayer. This was God's own prayer, so it was said. But it was also a prayer worthy of a typical *pharmakos*! Theophilus's studies had shown him that the Lord's Prayer derived mostly from various widely-known magical incantations. He recalled this all-purpose prayer now, piece by piece. He recalled that one should recognize that God is the presiding power on earth and in heaven. And that one should hallow God's name. And that one should respect God's will on earth, and recognize that divine will as heaven-sent. And that one should remain in the present. And that one should pray for forgiveness, and also practice forgiveness. And that one should shun evil. And that one should recognize God as the beginning and end of all things, throughout eternity. And that one should end all of one's activities with a mention of one of the many names of God, in this case a revered Egyptian name: Amen.

Theophilus mused: Perhaps there was something to this so-called Holy Land, and perhaps there was something to this so-called Lord's Prayer. For the prayer seemed to work! Theophilus felt quite a lot better after having recited it and having pondered it. He felt as though this Sea of Galilee, this so-called Kinnereth or Harp, hummed a pleasant tune to him.

He watched fishermen in their boats on the lake casting their nets, sometimes yelling and sometimes singing, and the sight and the sound were down-to-earth and pleasing. The fishermen reminded him that his quest was not so hopeless after all, because they reminded him of the insights that he had gained on Mount

Hermon. On Mount Hermon he had accomplished some important winnowing of fact from fiction. Some of the very earliest words written about Jesus had Jesus "passing along by the Sea of Galilee," where he saw the brothers Peter and Andrew fishing. He spoke just a few words to them and made them "fishers of men"; they became apostles. Only moments later Jesus persuaded another pair of fishermen brothers to become his apostles: John and James, who, it was emphasized were sons of Zebedee.

By Mount Hermon, the site of Jesus' Transfiguration, Theophilus had figured out that John and James, honored guests at the Transfiguration, were mythic copies of the Gemini brothers, Castor and Pollux, who were well known all over the world. John and James bore the strange sobriquet "Sons of Thunder" because the Gemini brothers were sons of thunder, being sons of Zeus who was everywhere known as a thunderer. All of these interpretations had hit Theophilus like a lightning strike, which was a traditional symbol of inspiration. John and James, in a flash, left their father Zebedee to follow Jesus. That was because they were symbolically leaving their father *Zeus*, among whose alternative names were Jupiter and the similar-sounding Zebedee. One of the Gemini was mortal, and the other was immortal. As copies of the brothers Gemini, the brothers John and James represented the capacity of humans to be both mortal and immortal. James was recorded as dying by the sword, but in the *Gospel of John* the risen Jesus hinted to the baffled apostles that John was immortal. Because the brothers James and John were special apostles who symbolized man as both mortal and immortal, they were honored guests at the Transfiguration, where Jesus demonstrated his identity as the symbol of the human capacity to be both earthly and divine. After the Transfiguration, John and James asked Jesus if they could sit to his *left and his right* when he came into his glory. There existed an obvious mythic parallel to this request on the part of the brothers. The parallel was that all over the Roman Empire there were depictions of the brothers Gemini placed to the *left and the right* of various deities!

The Gemini brothers when named separately were Castor and Pollux. Castor was mortal and Pollux was immortal. By way of making these Greek myth figures into Christian myth figures, it was emphasized in the *Book of Acts* that the apostle James was the *first* apostle to die, while the *Gospel of John* accorded to the apostle John the weird honor of being designated as a man who would *never die*!

So, the very beginnings of Jesus career were attaining a clarity which, as far as Theophilus's knew, no investigator of the life of Jesus had achieved before. Even the somewhat murky Sea of Galilee looked clearer now. Of course, just before enlisting the brothers John and James as apostles Jesus had enlisted the brothers Peter and Andrew. His experiences on holy Mount Hermon had clarified the nature of these major apostles too. The Greek names of these apostle brothers were key. *Anthropos,* "man," symbolized humanity itself, while Andrew's brother, being *Petros* or "stone," symbolized the material earth.

It all cam flooding back to Theophilus.

*Peter the rock was the material world itself!* Peter was Jesus' stumblebum chief companion and necessary starting point, i.e. his first apostle. He was the "wholly material," as opposed to the "wholly spiritual." He was the inevitable counterfoil to Jesus who represented the holy, because he was "man as a rock" who represented the worldly. He was the weak earthbound man who, on one important gospel occasion, could not rise to the anti-materialistic occasion by walking on water, and who, in perhaps his key historic and personal moment, steadfastly denied Christ three times. On that occasion a cock crowed three times; indubitably a cock would be in celebration at that point, because a cock symbolized earthly concupiscence and arrogance. And, more somberly, Jesus once said to this man, "Peter, Peter, Satan desired to have you, that he might sift you like wheat." That strangest of sentences did make sense. Peter anthropomorphized the lowly material world, ruled by Satan!

And Peter was called Simon Peter. He was a member of an array of scriptural storybook figures who all represented something unholy and faulty in the hearts of men. Simon Peter. Simon the Pharisee. Simon the Zealot. Simon the Leper. Simon the Sorcerer. Most memorably: Simon the Cyrene, who miserably carried Christ's cross that symbolized materiality. And most humbly: Simon the Tanner who dealt in skins.

And Luke in his *Acts* placed "Peter known as Cephas" in seaside Jaffa, which was the realm of King Cepheus. And there, Peter had visions of all of the myriad creature of nature, just as any proper Father Nature figure should! As part of the same little tale, Peter traveled to Caesarea to the house of a certain centurion named Cornelius, whose name represented the Horn of Plenty, the Cornucopia. Cornelius was the first gentile convert to Christianity, so he, in a sense, represented Christianity as a Horn of Plenty for all mankind. More Peter tales which all fit together.

And Peter was called the Son of Jonah, Jonah who spent a mystical three days in the belly of the grossest and deepest-diving of all God's creatures, the whale.

Peter's brother was Andrew, meaning "mankind." And certain lore claimed that Peter had a wife named Perpetua, meaning "in perpetuity."

Now, then. What was the *sine qua non* launching-place for "the way up"? The material world was that launching-place, of course! So, who but Peter the Rock would be necessarily appointed as "the keeper of the keys to the Kingdom of Heaven"?

"Upon this Rock I will build my Church!"

And lastly, there was the matter of that strange image at the end of the mystical *Gospel of John:* Jesus instructed Peter to tend to his sheep "till kingdom come," at which time Peter would be led in directions in which he had never expected to go.

Even the water of the holy Sea of Galilee seemed clearer to Theophilus now. For clarity prevailed now. Theophilus reckoned that if he had been able to come to understand the true nature of the leading apostles, then surely he could come to understand the true nature of Jesus too!

Clarity prevailed now, and its feel was exquisite. It occurred to Theophilus that Jesus' earliest-described work-of-wonder had taken place right here in Capernaum. It was the expulsion of a demon from a man. Theophilus could picture this "unclean spirit," this *spiritus immundus* or *pneumatos akathartos,* and he imagined this unclean spirit, within himself, as being the sum of all his doubts and fears. *"Obmutesce et exi!"* he cried. "Be silent and be gone!" These were the first magical words ever uttered by the great *pharmakos,* Jesus, who was fated to become known as the Christ. Now Theophilus desired the full force of this magic. So he shouted out the formula three times, a magical *three* times, and he shouted it out in the Greek in which it was first known to the world. *"Phimotheti kai ekselthe! Phimotheti kai ekselthe! "Phimotheti kai ekselthe!"*

Floating in a boat in the Sea of Galilee as Jesus had done, in the Holy Land where Jesus had lived, Theophilus prayed in the manner that had been taught by Jesus. He prayed the Lord's Prayer. Then he followed Jesus' example and attempted an expulsion of a demon. He attempted the expulsion of a demon within himself. For it occurred to him that the revolutionary nature of the Sermon on the Mount lay in its insistence on *internal* purity, rather the insistence on *outward* purity that people had generally settled for before. So Theophilus prayed to expel. And this expulsion felt cleansing. Together the prayer and the expulsion felt very cleansing indeed. There was cleansing. There was clarity.

Then all of a sudden Theophilus felt awash with amazement

and clarity. He wondered. Why had he not thought of a certain matter before? In all of his wanderings, and through all of his trials, this matter had never occurred to him. He had met so very many people. He had talked to so very many people. He had consulted so very many people Yet always there was one person he had failed to consult! For assistance on his quest, he had asked so very many people, but he had never asked the most obvious person! How could he have overlooked this? How? No more!

He stood up in his boat and spread his arms out wide with palms upward, in the prayer manner of the era.

For the first time ever, overdue though the action was, late-in-coming though the action was, he prayed to... *Jesus*!

# III ZADOK… THE RIGHTEOUS

*"Kai paragon para ten thalassan tes Galilaias."*

"And he passed along the sea of Galilee."

Theophilus walked along the western bank of the Sea of Galilee southward, heading for another town that could not be legitimately missed on his quest for the mystery of Jesus: the town called Magdala.

Frequently there were flocks of birds to be seen in the distance, all over a place called the Valley of the Pigeons. In his travels Theophilus had seen many places where people kept pigeons as a convenient source of food. And he remembered reading somewhere that Mary's offering of a pigeon as a purification sacrifice after Jesus' birth was evidence of her poverty. Beyond the Valley of the Pigeons there were caves of cave-dwellers to be seen, caves set inside a series of mighty cliffs.

Intermittently, sheets of wind-borne rain sprinkled the Sea of Galilee, producing quite pleasing splattering sounds and quite pleasing airborne aromas. Theophilus found this walk to be one of the most enjoyable that he had ever taken. This lake had the feel of a component of a Holy Land. This lake had the feel of a component of a Promised Land. A few times he went down to the shore to watch up-close as fishermen pulled in loads of fish, usually many loads of humdrum identical tilapia, but occasionally some larger and more exotic fish as well. He got a feel for why fish were symbols of God's infinite and never-flagging abundance. And why they were therefore symbols of Jesus.

While strolling, he gave in to an urge to burst out into song. He sang some psalms that he had learned. *Psalmoi* were what the Greeks called all music played by string instruments. As far as he knew such music was to be heard everywhere, and with a similar sound everywhere. However, something very deep and God-loving was added to such music when sonorous Hebrew incantations came into play. In Hebrew the psalms were Tehillim, "Songs of Praise." Theophilus was in a mood to praise God's earth. He recalled that the Jews referred to the Sea of Galilee as Kinnereth both because it was shaped like a harp and because it was endowed with some sort of mystical vibrational harmony. Theophilus reveled in soaking up this harmony. Kinnereth pulsated with life. Fishermen were pulling in catches all over this little sea. Theophilus recalled hearing, once or twice, that the name "Kinnereth" referred not only to harmony but also to fruitfulness.

Theophilus reflected that if someone wanted to set the life of a compelling figure like Jesus in a compelling place, literarily, this place would be an excellent choice.

Supposedly all of the psalms were written by King David, a rather disharmonious man, a man full of violence and guile, but also a man who was a marvelous player of the harp. A most multi-faceted character was David. The gospels went to great lengths to emphasize that Jesus was a descendant of David. Theophilus recalled that David was so imperfect that God forbade him to build a temple after he had founded the Jews' most holy city, Jerusalem, leaving that task to a more worthy, more holy, successor, namely Solomon. So why had the gospels emphasized that Jesus had had such an imperfect man as David as an ancestor? If there were one thing that everyone could agree on about Jesus, it was that he was perfect! Of course, King David stood for sovereignty over the nation of Israel, and that was why it was important for Jesus to have King David as an ancestor. The notion of the importance of this particular ancestry, Davidic ancestry, was still taken so seriously in Judea that anyone who made the mistake of loudly claiming descent from King David was liable to be executed by the Romans.

Then suddenly, as Mark might have inexpertly put it, "He arrived in those parts." Theophilus arrived in the little lakeside town of Magdala. This town was key. For the the all-important personage known as Mary Magdalene must surely have come from here, reasoned Theophilus. And not only was Mary Magdalene important, she was also depicted as young, so she was likely to have been one of the last of Jesus' followers to die. Moreover, some claimed that Mary Magdalene was the "apostle whom Jesus loved," who was cryptically mentioned in the gospel of John. Dare he hope?

No, as it turned out. No. In Magdala his hopes were quickly dashed. Magdala was small enough that he could make his inquiries in a very short time. No one had the least memory of anyone by the name of Mary Magdalene. Suddenly a large portion of Theophilus's psalm-singing harmonious feeling drained out of him. Galilee was proving to be one very frustrating portion of God's cosmos.

But here in Magdala Theophilus came upon an interesting tidbit of information or two. Magdala was famous for its salted fish. The town had been named for its sizeable landmark, the Magdala Nunaiya, the "Tower of Fish" where the enormous piles of fish intended for export were smoked. The town had been nicknamed Taricheae for its livelihood of salting these fish. Supposedly on these very shores, Jesus called his disciples "the salt of the earth," but warned that salt could easily lose its saltiness. The importance of salt to Taricheae at least partially explained the import of that little story that confused generations of Christians.

More importantly, here there appeared one major ray of hope for Theophilus's research quest. Nearly every citizen of Magdala that Theophilus questioned about Jesus had the same thing to say to him: "Go on to Tiberias and ask for Old Zadok." And that town of Tiberias was only a short distance away. As a matter of fact, Theophilus could see most of Tiberias as he gazed far south down the lake.

Tiberias was the largest town in Galilee except for a grand hilltop community in Galilee's center called Sepphoris. Both of these towns were Roman-built urban centers that had nothing to do with Jesus' biography as far as Theophilus knew. But he would be in Tiberias in quick time. The town lay a short distance off the main international highway that he had been treading since Damascus. This highway was the Via Maris, a thoroughfare which connected Syria with Egypt, mostly via the the Judean coastline. This Euphrates-to-Nile international highway had existed since the most ancient times. The fabled Kingdom of Solomon supposedly flourished by building fabulous cities on this highway, cities such as biblical Hazor and Megiddo and Gezer. However over the centuries those fabled cities of Solomon disappeared and were replaced by others.

While Theophilus was walking the highway, an insight about Jesus' sayings now struck his awareness, through observation and intuition. Jesus said, "Broad is the road that leads to destruction. Narrow is the road that leads to life." Apparently, in Jesus' mind the broad Roman roads of Judea existed for jaded urbanites, exploiters, pagans, idolaters and sinners. In contrast, Judea's narrow country roads, which were barely-perceptible footpaths, existed for simple unspoiled country folk and holy hermits. In the spirit of Jesus, Theophilus now took a shortcut down one such humble road.

He knew that Tiberias was a Roman-style town built by Rome's Judean client-king Herod Antipas, who was called a tetrarch because he ruled a sort of quarter-kingdom. Herod Antipas built Tiberias to flatter Emperor Tiberius, the monarch upon whom his career as a client-king depended. The part that this character Herod

Antipas played in Christian scripture was that he imprisoned and executed John the Baptist. Herod Antipas's palace, where perhaps John the Baptists had been executed, stood out glowingly and glaringly above Tiberias, serving as the local "Rome is indeed mighty" landmark that overlooked all.

As soon as Theophilus walked inside Tiberias' sturdy wall that stood against Bedouin marauders he saw that the town was indeed properly Roman. The elaborate southern gate led to a typical Roman *cardo,* a porticoed central commercial avenue that ran the length of the city, along the city's background hill. Herod Antipas's palace occupied most of the upper portion of that hill. Tiberias featured typically Roman temples, theaters, mansions, and streets paved with large flat stones. There was a strong Jewish presence which was made apparent by a number of mikvas, which were Jewish ceremonial baths that brought to Theophilus' mind the former presence of John the Baptist. Mikvas were baths that looked nothing like Romans' lush heated sybaritic baths; they were small, and equipped with a few small steps. They were typically located next to communal venues like synagogues or olive presses. For Theophilus, the most important aspect of Tiberias was that he knew that this was the only town in Judea that still contained a substantial number of Jews, and it was therefore a promising place for him to be asking questions.

This time, at last, Theophilus's questioning of locals bore fruit. It took him almost no time at all to find a man whom everyone seemed to know: Old Zadok. The man was sitting on his doorstep leaning on a cane, trying to catch a stray breeze from the lake. He was bald, white-bearded, nearly blind, and most promisingly ancient.

Theophilus whispered a word of thanks to the two gods that he lately favored, namely the Gemini, who to his mind were also the gospel brothers John and James. Then he addressed the ancient one. "Sir, I've been told that you might help me. I'm looking for any trace I can find of people who knew Jesus the Nazarene. I was just in Magdala, and I was surprised that no one there knew anything about Mary Magdalene.

Old Zadok squinted at Theophilus. His eyes were like the lake: not quite brown, not quite grey, not quite blue. They looked as though storms could brew there. He said, "Young Roman, did you come all the way to Judea for such a silly thing as to find Mary Magdalene? I'd say you might just as well be searching in your own country for that pine puppet whose nose grew long whenever he told a lie!"

Theophilus smiled broadly. "Now, sir, the gospel writers described Mary Magdalene."

"Then their noses must have been awfully long ones, even for Jews!"

Theophilus had certainly not expected this. The ancient one was very much alive. Theophilus asked him, "Sir, are you saying that Mary Magdalene simply never existed? That she didn't come from the town of Magdala that I just passed through?"

"That's what I'm saying, sure enough, young fellow. Don't

bother looking for Mary Magdalene. She is a fiction. Magdala is a very common name for a town. It means 'tower.' Now consider some Greek grammar. If a Mary were to exist and were to be named after a town called Magdala, she would be called Mary Magdalaia, not Mary Magdalene. The name Mary Magdalene is all wrong, and that's how we know we're talking about a legendary figure here. Here's how it works, son. In the Hebrew language *gadol* means 'great.' *Magdal* means 'the great one.' So we're talking about a 'Mary the Great One.' And 'Mary the Great One' is a figure of legend, just as she sounds to be. She has nothing at all to do with any town that's named Magdala after its tower! Watch how it works, son. Watch for a prefix that begins with the letter 'm.' *Kadosh* is 'holy.' Add the prefix 'm' and you have *Mikdash* which is 'the holy place.' *Mikdash*, 'the holy place,' is one word for the Jerusalem Temple. *Drash* is 'study.' Add the prefix 'm' and you have Midrash, which is the name we use for our Jewish popular legends that are worth studying. And Midrash is truly the applicable concept here. We're talking about the realm of Midrash when we talk about Mary Magdalene."

Theophilus stared into the lake-like eyes of Old Zadok that hardly seemed to notice him. His pleasure at finally encountering a worthwhile witness was amply mixed with the queasy feeling that all of his research might dissolve into a gobbledygook of Jewish folklorist mush, "Midrash" as Zadok had called it.

Zadok had demonstrated a surprising knowledge of obscure Italian folklore. Theophilus now attempted to show off his familiarity with the Jewish.

"Sir, I'm looking for the truth about Jesus. For my father's sake, since I believe he may have been a Christian." Theophilus had just mentioned one of the least important of his reasons for engaging in his quest, out of a suspicion that that particular reason might most appeal to this old fellow. "I've just come from the north shore of the Sea of Galilee where Jesus' ministry took place. I found out that there is no such place as Nazareth, and that no one has any memories of Jesus in the main town of his ministry, Capernaum. I'm beginning to wonder if I've been looking in the wrong place. 'A prophet is without honor in his own country,' they say. And Matthew said with regard to Jesus' home, 'He did not do many mighty works there because of their unbelief.' And Luke even said that the Galileans threatened to throw Jesus off a cliff because they were so offended by his preaching! What is going on here? Am I simply looking in the wrong place *completely*?"

"Young man, I wonder if you have the slightest inkling of how to look at all! Here you are, a Greek-speaking Roman on the Sea of Galilee. You see the sea and you want to build aqueducts and roads around it, and drain it of its marshes. I, a Greek-speaking Jew on the Sea of Galilee, in contrast to you, make use of the lake to make a story. In the story, Jesus comes to the lake and sees men fishing there: two brothers, Peter and Andrew. Andrew brings Peter to Jesus. 'Come, and I will make you fishers of men,' says Jesus. And they follow him. Young Roman, what do you make of this story?"

Theophilus could only shrug helplessly. Zadok sighed and shifted his position on his cane. "I thought as much, "he grumbled. "You only see fishermen and fish. And you'd probably like to build them an aqueduct!"

"Forgive me," implored Theophilus, "but I'm only looking for what's real. I'm most anxious for whatever you can tell me, but I can't pretend I'm not disappointed when I encounter only ghosts and chimeras. Mary Magdalene isn't real. Peter and Andrew aren't real. John and James aren't real. John the Baptist isn't real."

"Balderdash!" declaimed Old Zadok with force. "John the Baptist not real? Nonsense! *I myself was baptized by John the Baptist*!"

Theophilus' head whirled. To express his feelings in the mode of the old Jewish scriptures he would have said that he had been caught up into the seventh heaven, and, in the newer mode, that Jesus had turned the entire Sea of Galilee into wine for him. The miracle could happen! This search was not completely in vain after all! Theophilus excitedly blurted out his desire to hear more about the Baptist, and Zadok gladly complied.

"John was a sensation of his time, and I was at a very young and impressionable age. A very, very young and impressionable age. So I did the truly shocking thing, and went off to the River Jordan without my parents' permission to see John. He lived in the desert, nourishing himself on odd unsavory things like locusts, and dressed only in animal skins. He came to certain spots on the River Jordan to baptize, to wash people clean of sin. He was the most impressive man you can imagine, young Roman: strong shoulders, strong brow, strong chin, strong eyes, strong voice!"

"Sir, this is wonderful! I'm drinking in every word! But in that time and place you must have seen Jesus and the others who are mentioned in the gospels! What about them?"

"I only saw John the Baptist, son, so you'll have to content yourself with him."

"By all means! Please continue!"

Zadok did so.

"John was a 'voice crying in the wilderness.' The description is a fine one, even though it happens to be a mistranslation of Isaiah's description of a voice 'crying for a way for God to be prepared in the wilderness.' Meddlesome fools often mistranslate noble messages. 'Repent, for the Kingdom of Heaven is at hand!' is something that such fools have John say. But his true message was more along the lines of, 'Transform your whole way of thinking and you will see that the Kingdom of Heaven is present everywhere!' Noble. Noble. In general, the essence of John manages to shine through in the gospels."

"And do you think that Josephus' account of John the Baptist was accurate?"

"Hah! Josephus! The very image of a hack historian! Pus-filled, rotten, dung-heap carrion-crap Josephus! The man who should have been called 'Pestilential Shit-pile Turd-man' but was instead called 'Josephus'! A Jewish name, Joseph, that that reprobate perversely turned into a Roman name, Josephus! A man who was not even fit to be a feast for any vultures who might have had any degree of honor in their vulture-hood! A man whose writings might have value only in their slight superiority over a sponge-on-a-stick, for usage as an ass-wipe in a privy!"

Theophilus could not help but take a tiny step back upon hearing this attack which almost smelled. But soon he leaned back in towards Zadok, eager to hear as the old man calmed himself and continued.

"All right, as I settle down I can admit that Josephus' account of John the Baptist was adequate. Don't get me started on Josephus! That turncoat! That fake dreamer! But it's interesting. Do notice how amazingly *much* one can generally see in a name. Consider the name Josephus. What Josephus did best was *dream*. One night during the Jewish Rebellion Josephus dreamt that General Vespasian would become Emperor. Or at least so he claimed. And that dream-prophecy that he related to Vespasian saved his life and made his career as a Roman darling. In very much the same way, another Joseph, Joseph the ancient Israelite prophet, dreamed a dream for the Pharaoh that saved his life and made his career as an Egyptian darling. And if you look in the gospels at Jesus' father, also named Joseph, you'll see a very surprising thing. You'll see that that Joseph was an expert dreamer too! His dreams guided him to exile in Egypt with his wife Mary and son Jesus, to escape the rapacity of Herod. And dreams guided him and his family back to Galilee when it was safe to return."

Theophilus filed into his mind a reminder to find out more

about Jesus' little-regarded father Joseph. But for now he was far more taken with an opportunity to interview an eyewitness to the career of John the Baptist.

"What writer gave the most accurate description of the death and legacy of John the Baptist?"

Zadok replied, "It's hard to say. We don't know for sure what happened to John the Baptist. The man who executed John the Baptist was the ruler of Galilee at the time, Herod Antipas, a son of the infamous so-called Herod the Great. Herod Antipas was to be counted among the luckier sons of Herod the Great, because he somehow managed to avoid being executed by that vile father. Herod Antipas built this town, Tiberias, as his provincial capital. This town Tiberias was built to be a shameless bit of flattery of Emperor Tiberius. Herod Antipas's hope was that the gesture would encourage Tiberius to make Herod Antipas the king of all of Judea. But the ploy didn't work. Things rarely went well for Herod Antipas. John the Baptist was always the worst thorn in the man's side. John was ever critical, but he was also far too popular to eliminate. As you must already know, the deciding issue was Herod Antipas's marriage to a woman who was named with another confusing contemporary name, Herodias. The marriage was widely condemned as incestuous, because Herodias had been married to Herod Antipas's brother Philip. That's the Philip who was a rare example of a mild-mannered Herodian ruler, bless him. It's funny the things people will worry about, to the point of getting themselves killed over them! Like silly incestuous Herod Antipas getting married to silly incestuous Herodias!

"Herod Antipas and his wife Herodias were far from being the worst of the Herodians, but they were a very tough twosome nonetheless. Imagine how tough a bird Herod Antipas had to be, in order to survive the reign of his megalomaniac father Herod! Of course Herod Antipas and Herodias needed to kill John the Baptist, since he relentlessly attacked the very basis of their respectability. But we don't really know how they performed that deed, that murder, in the end. It was very important for the two of them to kill John *secretly*. Perhaps they did so right here in Tiberias, right up there in their palace which stands out to the eye, way up yonder. It's that building up there which you can easily see dominates the whole town. Or perhaps Josephus was correct for once, and Herod Antipas and Herodias brought John the Baptist to their isolated palace of Machaerus, way out in the desert. With Machaerus being as isolated as it was, imprisoning John there would have made a great deal of sense. The secrecy was such that all kinds of tall tales could arise concerning John's martyrdom. As for John's legacy, that's a very intricate topic indeed. For now just think of him as the *prodromos*, the forerunner, the man who insisted that being cleansed of sin is the necessary prerequisite for the salvation offered by Jesus."

Theophilus enthused, "How refreshing it is to have finally found a character from the gospels who is tangible and real!"

"Well, don't be too hasty to describe John the Baptist as such. The later the gospel, the more you'll find that authors have bent John all out of shape, mythologized him half to death. Luke used John in his gospel to magnify Jesus, by portraying the births of John and Jesus as happening at almost the same time, and to two cousins no less! That's all easily picked apart as myth. Luke put together a Jesus-conception story and a John-conception story, each of which was a typical conception story for a prophet, assembled from several sources. In a typical prophet-conception story, *God remembers and promises*. Thus you have John the Baptist's surely-mythical father Zechariah, bearing a name that meant 'God remembers,' and John's surely-mythical mother Elizabeth, bearing a name that meant 'God promises.' Zechariah and Elizabeth were an elderly childless couple who believed that they would never have children, just like the Torah couple Elkanan and Hannah. Like true prophets, John and Jesus were conceived magically rather than normally, and those conceptions were announced by the angel Gabriel. On learning of the magical conception of Jesus inside her, Mary sang a song that I believe you Romans call the Magnificat, and that song was very clearly derived from the song that Hannah sang under the same circumstances in the Torah."

Theophilus said, "There's much there for me to ruminate on later. But right now I want to ask you this. If you were baptized, then aren't you a Christian rather than a Jew?"

"I'm both a Christian and a Jew. As an outsider you can hardly appreciate how foolish were the fools who, over a long period of time, decided that there had to be a distinction. The damnable snobs of Jerusalem and Antioch, and so on, were to blame! Here in Judea we Jews who venerate Jesus call ourselves Nazarenes."

"Yes, I've heard that the Jews who venerate Jesus call themselves Nazarenes. And that their leader was James the Just, who was called a brother of Jesus."

Zadok spoke carefully and deliberately to correct Theophilus. "Nazarenes have never cared to have a leader. The man called James the Just was simply the most respected of the Nazarene holy men of Jerusalem. His famous *Letter of James,* which directly contradicted Paul in asserting that faith alone without works is barren, is one of the finest of the Christian writings. It's written in an excellent philosopher's Greek, and that fact should help to discount a certain popular claim. That claim is that James was a brother of Jesus. James was *not* a brother of Jesus, as is often declared. For evidence of that, have a look at the Gnostic *Apocalypse of James*, because it states *directly* that James was 'a brother of the Lord' *only in a spiritual sense!* A good man, that James the Just. The Temple priesthood, growing ever more corrupt as the Temple grew grander and grander, eventually just couldn't tolerate that man any more. The priests killed James the Just in a way that served to underscore the depths of their depravity. They threw him off the highest pinnacle of the Temple Mount, then gathered up his mangled body and beat him to death with clubs, and even stoned him for good measure too! That deranged act enraged almost everyone, including even the Roman governor Albinus who was absent at the time. Albinus deposed the High Priest on account of that terrible incident. James the Just was so respected, and this deed was so dastardly, that many have even claimed *that God destroyed the Temple a few years later to avenge the death of James the Just!"*

"Thank you so very much for this wonderful exposition! Nazarenes! There are Nazarenes! I've found my first Nazarene! James the Just is my first Nazarene! The term refers to a certain type of holy man, not to a resident of Nazareth! Those Nazarenes are exactly the kind of people I need to talk to!" Theophilus was ebullient. "Sir, you can't imagine how thrilled I am to hear that I'm going to learn about Jesus while I'm here in Judea after all! I haven't wasted my effort in coming here after all! You must tell me more about Jesus! Even if you never saw him yourself, there must have been other people whom you knew who saw him! Eyewitnesses to the life of Jesus whom you've talked to! *I've come all this way over a thousand miles of Roman road expressly for the eyewitnesses!"*

Old Zadok emitted a series of grunts and sighs that were so intricate that it was as though he were making up his own language. Then he turned to Theophilus with an intense look that stated in no uncertain terms that the younger man was errant and truant.

"Young Roman, no doubt your superficial knowledge of things Judean includes awareness of once certain very important fact. The fact that Jesus' followers *did not understand him*! Everywhere in the scriptures that is made abundantly clear. *People did not understand Jesus!* 'Other than in parables, he addressed them not,' so it is said. Jesus began his preaching career just after uttering an expression of indifference that his mother and his brothers were in his presence. In a society where family is *everything*, that indifference demonstrated, in no uncertain terms, and right from the start, just how totally *otherworldly* Jesus was! After making that curt anti-family statement, this new preacher named Jesus gathered disciples by the sea, *this* sea that sits right before us here, and proceeded to address these disciples *in parables*. So, here's the first parable: A sower sowed seeds, and some of these seeds fell on rocky ground, and some of them fell among thorns, but some of them fell on good soil and returned their bounty a hundredfold. Said Jesus, 'Do you not understand this parable? How then will you understand all the parables? He who has ears to hear, let him hear!'"

Theophilus rubbed his chin thoughtfully. "Sir, I fully take your point. You feel that my ethnic origins leave me unequipped to understand anything about Jesus. In your eyes I'm unworthy, being one of the *Kittim,* one of the foreigners who have often ravaged your land. But in the forgiving spirit of Jesus, surely you can't hold me personally responsible for the outrages that my people, the Romans, have perpetrated in this country for so long."

Zadok shook his head. "No, I don't hold you responsible for that. And *kudos* to you for knowing the term *Kittim* and the history of our land. But if various disciples who grew up with our Jewish traditions, which are replete with subtle clues and nuances, could not understand Jesus… then, well, I really don't see how *you* can! One day out there on the lake Jesus stilled the storm. But his disciples were not grateful or awed, they were only frightened. They did not understand him. Later they were terrified to see him walking on the water. Abject failures, all, were they, these foolish apostles.

They hardened their hearts and did not understand. Loaves and fishes? Again they did not understand. Near the end, in Jerusalem, they were all still utterly asleep. *Literally and symbolically asleep* were all the disciples at fateful Gethsemane, abandoning Jesus and leaving him all alone!"

"I don't deny that I've usually been baffled during this quest of mine. Over and over again I've been baffled. But I've persevered, and I know that through my diligence I've made great progress in understanding these things. For instance, when I was on Mount Hermon I experienced a revelation that explained much about the very first activities of Jesus."

In reply Zadok spoke words that reeked of the sardonic tones that were widely believed to have originated in Sardinia, and also reeked of the literary genre called satire that was well known to have originated in Rome. What he said was, "Well, well. A 'revelation.' Do tell."

Having been invited to do so, Theophilus related his experiences on Mount Hermon and his hard-won conclusions about the symbolic meaning of Jesus enlisting the fishermen brothers John and James on the Sea of Galilee. He had concluded that the brothers John and James were Jewish mythic equivalents of the mythic brothers Castor and Pollux, the Gemini.

Zadok's facial expressions went through so many permutations that it was, again, almost as if he were inventing a language. But the upshot was that his features softened. His attitude had changed. He said mildly, "Well, your revelation was not a bad one after all. Although I still doubt that you really have that which Jesus called 'ears to hear,' you may indeed have developed, let us say, *one* ear to hear! So, Roman, lend me your ear! I will now tell you the *inner meaning* of the prophet John the Baptist."

"Thank you, sir. You'll find that I'm not so ignorant of these matters as you're assuming. May I demonstrate this? I know that the Jewish scriptures end with the prophet Malachi prophesying a return of the prophet Elijah who will act as 'a voice crying in the wilderness.' So then... Mark began his gospel in such a way as to make it seem like a continuation of the Jewish scriptures! In Mark's gospel everyone keeps asking if John the Baptist is really a return of Elijah, but that question is never definitively answered, so the Baptist retains his mystery. Mark's John the Baptist was very much a copy of Elijah, being a 'voice crying in the wilderness' who lived rough, wearing a crude coat of camel hair. I've learned much about how a typical *pharmakos* or shaman operates. Now don't dismiss this supposition of mine offhandedly. Here it is. It seems to me possible that John the Baptist harnessed Elijah's departed spirit in order to work magic! And then after John was dead, Jesus harnessed John the Baptist's departed spirit, in the same way and for the same purpose! *In short: John the Baptist harnessed the dead Elijah's magic, and later Jesus harnessed the dead John the Baptist's magic!*"

Zadok pointed his index finger to the heavens. "John the Baptist was indeed a personage with a direct connection to the heavens, and therefore the gesture that memorializes him is this gesture. He was indeed, in some sense, the returned spirit of Elijah. Elijah is a figure so revered that when Jesus was on the cross and called to God, using the old name for God *Eloi,* some people thought that he was calling to Elijah! Now then, a holy hermit who exhorts people to cleanse themselves and transform themselves is a wonderful thing. But John, imbued with the spirit of Elijah, was much more than just another holy hermit. He wore only animal hair. Yes, the purpose of that was to emulate Elijah, but there was more to it than just that. He wore animal hair because that was the covering that God gave to *the first man*! You have just been given a great gift here, young man. Know that it has just been revealed to you, here and now, what John the Baptist was. What was John the Baptist? *John the Baptist was the spirit of primal man!"*

Theophilus nodded with the gravity that seemed to be expected of him, and remained silent. Zadok spoke.

"Josephus depicted a very dramatic moment when he had John the Baptist answer the question as to who he was. John the Baptist answered this question with the words, *"Enosh ani,"* "I am man." In many of Jesus' discourses which confounded his halfwit disciples, Jesus called himself Bar Nasha. This was the same as saying, *"Enosh ani,"* "I am man." Translators often mess things up prodigiously, as if they were reverse-magicians who make magic itself disappear! So, because of poor translation and poor interpretation, the term Bar Nasha has usually been completely misunderstood. That being the case, people generally think that Jesus kept calling himself the Son of Man. But in actual fact he was calling himself simply *Man*! 'I am man,' said he, over and over again, quite uselessly, to the non-comprehending masses! And when during a later inquest Jesus remained silent, as a good sage really should, it was *the inquirer himself* who provided the answer to the riddle. '*Ecce Homo!*' proclaimed Pontius Pilate. 'There is man! *Jesus was man*! *There you have it! Ecce Homo!*"

Theophilus had always thought that chills running up and down one's spine was a baseless cliché. But now that phenomenon was exactly what he felt. He had much to say, but abruptly he remembered what Zadok had said about the value of remaining silent. He let Zadok continue.

"John the Baptist did not generally baptize children. I was one of a fortunate few people: a child whom John baptized. It was considered acceptable to baptize children, but the act of baptism was really meant for adults, because the act was a *sacramentum,* a joining together of a whole ethnic group in a sacred cause. Baptism was the cleansing of Israel, a cleansing performed so that sorrowful fallen Israel could start anew, and rise and prevail. But as with all things of value, baptism had meanings on several levels. There was national salvation. But there was indeed also personal salvation."

"And there was universal salvation as well, I presume."

"Yes. Yes, you do show some modicum of promise in understanding these matters. I'm almost blind, so I can't look with you, but I want you to take a few steps over that way that I am pointing, and look over to the south where the Sea of Galilee ends and its waters flow into the beginning of the River Jordan. There's not much to see at this distance, but look anyway.

Theophilus went over and looked. No, there was not much to see. But he knew what tale was coming, so he had the chills up and down his spine again.

Recounted Zadok, "That was where John the Baptist did some of his baptizing. The gospels tell us that his main site of baptism was much farther downriver at 'Bethany on the other side of the Jordan,' a site located down in the barren lands that one finds past Jericho. That site has much symbolic weight, because it was where Joshua assumed leadership of the Israelites as they crossed into the Promised Land, and where Elijah ascended to heaven in a Chariot of Fire. What you see down there right now is the beginning of the River Jordan. It is our river, the Yarden. In Greek it is the Iordanes. The name means 'the going down.' Our River Jordan symbolizes something very profound. It symbolizes the 'going down' of divine creative energies into ever denser levels, down to the levels that created the material world. Observe the scenario. For the scenario is stupendous. Symbolically, the divine energies began at Mount Hermon, 'Mount Sacred,' with that mountain's pure snows that extend up into the heavens."

"A stupendous place indeed."

"Yes. From Mount Hermon down flow the divine energies into our own wondrous Sea of Galilee, a place of an infinite bounty of fishes, a place ready-made for Christ-miracles."

"I've been much impressed by the sea's inherent message of sheer abundance. Is that how I am to understand the significance of the miracles of the loaves and fishes? As a message of sheer divine abundance?"

Zadok huffed and puffed and almost spat. "You're interrupting one of my best dramatic discourses right now! But, all right I'll tell you anyway. Yes, the topographical-symbolic essence of the Sea of Galilee, which is abundance, stands behind Jesus' two miracles with the loaves and fishes, otherwise known as the Feeding of the Multitudes. But have an ear to hear this! The two instances of Feeding of the Multitudes were *two distinct instances*. When Jesus performed that miracle among Jews, after he had turned a few loaves and fishes into enough food to feed thousands, and everyone had eaten happily, all the scraps from the grand meal were placed into *twelve baskets*. That was the case because twelve symbolized the twelve tribes of Israel. But when Jesus repeated the same miracle *on the other side of the Sea of Galilee* things were different. Yes, look over to the other side of the Sea of Galilee now to get the flavor of the story. The other side looks the same, but over there the inhabitants have always been pagan. On that side one finds the Greek-speaking Decapolis, 'The Ten Cities.' When Jesus worked his miracle over there, the scraps from the grand meal were placed into *seven baskets*. That was the case because *seven* was traditionally the number of the gentiles. *Seven* was the gentiles' number because the Israelites defeated *seven* pagan tribes to conquer Canaan. The message of this second Feeding of the Multitude was not only that Jesus was the god-man who wrought abundance, but additionally that Jesus was the god-man who wrought abundance *for all people!*"

"Quite marvelous!" exclaimed Theophilus. "I'm sorry if I seem like an interrupting fool and a babbler, but I feel overwhelmed with a flood of information right now, after so many months during which my investigations yielded only the drops of water to be found in a desert! At this point I can almost feel the flood of the cosmic waters of which you've spoken! I believe I know how this story of yours progresses. The downward gush of the stream called 'The Going Down,' or the Jordan, symbolizes divine energies 'going down' to create ever more dense levels of existence. The levels are: first the heavens, then the earth, and lastly the lower realms like Tartary. The Dead Sea would represent that lowest realm of hell or Tartary, the realm of Sodom and Gomorrah, the domain of the Titans. Because of the nature of the Titans, I've often wondered if it was no coincidence that Jerusalem was destroyed by a man named Titus."

"You display a feel for this symbolic topology. The divine waters cascade downward to create worlds, from the subtlest to the grossest, in a progression of increasingly dense layers. From the heavens, to earth, to Tartary, just as you said. That is 'The Going Down.' True. But the next step in your understanding of the symbolism of the River Jordan is more important. I don't know if you've ever seen it, but in some holy texts Jesus *reverses* the flow of the Jordan. Joshua, too, did exactly this, using the magic of the Ark of the Covenant. This feat that is performed by certain outstanding prophets such as Jesus and Joshua is called 'the mastery of the waters.' This 'ascent backwards' of the cosmic waters that such major prophets as Joshua and Jesus can generate is termed the *anactorium.* Only the most potent of divinely-selected prophets can reverse the cosmic flow and achieve the *anactorium*, and it is all-important to do exactly that: reverse the cosmic flow. In this world-flood called the *anactorium*, this fabulous *kataklysmos,* the primal waters gush up from the primeval abyss located below the world's foundation stone, *eben shetiyah,* for the wondrous purpose of cleansing the world of its foulness and bringing the world back to God in apocalyptic spurting torrents. In this manner the cosmos is purified and renewed. Such it was with Noah. Such it was with Jesus."

"So baptism was invented as a purification rite and a renewal rite on all three important levels: the personal, the national, and the cosmic."

Zadok nodded an especially definitive nod. "It is so."

"I know something about magicians, sorcerers, healers, magi, wonderworkers, or whatever you want to call them. I know how they operate all over the world. Almost universal among them is an initiation that consists of a long sojourn alone in the wilderness, to face various demons and to overcome various temptations. So of course Jesus did this! Jesus did this, with his 40 days in the wilderness! Also almost universal is the arrival of a messenger-bird that symbolizes the establishment of contact with the heavens. That bird may appear on the head, or on the shoulder, or on a stick, or atop a very high pole, or whatever. Even the Roman army standards with an eagle on top have that cultic origin. Those standards have been a magical sigil with which to conquer the world!

"And so a bird came down to Jesus during his baptism! Jesus, being as ethereal as he was, experienced this universal holy bird as a *dove*. A dove hovered above him, representing the descent of the Holy Spirit upon him. I assume that part of the reason that it was a dove was that a dove connected Jesus with the Noah story that you mentioned. A pure white dove symbolized Noah's cleansing the world with holy waters. Exactly so, a pure white dove symbolized Jesus cleansing the world with holy waters! I always thought it strange that in all the Christian writings God spoke *only one single time*. But now I see how special was that time, how much of a key moment was the moment when Jesus arose from the waters after his baptism. Only at that moment, and at no other, did God speak to Jesus. God chose not to be original at that moment. Instead he quoted the second psalm that said, 'Today I have begotten you.' And then he called Jesus his son in whom he was well pleased."

Zadok allowed, "You did well with that long dissertation just now, son. I'm proud of you. I am well pleased. And I do believe that through my inadequate eyes I can almost manage to see how a messenger bird did arrive above *you* just now, and plop down a whole lot of inspiration on you!"

Theophilus took the odd comment as a sarcastic reminder to remain humble, and he bowed down a bit and smiled before he continued his oration. "Please forgive my enthusiasm at receiving this, shall we say, cosmic gush of inspiration after so much time spent thirsty in a desert. I'll continue, if I may, and I hope you'll correct me if I'm wrong at any point."

Zadok nodded and Theophilus continued.

"I've surmised that the gospel writers were driven by an urge to make John the Baptist ever less important, so that Jesus could seem ever *more* important. And they did this in an escalating progression. In the *Gospel of Mark,* John the Baptist was clearly an adept who was initiating a young apprentice, Jesus. Nonetheless, Mark had the Baptist declare that he was unfit to tie the laces of Jesus' sandals. Later, in the *Gospel of Matthew,* the Baptist repeated the sandal bit, but also went further, in a substantive way, and tried to dissuade Jesus from being baptized, since obviously Jesus could not be a sinner. The *Gospel of Luke* seems to have been written in the full flush of a competition-for-followers between a John the Baptist faction and a Jesus faction. Luke began his gospel with a lengthy tale that showed that John and Jesus were in complete harmony, and were also completely holy, right from the start, since both were born in supernatural ways, and at almost the same time, born to the cousins Elizabeth and Mary. But Jesus was undoubtedly the superior figure, right from the start.

"As usual, the *Gospel of John* did everything differently, reducing John the Baptist to a mere speechmaker, a speechmaker who proclaimed that the spirit-dove announced that Jesus was the Lamb of God, something which was a favorite *Gospel of John* term. The Baptist announced that Jesus will baptize the world in the Holy Spirit, which was favorite *Gospel of John* terminology. And, finally, the gospel-writer John had the baptizer John almost cringe with humility and state that he must decrease as Jesus must increase. So. All correct?"

"All correct. You're doing well, young Roman. Were you a Jew, I'm sure that by your thirtieth birthday you would be ready to read Torah in front of the congregation and sit in the seat of authority."

"Hmm?"

Zadok explained. "The gospels relate that after his initiation with John the Baptist, and after his initiation with the devil for that matter, Jesus had just attained the age of thirty. At that point he read Torah in the synagogue, and suddenly surprised the congregation by announcing that the spirit of the Lord was upon him. Then he sat down in the synagogue's 'Seat of Moses,' the seat which marks the presence of an authoritative teacher. This scenario is traditionally what happens when a Jew reaches the age of thirty, an age which was imbedded in tradition because David began his career at thirty."

"There's a fine image. There's a fine image. The way you just orally drew a picture of Jesus, namely Jesus coming into his own at the age of thirty. I can almost see him now. Almost. But not quite."

"Hmm?"

Theophilus wore a dreamy expression. He walked over to where he could get a good view of the Sea of Galilee, and spoke especially loudly so that Old Zadok could hear him.

"He was here, yet he was not here. That ever-elusive Jesus!

So many stories. But not a single eyewitness account! Jesus comes alive! And yet he doesn't come alive! It's so frustrating. He's so very alive and so very powerful. But ever out of reach!"

"Ah, Romans, Romans, Romans! Always wanting more! You've been given so much today, but all you can think of is your yearning for *more*!" Then Zadok seemed to catch sight of something familiar off in the distance, even though he was nearly blind. "Aha!" he shouted. You're quite a one, young Roman! I have a feeling that the way things often work for you is that things come to you as though they were coming from above! Like a message-bearing holy dove or something!"

Theophilus, querulously: "Meaning?"

"Look who's coming home now! Look who's approaching up the path!"

Theophilus looked. He saw a man who might be middle-aged or might be a little younger. The man wore the long brown hair and beard, and white eastern-style robes, and white turban, that were the hallmarks of how Theophilus supposed that Jesus had looked. He carried tools and looked tired, as though from a hard day's work. Most notable to Theophilus were the man's intense blue eyes. Those eyes reminded him of the Hebrew language, whose unique deep reverberations always seemed to him evocative of holy thunder out of the blue.

Zadok laughed hard enough to make Theophilus wonder if there might be a severe lack of amusements in this town. Zadok spoke louder and more enthusiastically than Theophilus had heard him speak before.

"All right then, you wanted a clearer image of Jesus! Feast your eyes on that image! There's your clearer image! I must be God, because here comes my *only-begotten son…* and he's *a carpenter*!"

# IV PELATHA… THE PARABLE

Zadok made introductions. "This is my son Uzziah. In truth he's not my only-begotten son, but he is my only *remaining* son, a son who, like Jacob's beloved son Benjamin, was born much later than the other sons. Only *he* remains to me. Life has been hard here in Judea. Now then, Uzziah, this is Theophilus of Rome, a wandering philosopher."

"Hold on there!" objected the wandering philosopher from Rome. "I don't remember telling you my name!"

Chided Zadok, "Surely you didn't think you were traveling incognito, did you? Just because the people of this region haven't been very forthcoming to you with information about Jesus doesn't mean that they're dumb hogs who know nothing and don't speak to one another! I knew for a long time that you were coming. After all, how absurdly noticeable can a person be, O eminently noticeable Theophilus? A Roman making hilarious efforts at singing psalms while walking along the Sea of Galilee! A Roman who comes all this way to Judea on a lark, just to ask a lot of questions about Jesus!

A Roman who wears a beard and plays the role of an itinerant philosopher without a care in the world, using a one-word Greek philosopher's name for himself instead of a proper Roman *praenomen, nomen,* and *cognomen!* The name Theophilus, 'lover of God,' no less! Talk about *noticeable!*"

Uzziah addressed his father without any effort at courtesy towards Theophilus. "So he's one of those so-called Judaizers among the Romans? Walking the land, to ask around about Jesus? And getting a little thrill by naming himself 'Theophilus' after that fictional wealthy patron 'Theophilus' to whom Luke dedicated his two books?"

Theophilus was miffed at this man's curt attitude, and corrected him without any effort at courtesy of his own. "My parents gave me the name Theophilus, as unusual as that may be for a Roman. I don't actually know why they gave me that name, and I would like to find out." Pondering for a moment just how sensitive was the issue of the discourteous dismissal of his name, he increased the level of his own discourtesy. "And how about you? As you correctly said, I walk around Judea asking questions about Jesus. I haven't yet touched on the interesting matter of Jesus being a carpenter. I understand you're a carpenter."

With Uzziah only willing to grunt, Zadok handled the question.

"My son and I are scribes, learned men, believe it or not. As you can see, our home is humble but by no means poor. When Jews filled this land, being a scribe was enough to guarantee a good living. But nowadays... well, it's very different. My son is quite an embodiment of Jesus, in a way, since he's both a rabbi and a *tekton*. A *tekton* was the profession that the gospels assigned to Joseph, and therefore presumably to his son Jesus. But the word has often been mistranslated. Because it does not mean carpenter! No! A *tekton* is not an assembler of furniture and carts and the like, but a genuine *builder*, something that you might refer to as a mason. This is a very high calling, this calling of a *tekton*. And it is a calling with many symbolic ramifications. That is the case with masons for one reason especially. And that reason has to do with the fact that there is nothing more dear to the memory of the Jews than the Temple of Jerusalem. Since the Temple was holy ground even while it was being constructed, while it was being constructed the situation in Judea was such that *every priest was a mason and every mason was a priest*!"

Uzziah interjected, "So now you've 'sort of' seen Jesus, since you've seen *me*. You've seen a *tekton,* and an 'only begotten son,' and a rabbi, and a man who is accustomed to being treated unjustly by Romans! So you've 'sort of' seen Jesus! So maybe now you've seen enough, and you can go back to Rome!"

Vexed by this escalating rudeness Zadok cut off his son sharply. Then there ensued an exchange in what was, to Theophilus, that bothersome guttural Aramaic that was to Theophilus the unworthy successor to majestic Hebrew. He was able to catch only some repetitions of the word *Kittim*. He waited quite a while before he judged it was time to put some of his hard-won skills at rhetoric to use.

"Please. Young friend and esteemed rabbi. And esteemed elderly friend and rabbi. I'll be the first to admit that you Jews have every reason to hate the Romans. What has happened in this land has been a tragedy of the first order. But aren't exactly such sad events the inevitable result of a lack of understanding? My friends, aren't we all obliged to do whatever we can do, to prevent such disasters from ever happening again?" Theophilus paused to think. And he could not resist the temptation to grimace and gesture theatrically. He had undergone long lessons in rhetoric, after all. "I don't know if it matters to you at all, but the fact is, and I say this not to be idly boastful, that whatever I write concerning my sojourn here in Judea may turn out to be of no small significance. Emperor Trajan himself has expressed interest in what I will write! And, what may be of no less significance, I'm acquainted with Trajan's heir Hadrian, and can even regard him as a friend. If you don't care, then I can't make you care. But I think that you yourselves have a lot to gain by helping me find out the truth. And the fate of future generations hangs on what happens here between us today. *Ha olam ha ba.* 'The world to come!'"

Zadok and Uzziah looked at one another. Then they did some more arguing in Aramaic, but briefly this time. Then the old eyes stared away. Zadok was pensive.

"Yes. Through the centuries, one after another, groups of outside marauders have rampaged through this land. So it has been for a thousand years. First came the Hittites, so that all subsequent invaders have been reviled with the name *Kittim*. Now you Romans are the *Kittim,* the worst and most bloodthirsty *Kittim* of all. So bloodthirsty were the *Kittim* known as Romans thirty years ago that nowadays Jews in Judea are a scattered remnant, morosely repeating to each other the tale of that catastrophe. Imagine, if you can, how this beautiful Sea of Galilee was once colored red with blood. Actually red with blood! Such has been the extent of human folly in this the land of Jesus. Imagine that! And now I think that the time has come to find ways to *move beyond all that*! So, a strange young bearded one-named psalm-singing philosopher has arrived in our land as a harbinger! So, O strange harbinger, come inside and share our meal!"

Theophilus bowed and expressed deep thanks, and the three men went into the house.

Inside as outside, the house was very white. The walls were charmingly irregular, and equipped with numerous accoutrements designed to make the place usable and homey: shelves, pegs, alcoves, tables, mats, baskets, bedrolls, bowls, amphorae, chests, pots, jugs, and woven stools. Theophilus saw all, because for some reason Zadok led him through all of the several rooms. Then Zadok told him the reason.

"We're going down into the storage area for just a little while. There's something we'll do there while our meal is being prepared."

Jewish teacher and Roman pupil descended. The storage area was almost completely dark. Zadok showed Theophilus a handful of objects in the last available beam of light.

"So, you want to know all about Jesus, and get a feel for him? Then surely you should be addressed in parables! Here is one of Jesus' parables. Have you heard of Jesus' parable of the woman with ten silver drachmas?"

"Yes, Zadok, I know the parable. I appreciate your setting up for me a re-enactment of that, since a re-enactment is what I guess you're about to do."

There was indeed to be a re-enactment. Zadok showed Theophilus ten silver drachmas in his open palm. Then he threw one of those coins down into the darkness, to the farthest part of the storeroom, and gave Theophilus instructions. "Now go down there and find that one silver drachma in the darkness. Rest assured, I'm not mocking you. Nor am I making you earn your supper! You'll see that there's a reason for this demonstration, strange though it may seem."

Theophilus felt his away around in the darkness of the storage room, somewhat discomfited by various types of dirt and various types of collisions, but before too long he emerged with the drachma in his hand.

"Well done! Keep the coin as an instructive souvenir," invited Zadok. "'Doing' is always better than mere 'telling.' You have just *lived* Jesus' parable of the lost drachma! A poor woman had ten drachmas, equivalent to ten denarii in the western half of the Empire, ten little silver coins that represent ten days of wages. Not a fortune, to be sure, but a meaningful sum. She lost one of the coins in a dark place. Then she found the coin, just as you did just now, and she did so with some effort and discomfort, but not a terrible amount of effort and discomfort. Then she rejoiced. The main point of this parable is that that one lost drachma meant far more to her than all the others that were not lost! You see, Jesus repeatedly had to justify something awfully controversial that he did. That controversial thing was that he accepted into his life people who were considered horrendous social outcasts: tax collectors, prostitutes, Samaritans, lepers, sinners, political zealots, skeptics, *Kittim*. As unfair as it may seem, God values redeemed sinners, *symbolized by a drachma that has been in darkness*, more than he values those who have always remained in the light. But parables always have several levels of meaning. This parable is not only about redeemed sinners, but is also about the necessity for *perseverance*. It is about the all-embracing truth of the dictum 'Seek and you will find'!"

"So true. So true," agreed Theophilus. "Very Socratic. And Platonic. And Aristotelian. I've been seeking throughout many lands and finding much. I've found myself engaging in Socratic dialogue with one teacher after another, and sometimes I find myself reflecting and really appreciating what they've taught me."

Unexpectedly, that information made Zadok laugh. "Ha! Perhaps that's not the best possible method, that Socratic method! Look at what a process of deterioration occurred a few hundred years ago in man's quest for enlightenment! Socrates taught Plato. Plato taught Aristotle. Aristotle taught Alexander. Alexander, who was called 'the great,' but who was really nothing but a brute! This was a process of wisdom dwindling, and then dwindling some more, and then falling down a hole! The hole of that barbaric Alexander! But you've just been given a lesson about searching in darkness. Try to reverse that Greek process of wisdom dwindling. Seek to be more an Aristotle than an Alexander. And more a Plato than an Aristotle. And more a Socrates than a Plato."

Now their dinner was served. Or, as Zadok had put it, also in the passive voice, "Our meal is prepared." The womenfolk of the household had made the three men dinner, and had then disappeared and did not partake. Their work was described in the passive voice. Theophilus knew that local custom was such that he was obliged not to notice the women or thank them. He also went over in his mind his knowledge of how sumptuous hospitality was the norm in this part of the world. He recalled that Christian scripture mentioned this norm in the first letter of Peter and the first letter to Titus. As part of the sumptuous hospitality a maidservant washed the men's feet.

"But you'll notice that our feet are not being washed with spikenard!" joshed Zadok. "In the episode of Simon the Leper's banquet in honor of Jesus, the gospel writers Mark and Matthew had a woman named Mary pour spikenard on Jesus' head. The gospel-writer John changed the story and had her pour the spikenard on Jesus' *feet*. And it was mentioned that the spikenard was worth 300 denarii!"

"The point being that the presence of Jesus was well worth that lordly sum of 300 denarii," surmised Theophilus. "A point well taken. Everyone is acquainted with the absurdly high cost of spikenard. The great Horace once promised the great Virgil a cask of wine in exchange for a tiny phial of spikenard. I can well understand the costliness of the stuff, since it really does smell like heaven."

"And it has the whiff of *legend* too! Tales should appeal to all of the senses in order to have a lasting effect! So in this case we have the sense of smell." Having said this, Zadok then turned more serious and uttered the prayer that would begin this meal, a prayer out of which Theophilus was proud to recognize one portion of the Hebrew: "Blessed are you, Lord God, King of the Universe, who brings forth bread from the earth."

At this point Theophilus was reminded of another all-male dinner, the Last Supper. In this current smaller version of the Last Supper, three men sat on leather mats on the floor, around bowls from which they partook of multi-variegated sustenance, using hunks of bread as tools. Even though the land of Judea was past its best days, the land was still a land full of luscious morsels: various mixtures of beans, chickpeas, leaves, gherkins, olives, oils, figs, dates, nuts, and, of course, plenty of fish. This seemed to be a special occasion, and so the garnishes were numerous too: mint, rue, dill, cumin, mustard. And above all, circles of fresh, hot, flat unleavened bread kept coming at the men. There was so much unrelenting copious bread in a typical meal in Judea that Theophilus could readily understand how Jesus could say, "Man does not live by bread alone," and everyone around Jesus would immediately understand that he was saying that man does not live by *material life* alone.

Theophilus commented, and complimented, "It seems as though I truly have arrive in 'the Land of Milk and Honey.'"

Zadok replied, "This is indeed a bountiful land when foolish humans will allow it to be. But there exists here in this land a matter meteorological which can became a matter theological. It is a matter that will help you understand a lot about Judaism. Sometimes the winter rains fail to arrive in Judea, and then this 'Land of Milk and Honey' becomes desolate, and people go hungry. I believe that that fact influenced the Jews to become a people who always live in fear of displeasing a judgmental and fearsome God."

"I'm most grateful, for both your 'Milk and Honey' hospitality and your information," said Theophilus. "I'm not at all clear on the reason why there's some element of mystery surrounding your, shall we say, theological lessons, but I'll gladly accept that. So tell me now, if I may be allowed to pry open some of the mystery, is there something about Jesus that goes deeper than the gospels?"

Zadok struggled to gnaw a hunk of bread as he spoke. "Hah! That's putting it mildly. You see, when Jesus quoted Isaiah repeatedly to the effect that many are those who hear but do not understand what they are hearing, he was making the point that one must develop a whole new way of hearing. That is the only way that one will understand the parables, the *pelatha*. And the parables are the heart of the gospels. 'He who has ears to hear, let him hear!' You must learn to understand symbol-talk. Learn to think metaphorically, Theophilus. If someone calls Jesus a door and a shepherd, that does not mean that he was a bunch of boards nailed together and stationed as a guardian in a pasture! Make efforts to *feel* the parables! *'For other than in parables he addressed them not'!"*

"Understood. But I still feel there must be more substance than mere symbolism to the gospels. There exists a feeling of genuine events being related there. Wasn't Matthew an eyewitness to the life of Jesus?"

Zadok looked up from his bread. "Matthew was no more a witness to the life of Jesus than I was. Matthew was a compiler of sayings and stories. And he was not much of a scholar. I knew Matthew."

At this point Zadok seemed to enjoy Theophilus' sudden look of jaw-dropped astonishment. He smiled broadly and continued.

"Some witness to the life of Jesus was Matthew! He never came anywhere near this country, Judea! I met Matthew on a few occasions in his own city, Antioch, where we were casual acquaintances at various religious gatherings and legal disputations. He kept very much to himself. I doubt that anyone who wasn't a fellow scholar ever got to talk to him. He was a long, lanky fellow, pale and sickly and perpetually hunched over as a scholar should be. But he wasn't much of a scholar, really. Take his description of Jesus' entry into Jerusalem, for instance: 'Jesus was mounted on an ass, and on a colt, the foal of an ass.' Matthew was so steeped in

Septuagint Greek that he remained unaware of the original Hebrew rendering of this quote from Zechariah, and he therefore took Zechariah so literally that he has Jesus riding on two *animals simultaneously*! Bloody fool!"

"Then there's that nonsense with the camel," added Uzziah, who had been waiting for a chance to make a smirking comment, any smirking comment. "Matthew has Jesus say that it's easier for a camel to fit through the eye of a needle than for a rich man to enter heaven. The saying certainly sticks in the mind, but before the ignorant fiddled with the saying the *kamelos* was actually a *kamilos*, a 'rope'!"

"But this man Matthew, whom you seem to think so little of, all the world proclaims him to be an apostle of Jesus!" exclaimed Theophilus.

"Oh, I'll come to that little detail," promised Zadok. "Right now we're having too much fun tearing apart Matthew's scholarship! We just *love* to do that, since we're scholars, you see! I didn't like Matthew much, to tell the truth. The blockhead even took a passage from the prophet Malachi and attributed it to Isaiah!"

Uzziah seemed enthusiastic for the first time, as he now had a chance to correct *two* fellow scholars at once. "Actually, Matthew lifted that passage from Mark and accepted Mark's false attribution of the quote to Isaiah without doing any checking. Eventually, gospel editors made a sort of compromise at this textual point by saying simply 'as is written in the prophets.' Be aware that an incompetent Jewish scholar is likely to mis-attribute everything to

Isaiah. That's a tribute to the immense popularity of Isaiah. Matthew made just such a false attribution to Isaiah with the *psalm* that goes, 'I will open my mouth in parables, I will utter what has been hidden since the foundation of the world.'"

Added Zadok," And Matthew falsely attributed to Jeremiah a quote from Zechariah that had to do with Judas's thirty pieces of silver. The trouble was, you see, that Matthew and Mark, second-rate scholars that they were, often took their scriptural quotes from popularized scriptural-quote lists. Later revisionists have had a devil of a time trying to harmonize Mark's and Matthew's quotes with the actual original scriptural quotes, and with each other!"

Theophilus opined, "I can only regard such slovenliness as astounding, in view of the fact that Matthew's whole view of Jesus' life was that it was the fulfillment of one old Jewish prophecy after another."

"Exactly so," agreed Zadok. "By the way, it was Matthew who invented that 'Nazareth' that I believe you mentioned.. Matthew says explicitly that Jesus went to live in Nazareth and thereby fulfilled the prophecy that says, 'He shall be called a Nazarene.' The desire to make Jesus a Nazarene was all it took to impel Matthew to invent a Nazareth! Yes, Matthew was constantly out to show that Jesus was a fulfillment of the scriptural prophecies. During the time of the fall of the Temple, which was when Matthew wrote, there was a crying need for that sort of thing, and there was a huge audience for that sort of thing. And so Matthew made a name for himself, after desperate Jewish refugees poured into Antioch after the destruction of the Temple. He not only made a name for himself, he also *made up* a name for himself: Matthew! He took the name Matthew for two reasons. First, in honor of the Maccabee patriot Mathias. And second because the name was redolent of scholarship, which is in Greek *mathemata*. The arch-patriot and the arch-scholar; that was how Matthew saw himself! There in Antioch sat an ambitious man making a career out of portraying Jesus as the messianic fulfillment of old Jewish prophecies. There sat that silly Matthew!"

"That was Matthew's only original accomplishment," asserted Uzziah. "Mark was at least original, though unskilled. And Luke was extremely imaginative, and skilled as well. As for Matthew, he stole nearly all his material from Mark and one other work, a work called *The Wellspring of Life*. Take one instance that demonstrates the difference between two of the gospel writers. Luke began his gospel with the dramatic multi-character lead-up to a wondrous birth. Drama! Poetry! Familial love! In stark contrast, Matthew began his gospel with an endless dull genealogy. All in order to show that Jesus was a fulfillment of Jewish prophecy, as usual. What could possibly be more boring? What a hack of a writer!" Uzziah smirked hard, and bit hard on a loaf.

Zadok got out some barely audible words while munching his bread. "Try to understand the mood of Matthew's time. The Jesus phenomenon threatened to overwhelm Judaism. Jesus had directly challenged Judaism by claiming that punctilious observation of the law did not matter, but that the contents of one's heart were what mattered."

"I'd say that that's the most appealing part of Jesus' message!" put in Theophilus.

"I can't disagree. But we Jews could not sit by and see the law toppled and disregarded. Matthew set out to make a name for himself by portraying Jesus as the *fulfillment* of the law rather than the destroyer of the law. One can't say he fully succeeded. A split has developed. Some of the Christians have gone far off in some awfully strange directions. Meanwhile here in Tiberias the Pharisees are meeting and laboring every day to make Jewish law more punctilious and Pharisaical than ever. They're writing a Talmud, a gargantuan compendium of law that is geared for making their control over Judaism complete. The Pharisees are gradually becoming the only teachers within Judaism, the only rabbis. And what else besides something like the Talmud can hold the Jews together now? There is no Jerusalem. Our own little Tiberias is the only town in the entire world that's controlled by Jews. How pitiful is that? Jews live in urban centers all over the world, often prosperously, but they're always threatened by complete assimilation. So the only thing that keeps Jews Jewish is an ever more, shall we say, Talmudic, adherence to strict religious laws. In a generation the Jewish-Christian split will be complete."

"Don't forget that Matthew played a part in forcing a split," inserted Uzziah. "He depicted Jesus as cursing the Jews for their rejection of him, and as saying that on the Day of Judgment God would show more favor to the pagan Phoenicians than to the stubborn Jews. Matthew depicted Jesus as enjoying great success in Phoenicia."

Zadok related, "Matthew's little vignette about Phoenicia was his way of getting back at various snob scholars and Pharisees. He said that Jesus went to Phoenicia for a bit of a rest, in other words to get away from those horrible Pharisees who were always gnawing away at him. But while Jesus was in Phoenicia a woman who was Phoenician-and-Canaanite-and-Syrian-and-Greek pleaded with him to drive a devil out of her daughter. This person was a mere woman and she was also, many times over, a foreigner. Thus, she was the lowest of the low, as far as the snobs and Pharisees were concerned! But Jesus just sat right where he was, not making a move, and healed the woman's daughter at a distance, purely through her having faith in him. What a revolution in Judaic thought was that! Unfortunately, at that point Jesus compared the woman to a dog that was getting crumbs that dropped from a table. Not so terribly nice of him, was that! But the story has some merit nonetheless. Such power of healing and righteousness, without any effort or ceremony, for the benefit of anyone who asked even if they were pagan, went against everything that the snobs and Pharisees stood for."

Theophilus held up his hands in a high shrug of exasperation. "I would have thought the whole mess to be a great deal more clear-cut. Either one believes Jesus to have been the long-awaited Jewish messiah or one doesn't! Isn't that so?"

Zadok sighed. "Ah, Theophilus, what are we going to do with you? You ask questions out of their turn, and we can hardly even begin to explain to you why you don't know what you're talking about! Be more patient! We'll see to it that everything becomes clear to you in its own good time! Your little speech a little while ago about universal brotherhood had its effect on me, and I'm determined that you shall learn what you need to learn while here in Judea. I'm too old to travel nowadays, but Uzziah will take you where you need to go. There are certain places where you need to go. Above all, of course, to Jerusalem."

Quite unexpectedly, Uzziah attempted to soften Zadok's already-soft chastisement of Theophilus. "Anyway, Theophilus, you deserve some clarification about the subject of the messiah. 'Messiah' has become a much overblown word. It means 'the anointed one,' and it basically refers to a king who is anointed to fulfill God's purpose. Wretched King Saul was a messiah, and he was anything but a paragon of virtue. Even pagan King Cyrus of Persia was called messiah, because he allowed the Jews to rebuild their Temple. And 'Christ' is, of course, simply 'messiah' in Greek."

"But let's not get into that now," suggested Zadok, mopping up the last juices of his meal with the last of his bread. "Instead I'll tell you how the hack scholar Matthew was transformed into one of the apostles of Christ. It happened only on papyrus. You'll have noticed that the 'apostle' Matthew is sometimes called Levi. The fact is, Levi was the real apostle. When Matthew's gospel became popular certain zealots began editing Matthew's name into the apostle lists in place of Levi. Matthew was himself a Levite, a lesser priest, so Levi's was the logical place for him to usurp. Thanks to that fiddling around with the texts, Matthew's book received the false cachet of an eyewitness account, and remains the most popular gospel partly for that reason to this day."

"Fascinating."

"There's much more to come."

Theophilus said, "Sometimes I think it all comes down to Mark, the first gospel writer. After all, Matthew just embellished Mark and that other lesser source that you mentioned earlier. Mark, on the other hand, was utterly original. How reliable was Mark in his account of Jesus?"

Zadok replied, "Not the slightest bit reliable. His account is saturated with evidence that he was writing somewhere far to the west and knew nothing at all about Galilee. But the fact was that Matthew hardly knew more. Look at their ridiculous misunderstandings about the geography of Galilee. Look around at what this land looks like. Look around! Look at the fertility of Galilee! You just had quite a fine Galilee meal, didn't you? In super-fertile Galilee those two fumbling storytellers Mark and Matthew placed such nonsense as sheep being lost in the desert and seeds being lost on stony ground amidst thorns! And they always used the term 'Sea of Galilee,' even though this lake's real name is Kinnereth, meaning 'harp.' 'Sea of Galilee' is just some sort of poetic rubbish. You won't find *anybody* saying 'Sea of Galilee' except for gospel writers! Jesus supposedly drove a herd of swine to their drowning at a place on the Sea of Galilee called Gadara. But Gadara is actually located many miles from the lake. Some early gospel manuscripts call the place Gerasa, but that only makes the situation worse, because Gerasa is *fifty miles* from the lake!"

"The value of Mark's account of Jesus' life seems to wholly vanish," sighed Theophilus. "And I had believed that Jesus was so active and so popular in Galilee. Why, there's a passage that describes how Jesus was so popular that he had to stand in a boat out in the lake over there, so that he could address the crowds pressing around him. And another passage has a man climbing a tree just to get a glimpse of Jesus through the crowds. And yet another passage has people in Capernaum lowering a paralyzed man through a rooftop to get to Jesus because the throng around the house was so dense."

Zadok shook his head. "Sorry. Never happened."

"So what are we left with? Jesus always seems to evade and disappear. Why wasn't Jesus ever mentioned by the three historians whom we would most expect to mention him: Philo, Josephus, and Justus of Tiberias?"

Explained Zadok, "Jesus did not make much impact on the times in which those three historians wrote. The impact came later. As I just got through telling you, it was the fall of the Temple thirty years ago that 'got the ball rolling,' so to speak, as far as Jesus' popularity was concerned. That was when Matthew described Jesus as the Messiah who made the Temple unnecessary. And, anyway, in a way that you'll be finding out about soon, Jesus existed outside of historians' purview. That's my opinion anyway. I can't really speak for Philo or Josephus. But I am Justus of Tiberias."

Theophilus stared blankly, and took some time to put his words together. "Uh, I'm sorry, Zadok, but I don't really understand what you're saying. Sometimes Jewish symbolism and metaphor are just too much for me! I haven't developed an ear for parable. Are you saying that you are an admirer of Justus of Tiberias? Or an adherent of Justus of Tiberias? Or inspired by the spirit of Justus of Tiberias. Or that you live after the model of Justus of Tiberias?"

"No! I'm saying that *I am* Justus of Tiberias! I am the historian who wrote by that name!"

Dumbly Theophilus let out with, "You are Justus of Tiberias?"

"Are you as deaf as *I'm* supposed to be at my age? *Stop asking me if am I Justus of Tiberias*! I've told you that *I am Justus of Tiberias*! I used to write history in Greek, and when I did that I employed that name! Look. 'Zadok' means 'righteous.' It is the equivalent of the Latin name 'Justus' which also means 'righteous.' So will you please stop belaboring the point now? I am that I am! *I am Justus of Tiberias*!"

"Of course. Of course. It's just that I'm astounded that you are the very man, Justus of Tiberias, who is known as a great historian of this land, Judea!"

"All right, then. Apology and praise accepted. Now then, to answer your query more directly. I would say that Philo of Alexandria never wrote about Jesus because he was basically only interested in philosophy. And Josephus never wrote about Jesus because that lowlife's only interest was in writing about things that would please the Romans. And I never wrote about Jesus because, over time, I learned a harsh lesson, in a harsh world. That lesson is: whatever you do, don't be contemporary! Write about antiquarian things! Write about old forgotten things, the farther back the better! If Moses doesn't turn out to be far enough back, then write about Abraham! If Abraham doesn't turn out to be far enough back, then write about Methuselah!"

Theophilus tried to adopt a genuinely reverent tone. "I'm very honored to have had you as a teacher. But I also feel some regret. I regret that a man of your knowledge and stature won't be accompanying Uzziah and me on my journey of learning."

Zadok waved a hand dismissively. "Not at all. I'm not really needed. Travel at my age would truly be an ordeal. You'll be in the best of hands with Uzziah. In many ways the younger generations are better versed in things mystical. Back in my day scholarship was perhaps a bit too stuffy, too mercenary and impractical. Picture something to yourself now. The platform for the Jerusalem Temple which you are going to see, called the Temple Mount, was possibly the largest object ever constructed by the hand of man. Have you absorbed that? *The largest object ever constructed by the hand of man!*

"The Temple drew innumerable pilgrims from all over the world. Not millions of pilgrims as claimed by Josephus, who was wrong as usual, but a lot of pilgrims. And that Temple was only one of many enormous building projects in the days of King Herod. In Herod's day, this was a thriving land of ongoing building projects such as the world had never seen. Many a Jew became, like Uzziah and like Jesus, a *tekton*, a mason, because so much construction was going on. Never before was there such a land. And there may never be such a land again. These masons, the builders of the Jerusalem Temple, were privy to many deep, ancient, esoteric secrets. After all, the Temple Mount was sanctified ground. A small Temple already existed there, and ritual never ceased during the entire course of construction. Thus, only priests were allowed to take part in the construction. Every priest was a mason and every mason was a priest! Has there ever been such a land anywhere else in history? Thus began a very special tradition. With the dispersal of the Jews to all lands this brotherhood of masons was scattered, but not shattered. They are an international brotherhood of masons that is the guardian of mysteries. You are in very good hands indeed."

Zadok proceeded to recite the prayer that ended dinner.

The guest and student decided that it was time to discuss his status as not so much a guest, but a student. "Now look, the two of you are doing so much for me that I would like to discuss payment to you."

Zadok waved a gnarled hand. "Wouldn't hear of it. Hospitality means everything in our land. But since you're our student we'll both be pleased to accept from you a book as a present at the end of your lessons, as is appropriate between teacher and pupil. That's all. What's most important is that we believe you're sincere and that you'll tell Rome the truth."

Uzziah suggested, "Go to bed now with one more Jesus

quote resounding in your ears: 'All that is hidden will be made manifest.'"

# V HANAN... THE GRACE

Theophilus slept as an honored guest on the flat roof of the little Jewish-Christian household, which was where a person could remain the coolest throughout the warm night. He was awakened in the morning by the sound of quarreling below him. He rose to see Zadok and Uzziah poring over their books and discussing something in excited guttural Aramaic. Several times he caught the Greek words "Dweller in the Crypt." An odd sobriquet for Jesus? wondered Theophilus. Or for himself?

Theophilus had found that he never tired of gazing out over the Sea of Galilee. He walked over to the spot where he had the best view. He immediately addressed Zadok when Zadok surprised Theophilus by walking over to join him in the viewing.

"I want to be sure that I've gotten all that I can out of Galilee before I leave the place. For instance, there remains the question of the town of Cana, where Jesus performed his first miracle. But I have a sneaking suspicion that you're going to tell me that Cana, too, is a purely mythical place, and I believe I know why."

"Then do tell, O harbinger."

"Well, I've found out a lot about the parallels between Jesus and the god Dionysus, especially when I was traveling through Asia, Syria, and Phoenicia. I discovered that Jesus' miracle at Cana, his turning of water into wine at a wedding, was a tale taken directly from a Dionysus rite of sacred marriage that was commonly celebrated at Sidon, even down to the exact wording of the tale. The setting was called Cana simply because the rite was a time-honored feature of life in the country of *Canaan*. The tale also adopted some language and motifs from the miracles of the Jewish prophet Elisha. But the main source of the tale was widespread mythology concerning Dionysus, a god whose temples at Andros and Elis and Teos each year *yielded wine instead of water*. A turning of the mundane into the wondrous! A fabulous story! A well-known myth like that simply had to be incorporated into the Jesus tales! And so it was indeed incorporated, as what's known as Jesus' first miracle: the turning of water into wine at the wedding at Cana."

"Right you are, my boy! You just summarized the essence of Jesus' miracle at Cana quite deftly! Now learn this one important thing. Maybe half of all of Jesus' miracles were written up so as to be miracles that echoed, yet superseded, the miracles of two much-admired Jewish wonderworkers: Elijah and his disciple Elisha. I believe that *all* of the stories of Jesus resurrecting a dead loved one were, in one way or another, based on the resurrections in the *Book of Kings* that were carried out by Elijah and Elisha. One of Jesus' resurrections was of the daughter of a man named Jairus, who was clearly a mythical character since the name Jairus meant 'he will awaken.' Jesus' healing of ten lepers was taken from Elisha's healing of just one leper, a leper named Naaman. It is quite telling that Jesus healed the ten lepers in the very same place where Elisha healed the one leper. Always Jesus had to be portrayed as outperforming Elisha. Elisha healed one leper, so Jesus healed ten! Jesus likewise outperformed Elisha when he fed a far larger multitude with far fewer loaves. Jesus fed not Elisha's paltry hundred people, but a multitude of thousands of people."

Theophilus was breathing heavily. "The famous loaves and the fishes by the Sea of Galilee. I may well never see this sea again, so I want to drink in the essence of it, as it were. Yes, there were allegedly still more Jesus miracles that occurred on this sea. I don't believe we've discussed them all. Do tell me about them now, in these final moments, won't you?"

"Very well. There is a psalm that sings of 'Those that go down to the sea in ships,' a phrase which is in Greek, '*Hoi katabainontes eis thalassan en ploios.*' In the psalm, the sea-goers become troubled and cry out to the Lord. One will find an echo of this psalm-episode in the gospels. In the gospels, people cry out to the Lord when the Sea of Galilee becomes stormy, so accordingly Jesus stills the waters. This shows that Jesus' powers are akin to the Lord's. As for Jesus walking on the water, in doing that he is once again showing that his powers are akin to the Lord's. That is because in the *Book of Job* the Lord himself walks on the sea. In Greek the words that describe the Lord walking on the sea in the *Book of Job* are: *'Peripaton epi tes thalasses.'* In the gospels Jesus does that walking on the sea *in exactly the same words!*"

"Well, whether or not any of those miracles actually happened, it seems to me that all of the Jesus miracles are accounted for as reflections of miracles that were performed by Israelite wonderworkers of old. Now, Zadok, please tell me if I am quoting correctly this snippet from Isaiah that previews many of the Jesus miracles. 'The eyes of the blind shall be opened and the ears of the deaf shall hear. Then shall the lame man leap as a hart... The dead shall rise, and they that are in the tombs shall be raised.'"

Zadok nodded. "Well done. Well done. You are able to correctly quote Isaiah. Theophilus, you'd do well to quote Isaiah over and over again, day and night, night and day. For a great deal of Jesus is in there, in that one book, the *Book of Isaiah*. Jesus is in there, the very Jesus that you are looking for. And always bear in mind that Isaiah was a *tradition* rather than a person. The *Book of Isaiah* was written over a period of some 200 years. Yes, it was a tradition rather than a person. The name 'Isaiah' means 'God's salvation,' exactly as does the name 'Jesus,' which was originally pronounced 'Yeshua.' And bear in mind that 'John,' or 'Yohanan' meaning 'Yahewh's grace,' is also not a man but a tradition. A tradition of grace. *'Hanan'* is 'grace.' I tell you that now because I know that the first place that you will be going to with Uzziah will be a place that pertains to the tradition of John." Then Zadok looked over to where Uzziah was preparing two donkeys for riding and two more donkeys for luggage. "And I see that you're just about to be on your way!"

The women of the household offered Theophilus a substantial package of tidbits to serve as breakfast and lunch to be eaten later on, as Zadok continued.

"I envy the two of you your ability to travel. You'll be wanting to get an early start. You'll leave most of your belongings here with me for the time being so that you can travel light."

"Why don't I just hire a carriage as I've usually done on this voyage?" asked Theophilus.

"Believe it or not, Roman roads don't yet go everywhere. You'll be needing donkeys to go to the place where Jesus came from."

"And that wasn't here in Galilee as everyone thinks?"

"No. Galilee was an embellishment to the life of Jesus. Mark wrote of a Jesus who lived in a nameless and timeless land, and when nowadays one looks inside the *Gospel of Mark* and sees specific mentions of Galilee a lot of what one sees is actually composed of later interpolations. Mark wrote quite vaguely about locales, and Mark's *seeming* to make Jesus a Galilean is mostly the work of later editors. But the main specialist in embellishments that made it seem as though Jesus came from Galilee was Matthew. After all, Matthew was writing for Antiochene refugees from the Jewish Revolt, and they mostly came from Galilee. All of the Jesus-embellishments make perfect sense if you look at them carefully. What's the geographical location of the Jews in their homeland? They live in Galilee and the Jerusalem area, with the Samaritans separating them in-between. So a potential messiah had better be born in the Jerusalem area and martyred in Jerusalem as well, but raised in Galilee, hadn't he?"

Theophilus nodded and looked at the donkeys. "All right. Very well. I'm beginning to have an inkling about what *wasn't* real in the story of Jesus. Now let's go see what *was* real! I used to think that Mark would prove to be the most reliable gospel writer because he was the earliest, but lately I've seen that misconception demolished. I should have known better. There was always so much evidence that Mark knew nothing about Judea, and that he may have done his writing as far west as Italy."

"Exactly so," confirmed Zadok. "It may be high time for you to forget Mark."

"And the same with Matthew?"

"Definitely forget him. He was more harmful than helpful. Just obsessed with making Jesus out to be a fulfillment of various old Jewish prophecies."

"What about Luke?"

Zadok paused but a moment. "Luke was a better writer than the others, but you certainly don't want to use *Luke* and *Acts* as the ultimate guidebooks to the life of Jesus that they were meant to be. The two Luke books are much better books than *Mark* and *Matthew*, but that only makes the Luke books all the more likely to lead you astray, strange to say. Eventually you'll see why those two books that began your quest, the two Luke books, are fatally flawed. There's much too much in them to talk about now. Suffice it to say, for now, that the Luke tales were a project of many hands with many different levels of skill. I've heard-tell that some 30 sources were used to compose the *Gospel of Luke* and the *Acts of the Apostles*! As glossy and captivating as the two works are, I can think of many examples of poor scholarship inside them. At one point in *Acts,* Peter proves his point to the Jews of Jerusalem by using a badly mistranslated passage from the Greek version of Jewish scripture in which the original Hebrew means something else altogether. And James' supposed speech in *Acts* uses a scriptural quote that was just as badly mistranslated. But why worry about these details? The fancy Luke books may serve well for others. You can do a lot better than them. You might as well throw away your scrolls of *Matthew*, *Mark* and *Luke* and save your pack animals the unnecessary weight in the future. I'll dispose of them while they're here with me, if you like."

"No thank you!" declared Theophilus with force. "But what about the *Gospel of John*?"

"Ah, now you're talking!" exclaimed Zadok, rubbing his hands together and enjoying Theophilus' look of utter astonishment. Uzziah was motioning to get the journey started, so Theophilus mounted a donkey during his next statement.

"Zadok, are you telling me that you approve of only the *latest* of the major gospels!? Zadok, you must be joking!" Theophilus reflected a moment. "Ah, but John's gospel is the gospel that has Jesus *spending almost no time in Galilee and doing almost all of his preaching in and around Jerusalem*! Now tell me: what is it about the *Gospel of John* that…"

There would be no completion of the question and no reply. Uzziah was whacking the donkeys to begin the journey. Zadok emitted a merry, "You're in good hands with Uzziah!" and waved goodbye.

Donkeys were slow. Theophilus knew that there was a strong possibility that he would never see Zadok again. He hoped for more words from him, and knew that out of respect for the man's age he would have to leave "the last word" to him.

Those presumed last words from Zadok came as a distinct surprise.

"And always bear in mind that when Jesus enlisted his first disciples down there on the lake, the wording in the gospels makes it clear that Andrew, alias *Anthropos,* was all people! *All people!*"

Now Theophilus had to raise his voice considerably to address Zadok, with little hope that the old man would hear.

"You know, I completely forgot to discuss with you all that I learned while I was up there among the fishermen in Capernaum! I spoke with a marvelous Roman officer named Michael who knew about all kinds of things that you wouldn't expect from such a man!"

Surprisingly, Zadok heard what Theophilus said. And surprisingly, cupping his hands over his mouth he was also able to make a reply endowed with impressive volume.

"I heard all about that Capernaum conversation of yours with a Roman officer, Theophilus! It reminded me of your improbable psalm-singing on the road! People told me all about that, and they thought that you were quite out of your mind! *Twice recently* you were out of your mind! A Roman officer who wore white, and *glowed with a strange light,* and was named Michael! You must be joking! Really! *Of course* there was no such person there conversing with you in Capernaum!"

Theophilus indicated to Uzziah that he wanted to turn back and discuss this queer matter, but Uzziah displayed nothing but determination to keep the little donkey caravan going.

Theophilus yelled, "I don't grasp what you're saying, Zadok! So who was this Michael fellow then?"

"Zadok yelled, "'Mi-ka-el' means 'who is like God'! Michael is the patron archangel of the Jewish people! You were speaking with the patron archangel of the Jewish people!"

"You can't be serious! I spoke with *a man*! He said he was a surveyor!"

Through cupped hands came Zadok's loud words, "Yes, of course he was a surveyor, you dolt! The Archangel Michael permanently surveys all the world, and is the guardian of the world's mystic energies and currents!" Then Zadok hollered a few last words to Theophilus. "Didn't this Michael of yours remain standing, never sitting down?"

And Theophilus hollered the last words that were audible to Zadok. "Yes, he was always standing! I did find that rather odd!"

Now the two men were almost too far apart for any hope of a shouted conversation. Zadok shook his head and looked down, and spoke mostly to himself. "Angels cannot sit, they only stand! They only stand! Ah, Theophilus, you have a lot to learn. A lot to learn."

Theophilus strained "to have ears to hear," and was just able to make out the last words that he would ever hear from Zadok, alias Justus of Tiberias.

Zadok shook his head again. "Ah, my dear Theophilus. Angels only stand! They only stand!"

# VI MIDBAR… THE DESERT

The Roman and the Jew headed south on their donkeys, in search of Jesus. At first they conversed amiably, a development which gratified Theophilus mightily, seeing as he had high hopes for the long journey ahead to be both pleasant and productive. But Uzziah virtually snarled at Theophilus as they passed the Roman stadium of Tiberias.

"The Romans slaughtered thousands of Jews in that stadium. That was before they decided to decorate their wonderful Roman roads with *crucifixions* of Jews, so that their barbarity could be on display to even more people. As you must be aware, Jews inhabit two distinct segments of what is loosely called Judea. Vespasian managed the slaughter of Jewish rebels here in Galilee, and like a good father he apprenticed his son Titus to do the same work in the other Jewish region: traditional Judea that surrounds Jerusalem."

"I hope Titus was a little more reasonable than his father," offered Theophilus weakly. "Vespasian was known to be both stern and ambitious, but Titus had the reputation of a very sweet-tempered man."

"It would have greatly interested the thousands that he crucified to hear that," sneered Uzziah.

Theophilus started to make a reply but stopped himself. He wanted to relate something that he had read: how Titus had taken down three of the Jews he was crucifying at the request of a friend, and how when given the very best medical care one of those unfortunates had actually survived. And he wanted to relate another incident that was well known. This was an incident of 188 years before, when one of the Jews' last kings, Alexander Jannaeus, crucified 800 of his fellow Jews while they were forced to watch the throat-slitting of their wives and children, all while hosting a drinking party and cavorting with concubines. Theophilus wanted to say that the world's problems were attributable not to the flaws of particular ethnic groups, but to the hardness of human hearts in general. And he wanted to say that that was the very core of Jesus' message. But he stopped himself and listened instead.

He listened while Uzziah related how he had personally witnessed the horrors of the suppression of the Jewish Revolt as a young boy. After he had talked about the experience for awhile he seemed to have relieved himself somewhat of a burden. Theophilus then learned that Uzziah was one of countless thousands of children who were orphaned in the revolt. Zadok was not his real father, but only a kindly stranger who took him in and trained him as a scribe. "Uzziah" meant "the strength of Yahweh," and was the sort of name that the Jewish people needed in that trying time.

"A scribe was really something back in the days before I was born, so I've been told. And Judea was paradise before the Romans came to pillage. Why in those days..."

Theophilus had long ago grown accustomed to closing down his auditory system when various "good old days" stories came along. Such stories seemed as innate to the human condition as fistfights. Everyone was trying to return to the Promised Land. It occurred to Theophilus, as he swayed on his donkey, that he himself was doing more or less the same.

Uzziah directed the donkeys to rough paths and made them climb and climb. He explained why.

"One last thing before we leave Galilee. We're going to climb to a great height in order to see something at a great distance, something that lies to the west. I want you to see Galilee's largest city, Sepphoris, off in the distance." He chuckled, and surprised Theophilus quite a lot by doing so. "I know you think I'm obsessed by the notion of Roman power gripping my land. Well, I think that with one last observation of that notion I'll be able to let the obsession go for a time. Behold! Look over there! Now we can see Sepphoris!"

At a distance, Theophilus was indeed able to see a great city on a hill. Apropos of it he pontificated a bit. "Well, that city may have been *exactly* what Jesus had in mind when he declared, in the Sermon on the Mount, that a city on a hill cannot be hidden. I suppose that Sepphoris was Jesus' idea of grandeur, with him being just a country lad. Sepphoris does, in truth, look pretty grand."

"Yes, I suppose that Sepphoris may well have been Jesus' inspiration for the phrase, 'a city on a hill cannot be hidden.' Not many cities are perched up high like that, so prettily. Sepphoris is perched up there like a pretty bird, and the name Sepphoris actually came from the Hebrew word *Zipporah,* meaning 'bird.' Josephus called Sepphoris 'the ornament of all Galilee,' and he *would* do that, after all, because he was the greatest pro-Roman Jewish turncoat that ever lived. Sepphoris was always as Roman as Roman could be. Herod Antipas used it as his capital before he built Tiberias. Sepphoris sided with Rome during the Jewish Revolt, and prospered greatly thereby. It became Rome's garrison city in the north. It was always Rome's bastard stepchild. It's completely imitation-Roman, with frescos, pillars, paving stones, and a whole lot of marble, rather the cheapest sort of marble as I recall. There's even a little theater, for acrobats, pantomimes, farces, and so on."

"Hmm," hummed Theophilus. "Jesus liked to hobnob with society's rejects, but I don't think he'd ever have gone *that* far! Acrobats and clowns!"

"There are rather worse rejects than acrobats and clowns living up there in Sepphoris, as far as I'm concerned! After the fall of Jerusalem the Romans allowed a few of the most subservient of the Jews of Judea to live up there and form a new Sanhedrin. And those Jews composed the Mishnah, which was a new religious text for a new breed of subservient rabbi. Maybe you know the difference between the Mishnah and the Midrash, or maybe you don't. The Midrash is a book of legends which loosely parallels the narrative in the Torah. In contrast, the Mishnah is strictly philosophy that is systematized in a fully Greek way, namely by subject matter. Sepphoris was so explicitly designed to forced Hellenization and Romanization down the throats of the Jews that it went through several official names that expressed exactly that process. First it was named Autocratis, then Imperatoria, then Dio-Ceasarea, and for a little while it was even named after Nero. A place can hardly sound more Roman than that! Well, I've made my point. I don't ever want to enter that city again. I don't even want to ever look at it from a distance again. Let's move on."

"One question before we go, Uzziah. You mentioned that Sepphoris is Rome's garrison city in the north. I've heard that there's another Roman garrison in Galilee, stationed at Armageddon. It's Legion VI Ferrata, the so-called Ironsides, a gang with a particularly grim reputation."

"Yes, sometimes you really know how to get me riled up! Armageddon is the ancient city of Megiddo, sometimes called 'Har Megiddo,' meaning 'Mount Megiddo.' That hill has always been a meeting place for armies and battles, and 'Megiddo' even means 'meeting place.' Megiddo lies way out there to the southwest, too far away to be seen from here. Yes, Legion VI Ferrata, the damned Ironsides, is stationed there, like a great rusty iron instrument ready at any moment to torture Judea. They have a particularly brutal reputation, so thanks a lot for mentioning them. Now let's move on."

The pair reached the River Jordan, which provided both a blessedly cooling midday resting place, and, further down, a pleasant overnight campsite. The next day Uzziah pointed out several places where John the Baptist had baptized in this pleasant, languid winding stream that was lined with its own miniature jungle.

Inspired by his liking for the River Jordan, Uzziah felt discursive.

"Rivalry was extreme between John the Baptist and Jesus, you know. "I don't mean between the two men, though. The rivalry existed between followers of the martyr John and the followers of the martyr Jesus. In the gospels you can see how the matter was eventually settled. John the Baptist declares that he's only a forerunner of someone greater than himself, someone whose sandal laces he's unfit to untie. Luke was not keen on Jewish traditions, so he made John the Baptist subservient to Jesus even in the womb, right at the beginning of his gospel! So John the Baptist has found his place. But his real place, and that of Jesus, is a place we will reach in not too many days."

They turned east, and in time reached a rise where they had a magnificent view of the endless brown hills of the desert to the east.

"A man feels close to God in such a place," Uzziah assured him. "In the desert. The *midbar!*"

"I've never seen a desert before. It's quite a compelling sight, really. By the gods, it truly is. Silently, the desert makes such a massive statement. 'I'm huge. I'm my own thing. I don't serve people. You can't bend me to your will! No, never!' I've heard of the tradition that in the desert one finds spirituality. Here Jewish holy hermits always came to be tempted by the devil and reject him. As did Jesus himself."

"Yes. It's God's place."

"Who else would want it?" Theophilus muttered, inaudibly, out of caution that Uzziah might by offended by inadequate respect for the *midbar*. He was becoming exhausted but he was not so exhausted as to be unappreciative of the desert's stark beauty. As they ventured further into the desert they were surrounded by reddish buttes and crags that jutted into an azure sky. That was all. Here nature's specialty was large-scale understatement.

Theophilus commented, "I've read that the philosopher Anaxagoras believed that the sun was actually a great fireball even larger than all of Greece."

"Somehow I find that remarkably uninteresting."

The travelers rested in some rare shade during the worst heat of the day, then pressed on.

"No, I've never been in a desert before," repeated Theophilus. "I'm so glad that this is one adventure I won't miss in my life. The sheer size of the desert is appalling. Does anyone know how far this desert extends?"

"This desert is harsh and unforgiving, but since time immemorial people have crossed it in all directions. It's home to Bedouins who don't find it inhospitable, but instead know it well, and love it. Those Bedouins are the Edomites of scripture, named for the redness of this land. Nowadays they're called by a different pronunciation of the same name, Idumaeans, and farther south they merge with related Bedouin people who are called Nabataeans and Arabs. As one proceeds much farther south the desert land is known as Arabia. Arabia stretches southward on and on and on. If one travels in a caravan to the end of massive Arabia, one comes to a well-watered paradise-land where baby Jesus' precious gifts of frankincense and myrrh are cultivated. Many adventurous Roman merchants have gone that far, and they named the place Arabia Felix, 'Arabia the Happy.' But to reach Arabia Felix one must travel far, and I mean really far. As far in yonder direction as Rome lies in the opposite direction."

Theophilus took a deep breath of the furnace's dry air. God's works were awesome.

Time stretched out like the desert. At times Uzziah became verbose to pass the time.

"I've heard that Arabia is mostly extremely barren, and is rich only in a few scattered places that God has favored with oases. Frankincense is so valuable that it gave rise to a myth of a vastly wealthy Arabia Felix. And that myth gave rise to an actual failed Roman invasion of Arabia. Ha! Imagine the Romans failing to conquer a land, and hightailing it out of there in their proud legionnaire thousands, dying of thirst! Me, I love to imagine that! The most favored part of Arabia is known as Yemen, and that name means 'favored,' and is a name that became Eudaemon in Greek and Felix in Latin. Frankincense is a brilliant white gum that is referred to as 'the pearls of the desert.' It drips from short prickly trees, filling the air with sweetness. That is when Arabia Felix really does seem to live up to the name Arabia Felix! It's a fabulous aroma that aroma of frankincense! The Arabs make frankincense into round cakes and transport those cakes by camel to Gaza. From there, the frankincense, as valuable as gold, is distributed worldwide to the wealthiest people of the world. Even more expensive is myrrh, derived from a thorny bush. Myrrh is less well known, and is used for embalming and as an ingredient in purported cure-alls. It spoke volumes about Jesus' preciousness to state that as a baby he was worthy of these three most precious gifts: frankincense, myrrh, and gold."

"Are there Jews and Christians in Arabia? What are the beliefs of the people down there?"

"Jews, yes. Christians, no. The complete lack of Christians would certainly explain the fact that Paul spent three years down in Arabia, and afterward never had anything at all to say about what he did while down there. As for me, I never took an interest in the gods of the Arabs. I do know that they have one main shrine, at the oasis of Mecca, which means 'shrine.' The Mecca shrine was placed where a stone fell from the sky, and that magical stone is still there, so I've heard. Inside the shrine there stand 360 idols, obviously one for each day of the year, and that's quite a few. Above all in Mecca, they worship three goddesses who are reminiscent of the Greeks' sacred threesome: the Virgin, the Matron, and the Crone."

Uzziah felt like lecturing at length at times, and this one was one such time.

"Long ago the Israelites came out of the desert to claim a

better land, a land flowing with Milk and Honey. That land was Canaan, which now goes under the name Judea or Palestine. The land of Canaan became the Israelites' land, but the gods of Canaan were not for them. Most of Jewish history describes the struggle to cast the statues of those alien gods down from their high places forever. Idols exactly like the idols in Mecca. The Jews brought with them from the desert the One True God. The *midbar* gave them the passionate conviction that there was One True God."

"I'm certainly willing to believe that the desert is the birthplace of monotheism," mused Theophilus. "No streams, no trees, no places to hide. This does not seem to be the kind of place that gods lay claim to little pieces of."

"I'm told that the tribes who live here consider only the god who brings *rain* to be a god worthy of worship."

"I'll worship him! I'll worship him!" croaked Theophilus through cracked lips.

"Yes, out here even a Roman is convinced. Imagine how it is for a Jew! Here in the desert we find our roots, Theophilus. This is where we come to find our God. Paul spent three years in Arabia, and seemingly never mentioned what he did there. Ha! Imagine that! *Paul* remaining silent! Paul who could never stop talking!"

At one point Uzziah stunned Theophilus by displaying a merry mood for a while, and then suggesting that they play a game to pass the time. "I promised to instruct you, and now I shall, in a manner that just came to me as an inspiration. I feel the spirit of Moses all around me here in this desert. It would behoove you to realize that Matthew constructed much of his gospel by having Jesus imitate Moses and supersede him at every turn. So here's what we'll do. I will mention an incident in the Torah. Then you will guess the Moses incident that Jesus mirrored, as that particular Jesus action appears in the *Gospel of Matthew*."

"An excellent idea. I'm ready when you are."

Uzziah began.

Uzziah: "In Torah. The prophet Joseph brings the Israelites to Egypt."

Theophilus: "In Matthew. The carpenter Joseph brings the Holy Family to Egypt."

Uzziah: "In Torah. The Pharaoh massacres boys. He commands that every Hebrew boy be thrown into the Nile. But he fails to kill Moses"

Theophilus: "In Matthew. King Herod massacres boys. Every newborn. But he fails to kill Jesus"

Uzziah: "In Torah. The Lord says to Moses in Midian, 'All the men are dead which sought your life.'"

Theophilus: "In Matthew. An angel tells the Holy Family in Egypt, 'They are all dead which sought the young child's life.'"

Uzziah: "In Torah. The Israelites go from Egypt to Israel."

Theophilus: "In Matthew. The Holy Family goes from Egypt to Israel."

Uzziah: "In Torah. The Israelites pass through the waters of the Red Sea."

Theophilus. "In Matthew. Hmm. I suppose the parallel is

Jesus passing through the waters of baptism."

Uzziah: "In Torah. The Israelites wander in the wilderness for 40 years, eating manna instead of bread. Says Deuteronomy, 'Man does not live by bread alone, but by every word that comes from the mouth of the Lord.'"

Theophilus. "In Matthew. Jesus is alone in the wilderness for 40 days, tempted by an offer to live on bread rather than on holy grace. Satan offers to transform stones, like these stones lying all around us here, into bread to assuage Jesus' hunger. Jesus' response is, 'For it is written that man does not live by bread alone, but by every word that comes from the mouth of the Lord."

Uzziah: "In Torah. The phrase 'Do not tempt God.'"

Theophilus: " In Matthew. The phrase 'Do not tempt God.'"

Uzziah: "In Torah. It is demanded: 'Worship only God.' Not the Golden Calf when it beckons."

Theophilus: "In Matthew. It is demanded: 'Worship only God.' Not Satan when he beckons. 'For it is written, 'You must worship the Lord your God and serve only him.''"

Uzziah: "In Torah. God gives the law to Moses 50 days after the first Passover.

Theophilus: "In Matthew. Hmm. Well, that giving of the law in the Torah would correspond with the Christians' Pentecost, which means '50' in Greek. Pentecost occurred 50 days after the Crucifixion. The correspondence with Torah would be that God gave mankind a new law, namely Christianity, 50 days after the first occurrence of the *Christian version* of the Passover, which was

Christ's Passion. Well, well, I actually just thought up that explanation for the invention of Pentecost, quite extemporaneously!"

"Yes, according to Luke in *Acts,* 50 days after the crucifixion God came as a whirlwind and entered the room in Jerusalem where the apostles were celebrating the Feast of Weeks, which was the Jews' celebration of Moses' giving of the law. God filled the room with fiery spirit, and the apostles began to 'speak in tongues,' meaning that they were inspired to chant in many different languages, astounding themselves. That exploit of theirs was a clear indication that the message of Jesus was meant to be propagated to all people the world over. And the entire incident was a clear indication that the Feast of Weeks was to be replaced by a new Christian holiday called Pentecost."

Theophilus mulled over what to say about Pentecost, and then mulled some more, for a very long time. Time seemed to be endowed with a tinge of sultry sluggishness in the desert.

"That incident of the Pentecost whirlwind and the 'tongues of fire,' taking place in crowded Jerusalem among old friends during an ancient festival. Hmm. That, and especially all the excited babbling makes me wonder. You know, that's all spirituality of a sort, but it all seems diametrically opposed to the spirituality of the desert. Here everything is so silently awesome and pure. When I was in Patmos I locked myself up in without any sort stimulation whatsoever, for nine days, and I found the experience to be most purifying. I wonder if I could benefit from spending a similar purification time in the desert."

"Most assuredly."

Theophilus continued, "But Jesus' time of 40 days in the desert is a most remarkable period of time. If he really did not eat during that time, then he did a fast that was at the absolute maximum achievable for the human body. That would demonstrate that his spirituality was absolutely of the highest sort."

"Most assuredly."

"And Jesus did what miracle-men and shamans all over the world do. They spend a long period of time alone in the wilderness, facing dangers, temptations, and themselves. That would be a typical beginning of the career of a healer and magician, a *pharmakos.*"

"You would know more about that than I would."

The men and donkeys plodded on. There came a time when Theophilus' burning ears detected a slight sound on the hot wind that wafted through all of this silent enormity. It was a tinkling sound. Presently the men caught sight of the source of the sound. It was a caravan in the distance. A line of camels was doggedly bobbing and striding. Their little bells made a charming sound. Coming closer, Theophilus could see that their look was charming too. They bore decorations of many colors, on their bodies, their saddles, and their loads. Their Arab riders wore clothes of many colors too, reminding Theophilus of the tale of the Arabs who took into slavery "Joseph of the coat of many colors."

Uzziah directed his own little caravan to the larger one. For some reason he felt confident that these particular caravan riders presented no danger. Through their black beards came smiles and gentle conversation. Uzziah brought his own little donkey caravan alongside the camel caravan, to travel with it for a time, and he chatted with the Arabs at intervals, to pass that wide-open desert time. As for Theophilus, he got into the rhythm of this near-silent procession and enjoyed his prolonged exposure to this bit of oriental exotica.

That night at the two men's campsite Uzziah showed Theophilus several white nuggets in the palm of his hand. He had purchased a small amount of frankincense from the caravan. Huddled by their little campfire, Uzziah lit the frankincense in a small bowl and waved the bottom of his robe to disperse the white smoke that it made."

"The aroma does indeed mesmerize a bit, doesn't it?" assessed Theophilus.

"I'd say it's a way of breathing-in the essence of Arabia. To Jews, barren Arabia is the somewhat ill-regarded land of Abraham's rejected illegitimate son Ishmael, the founder of the Arab race. But to those in the know, the story goes much deeper than that. They say that Arabia was once the Garden of Eden. The land has several ancient trees that are locally regarded as the Tree of Life, and there's also a town called Aden, which is just an alternate pronunciation of Eden. Moreover, Eve is said to lie in a tomb in Arabia, more precisely in Jeddah, a port whose name means 'grandmother.' Eve is called 'the Mother of All.' And then there's Lilith, after whom was named the Red Sea port of Eilat. 'Eve' meant 'life,' but 'Lilith' meant 'night.' Lilith was the 'night wife' or 'dream wife' of Adam. Lilith insisted on sexual intercourse exclusively *with her on top*, and there were also other ways in which she refused to be subordinate to Adam. So he abandoned her. Now Lilith lives on as a lone wandering spirit that is opposed to man's rules and man's civilization, a spirit devoted to death-throes and sexual abandon, a spirit who will come to a man in the night to seduce him away from decency."

"Now mysterious Arabia does indeed begin to intrigue!" interrupted Theophilus.

"Yes, Arabia is a land that does draw one in. You, for one, have begun to admire its sensuality, I see! The story goes that long ago God turned that land of Arabia barren in order to punish mankind for having become evil, in that mankind had become devoted to sensuality. In a way, then, Arabia represents mankind's suppressed sensuality. Ah, frankincense! Ah, Arabia of the nighttime demon goddess Lilith! Arabia the wasteland that somehow manages to defy God, and push up, through its sandy soil, all of that frankincense and myrrh! The Queen of Sheba is a spirit that rules Arabia, since she, too, is 'the Mother of All.' She stood for all that was nature-loving and sensual, so it was inevitable that legend would have her going on a memorable state visit to King Solomon, who stood for all that was sly and intellectual. And that makes me curious, Theophilus. Since you seem to enjoy learning through being tested: Do you know what mention Jesus once made of the Queen of Sheba?"

"Yes," came the reply." The episode is in *Matthew*. One day Jesus was feeling frustrated that the Israelites were not recognizing him as their true king. I suppose he was wondering why some Judeans would not travel the short distance to see him, so he mentioned how long a distance the 'Queen of the South,' meaning the Queen of Sheba, once traveled to see King Solomon. And then he dared to add, concerning himself, 'And someone greater than Solomon is here'!"

The next day, another hot trek in the sun had Theophilus remembering Jesus' brief encounter with the memory of the Queen of Sheba.

"Once again I've received a helpful taste of the life of Jesus. One day, Jesus made a comment about how far the Queen of Sheba traveled to meet with King Solomon, and everyone who was listening to him knew exactly what he meant. Apparently Jesus, and his listeners too, had an inkling of just how endless is travel inside Arabia. And now I too have an inkling of just how endless is travel inside Arabia!"

At this, Uzziah laughed far more heartily than Theophilus had ever seen him laugh before.

"O man of the Roman Empire! O man of the city! O man of luxury! You have absolutely no idea what a journey through the endless *midbar* really means! If someday you consult a map and see how ridiculously little terrain you and I have covered through this desert you'll be absolutely flabbergasted! Caravans trudge through this desert for weeks, or even months, at a time! You have no idea of this land's immensity, no idea at all! I wanted to give you just a little taste of it, and you've just had exactly that! A very little taste! But all along I've been playing a bit of a trick on you. All along we've been a duo of meek cowards who have been trekking quite close to a Roman road, a finely paved example of *your* world of Roman ease and modernity! That road is the Via Regia that goes straight down towards the heart of Arabia. We'll get to that road soon, and then your absurdly minor desert travail will be over! I'll take you swiftly down the Via Regia, and then we'll make a right turn back into Judea, just north of the Dead Sea."

Uzziah was as good as his word. Soon they were making good time down Rome's impressive desert-defying Via Regia, and there remained for them only one more night to camp out in the desert.

Theophilus watched Uzziah recite his sundown prayers, and upon seeing that he had concluded his prayer remarked, "It's a joy to listen to Hebrew, really. It's recognizably similar to Aramaic, but so much more sonorous. More like something that God what would want to listen to."

Uzziah smiled. "Hebrew has often been justly described as *fiery*."

"I wonder if language might be a clue, among many other clues, that people used to be far more godly in centuries past than they are nowadays. Hebrew is sonorous, while its offspring Aramaic sounds quite bland. Similarly, Homeric Greek is sonorous, while its offspring, the Greek of today, sounds quite bland."

"Well then, my friend, do recite for me a bit of Homeric Greek so that I can judge. That would be quite an appropriate amusement for an evening around a campfire, I would say."

Theophilus informed, "It's said that the very best reciters of Homer are to be found in Ephesus. I spent some time there, and I would agree. Imagine: they can even earn a living at it! In the marketplace, reciters of the Iliad wear red to represent warfare, and reciters of the Odyssey wear blue to represent the sea. I'm fed up with the idea of warfare. Therefore, I will recite for you the opening lines of the Odyssey. Singing of the clever man, and so forth!"

Theophilus stood by the fire to light up his face theatrically and made his recitation. That recitation lit up Uzziah's face in a way different from the way the fire lit it. The sing-song recitation echoed in the ears of the pair for a while, even seeming to echo off the darkening hills as well, before Theophilus broke the silence."

"You know, I think I'll treat you to another recitation. Reciting seems to be a nice addition to our final night under the stars. Very few people can do what I'm about to do. I'm going to recite to you something from a language that is as ancient as Hebrew and Homeric Greek. I'm going to recite something in Etruscan."

That rather somewhat bizarre-sounding recitation now rang off the hills. Etruscan did not seem to belong there. Theophilus mentioned that no one knew where the Etruscan language had come from. Then Uzziah made his critique.

"Hmm. I think tonight's point is made. As far as I'm

concerned the ancient languages had something that we can't quite put our finger on. We can't accurately say why, but they do sound to me like languages of people who were much closer to God. I'm glad that Hebrew is a large part of my life. Now for a good sleep. We've enjoyed lullabies with God!"

Theophilus expected to experience a different sort of sleep during this final night under the stars, and that did indeed come to pass.

Desert nights belonged to Lilith. Lilith came to Theophilus in a dream.

Lilith was by no means as dark as night, but she was dark. Her eyes blazed, and were dark. The most notable thing about her, at Theophilus' surprised first glance, was her extremely long black hair, because she was swishing that hair about provocatively as she danced, in a manner far more skillful than anything Theophilus had ever seen. And she knew how to gyrate her hips in in her dance so enticingly that it immediately occurred to Theophilus that she was the very inventor of enticing dance. She kept her hands behind her neck, all the better to display her perfect breasts and shake them in a perfect manner. She wore scant stringy garments that gleamed, but she stripped those garments from her writhing body in a manner that Theophilus had seen done many times before, but never done so well.

Lilith announced her identity by playfully mouthing "Lilith!" again and again with her darting tongue. Now Theophilus believed he was witnessing a dance by the very progenitor of seduction. He was developing an erection, and Lilith fixed her blazing eyes on that growing object and made it plain that she was offering her tongue as an aid to its progress in tumescence.

The dream goddess moved closer. She placed her long fingers in the darkness of her lower body's hair, and hummed singsong sounds of pleasure, and thrashed her tongue around ever faster, all the while still visibly offering that tongue to Theophilus.

"I will mount you now, beloved. I will mount you now, beloved. Now. Now." Lilith was speaking to Theophilus now without really speaking genuine words.

Then he heard other words. Genuine words.

"Get up now. Just get up now. Come on, now."

These were words from Uzziah. Theophilus awoke. Uzziah was shaking him awake. Now there was only Uzziah. There was no more Lilith.

Theophilus looked around, and saw everywhere the striking redness of a desert dawn.

"Oh, by the gods, that was one Hades of an encounter with a goddess!" he exclaimed.

"Yes, I know, I know. Lilith. You were with Lilith. It's good that we're getting you out of the desert now. Jesus was here in the desert and resisted temptations for 40 days. As for *you*, I don't know if *you* would even last for the time it takes a camel to emit four turds! Yes, better for us to head back into the Holy Land, *right now!*"

Theophilus decided not to ask Uzziah how he knew that there had been a visit by Lilith. He watched in silence as Uzziah reached into packs and took out their last desert breakfast. It was very much a desert breakfast, consisting solely of dates, but plenty of dates.

After breakfast, they did not need to walk long before they observed from a hilltop the very best geographical feature that could have punctuated the end of their sojourn in the land of the lost.

Theophilus spoke the obvious when he saw the distant long string of bluishness in the brownness of the desert.

"The Dead Sea."

The lifeless, worthless, joyless salt sea seemed like an exclamation point set in place to emphasize the scene of desolation.

"The Dead Sea covers the long-dead sin-cities known as Sodom and Gomorrah," informed Uzziah," cities that were violently destroyed by God for their wicked ways. What could be more appropriate than for the Dead Sea to be those cities' tomb? That sea is sheer death and hellishness, after all. But hail to you, O sea of death and hellishness! For you welcome us back to the Holy Land!

# VII ESSENES… THE HEALERS

"And now comes the time to tell you about one of the holiest bits of terrain in the Holy Land. That's the terrain we'll be passing through now."

Thus did Uzziah begin his exposition on an area that he called "Bethany beyond the Jordan."

"Once my father mentioned to you this area, which we call 'Bethany beyond the Jordan.' Look over there and see where the Jordan River finalizes its existence in an odd way, by pouring its luscious sweet water, to be shamefully wasted, into the salty Dead Sea. The symbolism seems ill, but nonetheless the site is holy. And the site was holy long before it became the traditional site of John's baptism of Jesus. The site was holy because of two mighty scenes that took place there centuries before the time of John and Jesus. Firstly, 'Bethany beyond the Jordan' was the place where Joshua assumed leadership of the Israelites as they crossed into the Promised Land. And secondly, it was the place where Elijah ascended to heaven in a Chariot of Fire. We can't precisely pinpoint the sites of these events anymore. But be aware that we're walking on very holy ground, even if we're *anywhere* near those holy places that commemorate Joshua and Elijah."

Asked Theophilus, "Might I venture a guess? You say that this spot is holy because here Joshua assumed leadership of the Israelites. I wonder if Jesus' baptism story is associated with this spot because here his ministry truly *began*. It began with that baptism. Here, with that baptism, Jesus assumed leadership of the Israelites, in reflection of the way Joshua assumed leadership of the Israelites. And it's interesting that 'Joshua' and 'Jesus' are just two forms of the same name. This spot assumed extreme importance the moment that the Holy Spirit descended on Jesus in the form of a dove, and God told him, 'This is my son in whom I am well pleased.'"

"Your guess is an excellent one. Yes, Jesus assumed command of the Israelites in the same spot where Joshua assumed command of the Israelites. Yes, I like that. By the way, that statement by God at Jesus' baptism echoed God's statement in a psalm that was addressed to any newly enthroned king. 'You are my son. Today I have begotten you.' The title 'Son of God' was an important one. But Jesus was by no means the only 'Son of God.' Many people who were especially favored by God were called a Son of God on account of that favor."

Next, Uzziah led Theophilus to a height where the two of them could enjoy a full view of the small brown oasis town of Jericho. Theophilus knew something about this community and was quick to say so. He was tired of only listening, and was in a mood to do a bit of lecturing himself.

"Fabled Jericho! Jericho the splendidly ancient desert oasis! It's known as Hierichous, on Roman maps. It's the luxuriant town of eternal palm-filled summer, where King Herod built himself a magnificent palace where he could escape the bite of winter. I do believe that even from up here I can pick out that palace of Herod's, though it looks as though upkeep on the place has been rather meagre since Herod's time. What surprises me is that many of the other houses in Jericho look virtually palatial too."

Uzziah explained. "King Herod wasn't the only extremely wealthy person who wintered in this land of southern Judea, which, in good times, is definitely a Land of Milk and Honey. It has always been the case that many other wealthy men besides Herod have built fine winter homes in Jericho. Many who can afford it come here to enjoy a winter of languid, pleasant luxury amid the palms. This is the region of Sodom and Gomorrah, you know, and Jericho bears some resemblance to those two immoral cities. Jericho has always stood for selfish human indulgence in sin and materialism. Maybe that characteristic of the town has something to do with the fact that the very name 'Jericho' connotes the sensuality of the moon. Do you know how the symbolism of Jericho works? Notorious Jericho's walls come tumbling down, in a metaphorical sense, as soon as one has attained a countervailing taste for spirituality. Then stone topples! Then spirituality prevails!"

"Well, that certainly is a fascinating interpretation of the legend of Joshua making the walls of Jericho come tumbling down!" allowed Theophilus.

"When Jesus was in Jericho he stayed at the house of a certain Zacchaeus, who was a tax collector. He stayed with that particular man in order to emphasize, as adamantly as possible, that he was on a mission to address *sinners*. For who was a better example of a sinner than a tax collector? In Jesus' time those people were particularly rapacious and despised. Zacchaeus was a Roman dupe, and a sinner, and a tax collector, living in Jericho, a city exceeded only by Sodom and Gomorrah as 'the city of sin'! And it was emphasized that Zacchaeus was a particularly small man. I think that one can read that description of him as small as a symbolic statement of materialistic inclination too. For why else would a gospel writer bother to mention the man's size? Moreover, Jesus was on a mission to address the spiritually *blind*. So for that reason, while Jesus was here in Jericho he healed Bartimaeus. a blind beggar."

Theophilus inquired, "Do you think it possible that Bartimaeus was a fictional character? I have thought so because 'Bartimaeus' means 'son of Timaeus,' and *Timaeus* was Plato's most mystical book, the one which talked about the Demiurge, the moon-ruler and the crude ruler of the material earth."

"That's an interesting hypothesis, but the fact is that 'Bartimaeus' is traceable to Aramaic for 'son of filth.' To put it less delicately, one might well say that 'Bartimaeus' really means 'stinky'! That certainly would have been a fitting name for an actual beggar! But I surmise that this fellow Bartimaeus did indeed exist only as a symbol. I surmise that he was invented as a symbol of how the lowly material world, as represented by that damned city of Jericho, is *filthy* and *stinks!* And is *blind!* Jericho represents the lowly material world, so its denizens according to Christian lore were Zacchaeus the small and sinful man, and Bartimaeus the blind and smelly man. And to further emphasize Jericho's role as a seat of materialism, the gospels described how when Jesus finally went to Jerusalem to meet his end in the Passion, the walk that he took was, precisely, *the walk from Jericho to Jerusalem! The walk from Jericho to Jerusalem!* That was a highly meaningful itinerary! From the most lowly to the most heavenly!"

"Is there any reason for us to go into Jericho to inspect it," asked Theophilus.

"No. We won't go into Jericho. As Mark said, in his strange clipped way, 'And they came to Jericho; and as they went out of Jericho...etcetera.'! Ha! As far as Jericho was concerned, Jesus just came and went in an instant! I don't like the place. Just like Jesus didn't like the place. No. Jericho makes me feel *queasy*. Today I'm going to take you to an entirely different Jesus-place that always makes me feel *sanctified*. We're going to go to Qumran."

Theophilus offered, "I've seen some texts that add the words that are usually missing in that strange Mark passage that you just mentioned. The full text reads, 'And they came to Jericho and the sister of the young man whom Jesus loved was there, along with his mother and Salome, but Jesus refused to see them. And as they went out of Jericho, etcetera.' What do you suppose that strange little episode in Jericho meant, and why was it destined to be excised from most texts of *Mark*?"

"That may become apparent later on," replied Uzziah mysteriously.

Soon they were in Qumran, a semi-arid hilltop ruin near the Dead Sea, which, on Theophilus' close inspection, looked like a long-abandoned fort. A layer of ashes that appeared fresh in the crisp desert air seemed to confirm the supposition.

"This too was the Romans' work, these ashes I mean." Uzziah's old snarl had crept back into his voice. "During the Jewish Revolt the Romans wrought their customary complete destruction here, even though there had been no revolt here at all, and there was therefore no justification at all for repression. This was nothing but a home of peaceful holy hermits."

Theophilus' throat was becoming dryer than ever. He believed he could scarcely speak. "Is... Is this Jesus' place? Finally? Jesus' place?"

Uzziah lumbered slowly among wrecked walls and dug here and there in the ashes. He discovered a Roman arrowhead, inspected it, and hurled it off the hill. Then he returned to the ashes.

"Yes. This is Jesus' place. And the Baptist's. Perhaps it would have been mine as well, but I was born too late. Come. I'll show you what once existed here."

Uzziah apparently knew Qumran well. He pointed out the settlement's perimeter and asked, "Have you heard of the Essenes?"

"Yes. I've read about them in Josephus and Philo and Pliny. I was beginning to suspect that this place you've brought me to was the home of the Essenes."

"Yes. This was their home. The Essenes. The 'healers.' They were so named not so much for what they could do for bodies as what they could do for souls. Sadducees ruled the Temple, collected tribute, genuflected before their Roman masters, lived in luxury, and scoffed at the masses. Oblivion is their reward. Pharisees told men that salvation could be theirs through unstinting observance of the law. They have survived. And now they're constructing a second Mount Sinai of laws. They're doing so at Tiberias and Babylon, by writing a Talmud. But then there were the Essenes. They were the Jews who returned to the desert to find their God!"

"Do Essenes still exist?"

"They are of yesterday, Theophilus, they are of yesterday. Perhaps they managed to hide some of their writings from the Romans in the hills. But they do live right here!" Uzziah pounded his chest. "They live here in my heart, and in many other hearts! Good men came here to live in blissful isolation from the wicked world. They have their reward now, I'm sure, and they've left something for all of the rest of us as well."

Uzziah proceeded to describe how the all-male monastic community of Qumran had been set up. Central to the design was an elaborate system of cisterns that had been fed by an aqueduct that led from cisterns in the mountains.

"You can still see how Qumran was crisscrossed by pools,

channels and cisterns. Healing water. Purifying water. The stuff of life. Essenes practiced full immersion baptism, for the purpose of full purification from sin. I don't believe that baptism was ever something that was *invented*. No, it was never invented. Surely some form of baptism has always existed as long as humans have existed. Essenes practiced baptism for the sake of purity, and they dressed in white to emphasize their purity."

Uzziah guided Theophilus through the remains of the Essenes' scriptorium, kitchen, pottery factory, assembly rooms, and laundry. He proclaimed, "The Essenes had all that they needed, and they honored God by not craving more. Jesus blessed 'those who are poor in spirit' because the people who are the most blessed are those who accept poverty for the spirit's sake. That's what's meant by that somewhat confusing phrase 'the poor in spirit.'"

Uzziah explained the Qumran community's hierarchy. "A so-called Teacher of Righteousness was the leader, assisted by a Council of Twelve. Two further titles of officers were 'overseer' and 'elder.' The Greek forms of those two words are *episkopos* and *presbyter*. Now I have heard that the Christians use those two terms rather haphazardly and interchangeably as 'bishop' and 'priest.'"

Uzziah ambled along further, picked at the ashes, thought, and spoke earnestly. "I could talk to you for days about the Essenes, but I'd best tell you only a little now. And it's best that at this point you ask me no questions. Here, new initiates received a new robe of purest white. This should bring to mind Jesus at his Transfiguration. Here, light versus darkness and the existence of a Wellspring of Life were the central themes of preaching. Of great importance here was the all-male ritual meal that observed a strict seating order, a meal which you will find in *Luke*. Here, a messiah was foreseen, and he was to preside at a banquet where ritual sacrifice would be reinstated."

Theophilus was swallowing hard. "You're pressing me, Uzziah. I want to drink from this 'Wellspring of Life,' and you keep me thirsty with tiny drops of dew. But all right. I'll trust you and not ask any questions. Nonetheless, I can make a statement. Jesus was a man like others! He couldn't have been *born* here in this all-male hermitage! And I don't think it's likely that he *died* here! So in what way was this Jesus's place?"

"You'll drink your fill from the wellspring when we go to the place where Jesus *did* die! Oh, and one more thing. You'll hear most people refer to this place as Sekhakha. Qumran is the special holy name for the place. Qumran means 'arched doorway.' Such an arch is a thing of reverence to us masons. It is reminiscent of the vault of the heavens, and of the human skull, and of much more. The Jerusalem Temple was fronted by two great pillars. And a concept called 'Shalom,' 'Heavenly Peace,' was considered the sacred Keystone that could unite those pillars."

"Wasn't the Temple's centerpiece an Ark rather than an arch? And wasn't Jesus sentenced to die at the Temple? And didn't he die at the Place of the Skull?"

"Onward."

As the men and their donkeys climbed out of the furnace that was the Dead Sea region, Theophilus noted, "You've led me from Galilee to the environs of Jerusalem on a very indirect route that bypassed Samaria. Did you do that on purpose or not?"

"We Jews avoid Samaria as a matter of course, to avoid trouble. Between Jews and Samaritans there is mostly just trouble. But you raise the question at the perfect time. Jesus, a person much better than you or I, made a point of traveling through Samaria and talking with the Samaritans, things which Jews would normally not do. He did this because his message was universal love. Jesus' parable in *Luke* about the Good Samaritan makes the point memorably. This story took place *on this very road!* It took place on this arid and difficult road between Jericho and Jerusalem! In the story, bandits attacked and robbed a Jew, and left him for dead by the road. Many other travelers passed by the helpless man. Only a Samaritan was good-hearted enough to help the man. Even though Jews and Samaritans were supposed to be sworn enemies. Jesus taught a whole new relationship among human beings. Ah, look now Theophilus! Perhaps guided by the angels of Israel we have just now come to a well! That's our signal to discuss another of Jesus' encounters with Samaritans."

The men watered themselves and their donkeys at this well that blessed an otherwise barren terrain. One of the things that this journey was teaching Theophilus, through experience, was how wells were automatically supremely blessed objects in this part of the world. He voiced this observation and went on to say, "Let me guess. I believe you're finding our arrival at this well fortuitous because we were just discussing Samaritans, and Jesus had an important encounter with a Samaritan woman *at a well*!"

"Precisely. Let's slake our thirst for insight here at this auspicious setting, this well. Jesus had his encounter with a Samaritan woman not by just any well, but by a specific venerated ancient well: the well of the prophet Jacob. This well was located at the center of the land of the Samaritans. And the center of the land of the Samaritans was a place where Jesus, almost alone among Jews, was brave enough to travel. There at Jacob's sacred well, Jesus asked a Samaritan woman to draw water for him, and she could not believe her ears, because Jews were usually so antagonistic towards Samaritans. But she drew water for him, and he thereupon promised her that the water that he would draw for her, *in return*, would be the very water of the divine! He was promising that all who drew from that promised wellspring of the divine would find bliss within 'the brotherhood and the sisterhood of the divine.' He was talking about very deep wells indeed! The Samaritan woman could hardly believe the extent of those wells' profundity!"

"I'll conjecture now that it's a matter of cosmic waters, like the cosmic waters involved at Jesus' baptism."

"Yes. To be sure. Now, be aware that Jesus' well-scene in Samaria existed within an old tradition encompassing many other scriptural well-scenes. This scenario was always a scriptural staple: a divinely-inspired man meeting a divinely-inspired woman at a sacred well. I'll give you the four main examples of this timeworn scenario. Abraham's servant and Rebecca... at a well. Jacob and

Rachel… at a well. Moses and Zipporah… at a well. Elijah and the widow of Sarepta… at a well. The same story kept repeating itself. Here's the heart of that story: *A young hero journeys to a foreign land and finds sustenance at a well*! Hah, I can see *you* in this tale, my young friend! At the well, the young man asks an unmarried local woman for a drink. But it quickly turns out that *it is the young woman who is really in need of sustenance!* At this point, the young man turns out to be a great prophet who is capable of providing unending sustenance. In Jesus' case, he offers the Samaritan woman a spring 'always welling up for eternal life.' The woman is amazed at the prophet's insight about her, and certifies him as a true prophet, in the hallowed tradition of well-scene prophets who have come before."

Theophilus nodded enough times to certify that he had absorbed the meaning of the hoary story of the well, and then had something to add. "I seem to recall that the Samaritan woman at the well declared that she and Jesus could have nothing in common, because he worshipped in Jerusalem, and she, as a Samaritan did not."

"Precisely. Now onward to Jerusalem to see what *that's* all about!"

# VIII DEBIR... THE ORACLE

Now Uzziah explained the significance of Jerusalem. He maintained that merely approaching the most holy of cities instilled a quickening into his blood. The Temple, or nowadays the bare plateau where the Temple had previously stood, was everything to the Jews. To them the world was a set of concentric circles of decreasing holiness. At the center was the Temple's Holy of Holies, whose name, *debir*, indicated that it must once have been an oracle. Next came the Court of Priests, then the Court of Israelites, then the Court of Women, then the Court of Gentiles, then the rest of Jerusalem, then the rest of the Promised Land, and finally all the rest of the world. Such a compacting of holiness in Jerusalem was enough to explain Uzziah's excitement at nearing the place.

The travelers were now leaving barren terrain behind them. As they entered once again the Land of Milk and Honey, there was, once again, as had been the case days before in Galilee, actual milk and honey to be had. And in addition to the milk and honey there were lovely vineyards full of grapes.

Uzziah clarified the matter of the grapes.

"Those who have worked with grapes know the hard truth about this wonderful fruit. The hard truth is that grapes require a truly enormous amount of care. Tender loving care. That was why Jesus could make a cogent point by saying, 'I am the vine.' The vine is the indispensable *parent* of the grapes, so by saying that he was the vine he identified himself as *the provider of infinite tender loving care for all mankind!*"

Theophilus nodded, and then observed, "Now, in this marvelous Land of Milk and Honey, we're among not only vines, but also fig trees. Why on earth did Jesus, the provider of tender loving care, actually *curse* a fig tree at one point?"

"Someone who really knew Judea well must have written that parable about Jesus and the fig tree. It's odd, because that parable was incorporated into the Jesus story by gospel writers who often demonstrated that they hardly knew Judea at all. A fig tree is a plant which, at the right time of year, puts out an abundance of beautiful, shapely dark green leaves, making itself look as though it is bearing much fruit. But at that time of year the fig tree is just a *deceiver*; for in fact, it is *not* bearing any fruit at all! So you can now see the whole point of the Jesus-and-the-fig-tree story. Jesus was cursing a plant that had a reputation for being *hypocritical*! This statement was Jesus' subtle way of cursing *the priesthood of Jerusalem*, which was outwardly so finely-attired and holy, but inwardly so totally worthless! On another occasion Jesus compared such rubbish-people to tombs which were whitewashed on the outside but full of corruption on the inside. It's a shame that these statements by Jesus are likely to be nothing but a source of confusion to people who have no familiarity with things like Judean agriculture or Judean tombs!"

Theophilus commented, "I'm equally confused by Jesus' other mention of a fig tree. There were two of Jesus' twelve apostles who were close friends, and who were usually together. They were Philip and Nathaniel. Philip brought Nathaniel to Jesus, upon which Jesus said to Nathaniel, 'Before Philip called you when you were under the fig tree, I saw you.' What was that all about?"

Uzziah's response was, "Jesus was using a Jewish figure of speech when he said that. The phrase 'sitting under the fig tree' meant that Nathaniel was a man who studied Torah. Jesus also called that fellow Nathaniel a 'true unimpeachable Israelite.' Quite a fine character this Nathaniel must have been to have received such praise from Jesus! Yet he has thoroughly disappeared from people's memories! Too bad. Nathaniel never managed to have many stories built around him. Nathaniel stood in contrast, a sort of Hebraic contrast, to his friend Philip, who, with his Greek name, was the most *gentile* of the apostles. He was a Jew, as were all of the apostles, but he was the one among the Twelve Apostles who was the most gentile. The tales of Philip's later worldwide travels confirmed that gentile nature. Nathaniel was the apostle who quipped, 'Can anything good come out of Nazareth?' Which was odd, since he himself was from Bethsaida, meaning 'fishing camp' or 'hunting camp,' which was really a way of saying 'any old place.'

Nathaniel seems to have been a personification of the 'salt-of-the-earth' average Israelite, and that stands to reason because he seems to have been the same character as the apostle Bartholomew, whose name meant 'plowman.' I wonder if the gospel character Nathaniel was meant to echo the Torah personage called Nathan. In the *Book of Samuel,* the prophet Nathan had his big moment when he explained to King David that as soon as he became king he also became a Son of Yahweh. Jesus was supposed to be a King of Israel and a Son of Yahweh, just as was David. So it's small wonder that Jesus obtained his own echo-version of Nathan, namely his apostle named Nathaniel!"

"So Nathaniel had to do with Jesus; appeal to the Jews, while Philip had to do with Jesus' appeal to the gentiles. I guess it makes some sense for these two apostles to be presented as pals. Very Jewish indeed are these stories. It seems to me that everything about Jesus was an inevitable circling-in on Jerusalem, for a divinely-ordained mighty climax, a climax as the King of Israel and the Messiah."

"You are correct. It was exactly so."

Soon a Roman military presence became apparent along the road that the travelers were using. Since the crushing of the Jewish Revolt, the Tenth Legion had occupied the district around Jerusalem, and a praetorian legate of that legion was in place to uphold martial law. A Roman's traveling into this district with a Jew aroused some suspicions, but that particular Roman's imperial letter worked wonders in turning suspicion into hospitality. Theophilus made no attempt to hide the fact that to him a Roman military presence was reassuring. Uzziah, meanwhile, looked as though he would have preferred a nest of scorpions.

The mismatched pair rode into Bethlehem, a sleepy suburb of Jerusalem that had lost its "mother city," Jerusalem, and therefore slumbered all the more. Theophilus brushed away some flies and inspected the perfectly ordinary collection of square earthen huts. Uzziah showed every sign of intending to simply ride through the town and ignore it.

"Obviously I'll be wanting to tarry here in Bethlehem and discuss the place!" declared Theophilus. "I'm here to research the life of Jesus, after all!"

Promised Uzziah, "We'll make a stop here after we've visited Jerusalem. For now we'll just take a brief look at the place. I have my reasons for doing our itinerary in such a way."

Theophilus experienced an odd feeling. Outwardly, Bethlehem seemed to have nothing to offer. Yet he felt pulled towards it, and kept gazing at it longingly as they began to pass it by. "Might you at least have *something* to tell me about Bethlehem now?" he asked Uzziah.

"Certainly. I'll tell you quite a lot in fact. Our nation's traditions have long predicted the coming of a 'Messiah ben Joseph' and a 'Messiah ben David': a messiah who is a son of Joseph and a messiah who is a son of David. Jesus was made into a son of Joseph by the simple naming of a name: Joseph, the purported adoptive father of Jesus. And Matthew's elaborate genealogy demonstrated

Jesus' descent from David. And note that Jesus is supposed to have begun his messianic career at the age of thirty, exactly as did King David and the patriarch Joseph. Now then... Messiah ben Joseph is to gather the lost tribes of Israel and march on Jerusalem against the heathen, and there he will save the people of God with his spilled blood. Then the world is to be ruled by Messiah ben David, lord of New Jerusalem. Here you see clearly the need for both a martyrdom and a 'second coming' in Christian scripture. But for the moment let's concentrate on Jesus' purported adoptive father, Joseph."

"You say 'purported.' So this elderly carpenter named Joseph who married Mary did not exist?"

"No. He was a necessary manufacture. And a clever composite. Consider the carpenter Joseph's legendary inspiration, the original Joseph who is found in the Torah. This was the prophet Joseph who organized his twelve brothers, the twelve sons of Jacob, and was, thus, the organizer of the Twelve Tribes of Israel. The story of Potiphar's wife showed this Torah-man Joseph to be a model of chastity. Exactly such a model of chastity was the carpenter Joseph who married Mary and yet allowed her to remain a virgin. Crucial to the story of the first Joseph was the fact that he was a Master of Dreams. That mastery eventually made him the master of Egypt. Look at the meager plot lines in the gospels involving the second Joseph, the stepfather of Jesus, and you'll see that he was the same: a Master of Dreams."

"Yes, quite so! A dream instructed Joseph to flee with Mary and baby Jesus into Egypt!" recalled Theophilus.

"Yes. That happened so that there could be fulfilled a prophecy from the prophet Hosea in which God said, 'Out of Egypt I have called my son.' Prophecy fulfillment: that was perennially the gospel writers' task! Luckily for those who want to understand the process, Matthew liked to explicitly quote such Torah prophecies in his gospel. He did so, for instance, with the prophecy that prompted him to fabricate the tale of Herod slaughtering the Jewish infants. And if you like Luke's touch about Jesus being born in a stable, then you must, as so often, thank Isaiah. Isaiah said that an ox and a donkey recognized the Lord but Israel did not. Moreover, Isaiah was responsible for the most important tale concerning Jesus' birth."

"The virgin birth tale?"

"Yes," concurred Uzziah. "No virgin birth ever took place here in Bethlehem or anywhere else. But Isaiah said, 'Behold a young woman will conceive and bear a son, and shall call him Immanuel.' Matthew, steeped in the Septuagint as he was, accepted the Greek mistranslation *parthenos* for the Hebrew *alma*, thus transforming Isaiah's 'young woman' into a virgin. So Matthew's convoluted storytelling made a virgin conceive miraculously, though Isaiah's prophecy had indicated nothing of the kind. Isaiah originally meant to refer to the speed with which God's help would arrive in the contemporary situation. In other words, *a woman not yet married* would eventually be naming her son Immanuel, meaning 'God is with us.' This second name for Jesus, Immanuel, exists, but for some reason is hardly ever used."

"Then Mary too is a fiction?"

"You haven't earned the right to conclude that yet. There's much more to Mary. There are many more Marys. They'll be waiting for us in Jerusalem.

"Ah, yes. Many Marys. Mary Magdalene. And Mary the mother of Jesus. And certain other Marys who add a lot of confusion to the tale. And somewhere around here there also lived Mary the sister of Lazarus."

"Yes Mary's and Lazarus's town, Bethany, is not far away from here. But like Bethlehem, Bethany is a place which we'll visit *after* we have visited Jerusalem, and where we'll conduct a thorough study of many things of great interest. For now, as I've been so fond of saying for a while now: Onward! One's blood has to quicken in one's veins now! Now I can see in the distance what remains of dear holy Jerusalem!"

# IX MIKDASH... THE TEMPLE

Uzziah seemed to want to wrap himself in Holy Scripture as he passed the multitudes of legionnaires who so prominently polluted the holy district, holy Jerusalem. Indeed, one feature of these troops' presence was unexpectedly disconcerting: the soldiers who had obliterated the holiest city on earth were now stationed all around that city displaying banners of the Tenth Legion. So everywhere there glittered the Roman numeral X. That omnipresent numeral X seemed to symbolize a crass Roman crossing-out of Jerusalem.

Throughout the two-man journey Uzziah, originally quite brusque, had become more loquacious. But today something inside him needed to burst forth. Today would be a day when he would speak like a Noah flood.

"Isaiah was the favored prophet at Qumran. Shortly, I'll be quoting you a great deal concerning a certain man whose coming was predicted by Isaiah. This man was called the Man of Sorrows. The Man of Sorrows was despised, yet carried our human sorrows and bore our human grief. And he was bruised for our iniquities, and saw to it that with his wounds we are all healed. In Luke's *Acts of the Apostles* you can find confirmation that Jesus was none other than this Man of Sorrows, the very figure who was continually mentioned by Isaiah. You may recall that because of something that was predicted by the prophet Zechariah, the Man of Sorrows entered Jerusalem, well, much like the two of us: 'mounted on an ass, and on a colt, the foal of an ass.' I believe that Jesus entered Jerusalem mounted on a donkey because all Judean kings did *exactly that* as part of their coronation ceremony. And because of a passage in one of the psalms that they loved to sing at Qumran, the Man of Sorrows entered Jerusalem surrounded by crowds who were *waving palms*. Today we'll do without people waving palms at us. And we'll do largely without any people at all for that matter! Since Jerusalem is now not a city but a ruin. There's hardly anyone here to sing out to us that word that came from the same psalm that the palms came from: the word 'Hosanna!' We're not Jesus, after all. The word was ideal for Jesus. 'Hosanna' was literally 'Yahweh save us,' and, after all, 'Jesus' was literally 'Yahweh saves.'"

The four-donkey expedition arrived at the crest of a hill and Uzziah pointed down. He announced, "We'll scope out Jerusalem from here atop Mount Scopus. There it is at last: Jerusalem!" His every syllable echoed with sadness. Theophilus was appalled. He could discern no holy city, nor any city at all, but only a few more of the familiar tan, rock-strewn, scrub-covered hills of Judea, plus a few barely-intact tumbledown buildings that were overshadowed by omnipresent ruins. Overshadowing all, however, there stood a curiously enormous man-made plateau.

"Most visitors can't believe this place was ever a great city," Uzziah told Theophilus, leading him to the shade of a lone tree. "Let's sit here. Let's sit silently for a few moments and think about what man does to man. Then I'll tell you all about the Jerusalem of old."

Theophilus stared, unbelieving, at the near-wasteland where one of the world's most famous cities had stood just thirty years previously. Only one thing in the dusty-dreary environment was notable. But that one thing was extremely notable. It was that enormous plateau, the Temple Mount. Theophilus knew that this was the massive foundation that Herod built to hold one of the largest constructions of all time. Upon completion, that construction, the Temple of Jerusalem, was four times the size of Athens' Acropolis. The mammoth foundation of that-which-once-was still hulked over the scene. Admiring that bare platform for its sheer hugeness, Theophilus could well understand Josephus' rapturous description of the Temple that had once stood there: "immense, incredible, amazing," and "the most spectacular creation ever achieved by the hand of man." Even curmudgeonly Tacitus had called the Temple "more remarkable than any other human work." Josephus wrote that from a distance the Temple looked like a snowcapped mountain tinged with gold. According to a much-repeated story, when Titus razed Jerusalem he left completely intact only the impressive Temple Mount, expressly in order to make known to future generations that a great city had really once stood here, a city which had been completely destroyed because it had dared to defy mighty Rome.

Then Theophilus noticed that he was at risk of missing much valuable information while in a rapture. Uzziah was making good his promise to tell all.

"Jerusalem in its heyday, the Jerusalem I knew thirty years ago, was one of the largest cities in the world, with a population of some 100,000. In addition to that huge number, some 100,000 more people would pour into the city during each of the pilgrimage festivals. They say that during those festivals there was hardly a language of the world that could not be heard spoken in Jerusalem. They say that the Temple was the greatest edifice on earth because it needed to accommodate more people than anyplace else on earth ever needed to accommodate. You might well wonder how our now-somewhat-desolate Judea could support so many people and such a grand construction project."

"True. I'm wondering."

"Well, part of the answer lay in the vast income that Judea took in from Jews from all over the world, Jews who paid a Temple tax and also came here on pilgrimage and spent freely. But King Herod's Judea was a notably prosperous place even aside from that tremendous pilgrimage income. Horrible though Herod was, his realm knew an unprecedented prosperity under his rule. Roman rule had just united the world, and Judea enjoyed fabulous prosperity based on its centrality in the world's freshly-founded trade in luxury goods. Judea acted as a central entrepot in the luxury goods trade, including, interestingly, items like gold, frankincense, and myrrh. And Judea itself produced many luxury goods in plantations that were newly established near the Jordan River: herbs, spices, scents, medicines, balms, fish sauce, olives, figs, and the world's best dates.

"Nowadays the Temple Mount dominates ruined Jerusalem, just as it used to dominate Jerusalem when the city was a thriving metropolis. That one small but long hill that you see over there at the southeast corner of the Temple Mount, that hill called Ophel, made up the entirety of the small ancient Jerusalem of David and Solomon. Ophel brought Jerusalem into existence, because Ophel contained the region's only source of water: the Gihon Spring, the spring that fills the Pool of Siloam. Ophel led up to the highest point in Jerusalem, where, naturally, David and Solomon built their royal palace and Solomon built the First Temple. All of that is well known. But in the past century the upheaval involved in the construction of the Temple Mount wiped out the original look of the original Jerusalem. Herod constructed that huge Temple Mount as a base for one of the most prodigious feats of architecture of all time: the Second Temple, or Herod's Temple, which is usually referred to as simply 'the Temple.'

"Herod was a despicable tyrant, but he gave the Jews the most impressive of all the world's temples. I wish there were a way I could convey to you its splendor. Yes, I saw it as a boy; one of my fondest memories. To behold the Temple was the highlight of the life of a Jew. A splendiferous highlight. The one and only story the gospels tell about the childhood of Jesus concerned one of his visits to the Temple. His parents thought he was lost, and when they finally found him they found that he was amazing elders in the Temple with his wisdom. And at that point he told his worried parents, 'Didn't you know that I would be in my Father's house?' The Temple shone with light of white and gold like a vision of heaven itself. From some perspectives it could have been mistaken for a snowcapped mountain. I'll be a living wonder if I grow very old: I'll be one of the last of the Jews to have laid eyes on the Temple, the great *Mikdash!*"

"Did you see the inside of the Temple as well?"

"Yes, and more than you yourself would have ever been allowed to see, my friend. You, nosy though you may be, would have had to content yourself with seeing the enormous outer courtyard where access was allowed to gentiles. Logically enough, it was called the Court of Gentiles. There, sacrificial animals were sold and money was changed. The gates to the inner courts bore warnings that gentiles who tried to enter the inner courts would be executed, and even the Roman governor respected that rule. Beyond those gates was the Court of Women, an area of moderate size which was as far as Jewish women were allowed to go. Beyond another set of gates was the narrow Court of Israelites. That was as far as I myself could ever go. That narrow space was where the sacrifices took place, on a high square altar of sacrifices on the left, while a chorus of priests sang like angels atop a platform on the right.

"If one was a male Jew, and therefore privileged enough to

be present in the Court of Israelites, one would behold, at center, the grand bejeweled gates that shut in the highest and most holy site in Jerusalem. That site was the Sanctuary, the *Hekal*. This Sanctuary was the great white-and-gold building, facing the sunrise in the east, that was accessible only to priests. The Sanctuary or *Hekal* was the Temple proper, and was said to be modeled on Solomon's original First Temple. Within that *Hekal* were the golden candelabrum, or menorah, and the golden table that held 'showbread.' These were among the objects which thirty years ago the Romans stole and carried to Rome in triumph. And at the rear of the *Hekal* behind a fabulous high veil was the small square room called the Holy of Holies, which was entered only by the High Priest, and only on one day a year, Yom Kippur."

Theophilus squelched his urge to inform Uzziah that he, as a casual Roman tourist, had once strolled inside Vespasian's temple in Rome and viewed the golden menorah and golden table, the very objects that had previously been denied to Uzziah and nearly every other Jew as too sacred to behold. Theophilus did not want to mention that these items had become curios for the delectation of visitors to Rome, and had thusly become desecrated in the eyes' of Jews. Instead of offending Uzziah in this way he asked, "Where was the place where Jesus drove the moneychangers from the Temple?"

"Imagine an enormously long building that ran along the entire length of the southern end of the Temple Mount. That was the Grand Portico. The Grand Portico was an exceptionally long version of a typical multi-columned Greco-Roman basilica, a place for the conduct of a city's most important business. One could enter that place from Jerusalem's busiest street, at the southwest corner of the Temple Mount, on an overpass which happened to be supported by the largest arch ever constructed. Besides being exceptionally long, the Grand Portico had columns that were so wide that three men could barely join hands around them. A person generally entered the Temple not via that southwest corner overpass, but via an extremely broad staircase that fronted the Grand Portico. That very broad staircase was for entering the Temple grounds, and there was another narrower staircase for exiting."

"So if one wanted to very definitely follow in the footsteps of Jesus the ruins of those staircases would be the place."

"You might say that." Uzziah seemed eager to move on to other subjects. "In the Grand Portico's lower levels, and spilling out into the Courtyard of the Gentiles, were the moneychangers and their caged sacrificial animals that were for sale. The underground animal caverns were huge. It's still possible to explore them. I tell you truly that in this world very quickly, very quickly, truth tends to be forgotten. That being the case, I've heard that some people now mistakenly refer to the still-extant sacrificial-animal caverns as Solomon's Stables. Now, having heard all this, you can visualize Jesus' enraged driving of the moneychangers from the Temple. That would have been the act that would have meant execution for him. The moneychangers were very controversial. Jews came as pilgrims from all over the world to make their offerings at the Temple, thousands upon thousands of them. Only a special Temple coin was permitted as an offering, so changing pilgrims' coinage was an important ongoing business. And the business of selling sacrificial beasts was even more lucrative. The poor would usually buy a dove to send to sacrifice, and those who were a bit more well-off would usually buy a goat for the same purpose. The din and clatter of moneychangers and animal sellers was incredible, and, to many, it was also horribly unseemly. One can well imagine Jesus being so offended that he would commit violence, for the one and only time ever recorded. A place of so very many wonders, in so very many ways, was that Temple. So much confusion and commotion. Yet the very purpose of the almost continuous sacrifices was to bestow peace and order on the world! This is, after all, Jerusalem, Ur-Salem, the Place of Peace!"

Uzziah looked distant and dreamy, as though something vital had just occurred to him that had never occurred to him before. When he spoke on, his voice sounded very much like the voice of a prophet.

"Hmm. Animals and commerce. Commerce and animals. Such was the vast subterranean labyrinth of the Grand Portico, much like a *kataluma*, the animal-filled cellar where Jesus was supposed to have been born. And such was the vast courtyard that adjoined the Grand Portico. A model of the world itself, that's what it all was! It's well known that the holy Temple precincts were a model of the Garden of Eden. In the first book of the Torah, God placed cherubim east of Eden to guard the Tree of Life, and for that reason cherubim were decorative motifs all over the Temple, along with innumerable plants. In the *Letter to the Hebrews* the Temple is called 'a shadow of good things to come' and 'a picture of the true.' It was, you see, a model of life. Such was this Temple with its innumerable underground chambers with innumerable mysteries. It was the *Mikdash,* the 'place made holy.' Within the Sanctuary or *Hekal* a great veil hid the Holy of Holies, in imitation of the veil that obscures from us the origins of life. When Jesus died that veil supposedly ripped of its own accord. *Suddenly there was no more veil!*

"Beneath the Holy of Holies was said to be the foundation stone, the very spot around which the material world was constructed. That stone held down the waters that flooded the world in Noah's time. Interestingly, beneath the Temple there were vast networks of cisterns to supply the large amount of water used in the Temple for ritual purposes. And the foundation stone was the stone upon which Abraham made ready to sacrifice Isaac. It was always said that at the end of time the dead will awake from the grave and look towards the site of the Temple from across the Valley of Kidron, also known as the Valley of Jehoshaphat which means 'God judges.' Then the Messiah will enter the Temple in triumph through the Eastern Gate, also known as the Golden Gate, the gate that led directly to the Sanctuary entrance and which let in the sunrise. Then the Temple will not be like other structures, for it will have windows that will allow light to shine *out*! The Temple will then have a light that will shine *out,* yes! For at that time there will have returned to Jerusalem the object that was missing from Herod's Temple, the Ark of the Covenant!"

"And what will that mean?"

Uzziah seemed go into a trance, and then to come out of it in an instant. "Ah, enough for now. These tales could go on endlessly. The Temple is involved with so many symbols. Did I say *many* symbols? I should say *all* of the symbols that exist, really!"

"It's almost beyond belief that so grand a structure could perish so utterly," said Theophilus. "It really makes you wonder."

"Rome was determined to leave nothing here. Rome's patience with Jews was at an end. Even in the best of times when the Temple was at the height of its greatness a cohort of Roman soldiers hovered over us Jews, waiting for trouble. Those soldiers were ensconced in the Fortress Antonia which sat like a great square tumor over in that far northwest corner of the Temple courtyard. The Romans insisted on keeping the Temple's vestments and ornaments there in the Fortress Antonia when they were not in use, and they even controlled the Temple's water supply, much of which was to be found in the Struthian pools. Beyond the remains of the Fortress Antonia you can see the remains of the five porticoes that surrounded the the Pool of Bethesda, whose name means 'House of Healing.' According to John's gospel, in that pool Jesus healed a man who had been loitering around the healing pool for 38 years because he was paralytic. Supposedly, the Holy Spirit descended suddenly and unpredictably on the Pool of Bethesda from time to time, and whoever plunged into it first, at such a time, was instantly healed of any ailment. The poor paralytic, crippled as he was, never managed to be that first person. So Jesus took pity on him and healed him. Because Jesus had the audacity to perform that healing on the Sabbath, right then and there the religious authorities decided to kill him. That tale of John's about the Pool of Bethesda directly parallels a tale in the *Book of Kings,* wherein the authorities decided to kill a prophet for having the audacity to heal on the Sabbath. Realize how tense were the politics of the time, and how small a thing could set off disturbances. There in the Fortress Antonia the Roman procurator and his cohort of legionnaires sat during every pilgrim festival, brooding over the Temple, alert for any disturbances."

"Is that where Pilate would have tried Jesus?"

"No, not there. Let me direct your attention to the other side of the city, the western side, the side occupied by the city's wealthy inhabitants. It was also known as the Upper City. That western side received all of Jerusalem's fresh air. The poverty-stricken Lower City in the southeast consisted of valleys and alleys that received the city's runoff water and the accompanying waste. And the Lower City had the ever-burning waste dump called Gehenna, which became a synonym for Hell. In the remains of the Upper City you can see a series of three tall military towers that the Romans have left standing for their own use. Those three towers are all that remains of Herod's great Jerusalem palace. After Herod's death the Romans converted that edifice into a palace for their procurator or praetor, calling it the Praetorium. There in the Praetorium, Pilate would have judged Jesus in a hall called the Stone Pavement. That whole quarter of the city, the Upper City, the quarter for the administrators and the wealthy, was readily distinguishable by its many fine white houses with bright red roofs. Jerusalem in those days had many, many wealthy citizens. You can still see outlines of the intricate halls and baths that they built for themselves.

"Literally a stone's throw away from Herod's palace which became the Romans' Praetorium you can still see the outlines of what was a massive rectangular house fronted by a massive rectangular courtyard. That was the High Priest's House, where the High Priest Caiaphas would have tried Jesus. That thoroughly vile and thoroughly despised Caiaphas lasted longer in office than any other High Priest, because he somehow found ways to get along with that thoroughly vile and thoroughly despised Pilate. It was in Caiaphas's courtyard that Peter skulked around, not daring to go inside to witness whatever confrontation Jesus was having with Caiaphas. There, bystanders questioned Peter because he was skulking, and in frustration he denied Jesus three times, in synchronization with a cock that was crowing three times. A cock symbolized self-centeredness, of course. Peter was showing himself to be guilty of this self-centeredness at the most crucial time when self-centeredness should have been discarded. The 'cock crow' was also a way of describing the three trumpet blasts that signaled the beginning of the Temple's liturgical day. The gospels were making the point that Peter represented the beginning of *an entirely new liturgy!* One of the many things that a cock can symbolize is the first 'dawning' of spiritual consciousness."

Asked Theophilus, "Would the Sanhedrin have tried Jesus in

Caiaphas's house?"

"No. The Sanhedrin would have tried Jesus in their meeting hall that was part of the Grand Portico. The Sanhedrin met in a chamber called the Chamber of Hewn Stone. Their number was supposed to remain limited to an astrologically auspicious 70. They met sitting around a large semi-circle that was half on holy ground and half on profane ground. The Sanhedrin has a terrible reputation nowadays owing to the Jesus episode. However the Sanhedrin actually operated nobly, with some excellent safeguards. They convened in a semicircle so that all members could see all other members. Students and disciples sat opposite the members of the Sanhedrin. The youngest members of the Sanhedrin voted first, so as to avoid their feeling pressured as to how to vote. One secretary recorded for the defense, and another secretary recorded for the prosecution. Another excellent custom was that any liberation of a prisoner was immediate, while any execution of a prisoner had to wait for the next day.

"But we're getting ahead of ourselves with Jesus' trial. Let me tell you more about the Temple. 'Vanity of vanities, all is vanity,' say the scriptures. The Temple was completed in all its details just in time for its destruction, thirty years ago. In fact, the sudden surge in unemployment that came with the end of construction played a role in aggravating the fatal political situation that led to disaster. Tensions were so bad that anything could have set off the conflagration. You've heard about the incident that started all the trouble, the incident of the Greek youths in Caesarea who taunted the Jews by sacrificing a cock in front of their synagogue. But more important than that nonsense was the corruption of the procurator Florus. Florus illegally appropriated money from the Temple, so to take a stab at him jokesters went around with a begging basket requesting money for him. He was not amused at those antics, and he demanded that the jokey culprits be produced. But they were not produced. One thing led to another, and before long the Temple priests expressed their displeasure at Rome by halting sacrifices to the Emperor. That was the crucial misstep. In the eyes of the Romans, that misstep amounted to treason and a declaration of war. You can see how insipid little things that are piled up one upon another can lead to a cataclysm!

"So things began as simply idiotic, as the ill-advised humor of some idiots sacrificing a cock in front of a synagogue, and other idiots walking around with a begging basket, and other idiots further antagonizing the Romans, but then things gradually turned violent. The violent aspect of the rebellion broke out outside the Praetorium where Roman authority in Jerusalem was ensconced. There, rioters transformed themselves into genuine rebels. Suddenly the rebels found, to their delight, that they could beat the Romans! They took the Praetorium, and eventually they also took the Fortress Antonia and massacred the troops there! So then the Roman troops in Jerusalem held only the three massive towers of the Praetorium that you see right there before you. In the next act of this tragedy, rebels promised those troops safe passage out of the city. So those troops withdrew. And the rebels slaughtered them forthwith.

"Thus began three years of rebellion throughout Judea, rebellion which culminated in high tragedy here in Jerusalem where it had begun. You've read Josephus. You know how the situation worsened and worsened, eventually sinking to the lowest levels to which mankind can sink. Faction fought faction. Plundering. Burning. Massacre. Starvation. Cannibalism. So the rebels had largely defeated *themselves* by the time that Titus and his legions arrived to survey the scene from right here, from Mount Scopus, 'Mount Observation.'

"The Roman legions attacked with their customary tight order and determination. The Jews made their last stand in the Temple precinct, fighting like wild beasts. But the Romans came on in their tens of thousands, wave after wave of them, methodically battering at the walls with all of their clever machines, their catapults and siege towers and whatnot, and using the rubble from the battering to construct an enormous ramp. In the end they slaughtered the Jews of Jerusalem both methodically and savagely. Massacre. Starvation. Multiple firebrands that were used to start multiple conflagrations. And finally: scenes of captives crucified by the thousands in imaginative poses, imaginative poses that were thought up purely for the purpose of inflicting the most thorough possible revenge. Then the Romans flattened this city so that it could be nothing more than a memory. Titus even uprooted the ancient olive trees. Over there you can see a barren hill that used to be called the Mount of Olives. Concerning the Mount of Olives, Zechariah pronounced, 'On that day his feet will stand on the Mount of Olives, which is opposite Jerusalem to the east.' This passage became the basis for a widespread belief that the Mount of Olives would be the very place that would see the coming of the Messiah. And so it did! For Jesus was there, in a particular garden. You know the name of this garden."

With a trace of melancholy, owing to the complete aridity of what had previously been a garden, Theophilus murmured, "Gethsemane."

"Yes. Now let's walk over to Gethsemane."

# X GETHSEMANE...THE OIL PRESS

Uzziah preached at Gethsemane.

"Yes. Gethsemane. It certainly does not look like much now. But a beautiful garden really did once stand here. I saw it. From here Jesus would have gazed out over the Temple complex, having a full view of the vast Court of the Gentiles. That court was completely surrounded by colonnaded porticos, porticos where Roman soldiers often stood at attention to remind everyone who was the true master of the place. The gospel of John depicted Jesus walking back and forth in the portico that was nearest to the Mount of Olives, the Solomon Portico, walking back and forth and casually philosophizing like some Greek philosopher in a *stoa,* and declaring, 'I and the Father are one.' That was one of the more pleasant memories of Jesus in Jerusalem. But all the world knows how up here in Gethsemane Jesus' situation became dire."

Theophilus now made an interruption to the monologue. "I've thought much about this Gethsemane episode in the Jesus drama. Gethsemane seems the perfect dramatic setting for Jesus to suffer his most agonizing hour of doubt, in his last hour of freedom. *'Get'* is 'press' and *'shemen'* is 'oil.' Gethsemane is 'oil press.' This was the perfect setting for Jesus to be *squeezed to his limit,* and to begin to offer up his essence! He asked that the bitter cup be taken from him. He sweated blood. His disciples, who never understood him or provided much help to him, were all asleep. Symbolically, they were all asleep!"

Uzziah nodded assent and further enlightened Theophilus on this topic. "The prophet Elijah provided much of the inspiration for this episode on Gethsemane. Elijah was an outcast who sat brooding under a tree, just as Jesus must have been sitting under a tree when he prayed for deliverance here at Gethsemane. In both cases, an angel appeared on the scene to provide strength. For both Elijah in the Septuagint and Jesus in the gospels, the word used to describe this angelic help was *enischuon.* The gospel writers constantly introduced tidbits of Jewish history to string together Jesus tales. When Jesus was arrested at Gethsemane, Peter, acting in an uncharacteristically decisive manner, cut off the ear of one of the High Priest's servants. This action took place to illustrate symbolically, at this moment of high drama, that the High Priest had no legitimate jurisdiction. That was the case because any blemish made a man unfit to serve as High Priest. In a certain historical account, a man named Antigonus, who was in rebellion against Herod, bit off the ear of Herod's High Priest, John Hyrcanus. The gospels echoed this well-known episode by having Peter cut off the ear of one of the High Priest's men. And the gospel writer John, writing the latest of the gospels, had Jesus *heal that ear* that Peter's sword had severed, thus throwing in *one last miracle* for Jesus!"

"To my mind, it seems a silly story, this severing of an ear, a story that should itself have been severed from the gospels. Something far more important than ear-slicing happened here at Gethsemane. Here Judas betrayed Jesus!"

"And with a kiss," added Uzziah, surprising Theophilus by imitating the deed against the air. "False love. False love. But mainly the kiss of Judas was inserted into the Gethsemane story in order to make the story reminiscent of an incident that took place in the second book of the prophet Samuel. In that incident, Joab, betraying Amasa, kissed him... but also disemboweled him! That disembowelment neatly foreshadowed the story of Judas's suicide, in the course of which Judas' intestines fell out. Have you ever wondered why that Judas-kiss and that Judas-betrayal was necessary in the logical flow of the Jesus story? Why would the priests need an accomplice simply to find Jesus, who was so well known to everyone, and why would Judas be willing to become that accomplice?"

"I've studied the matter carefully, but one can't really piece together a sensible scenario about that strange character Judas from the gospels."

"Indeed one can't. Luke claimed that the devil got into Judas. Other versions, Matthew's and John's versions for example, made Judas simply money-hungry. But how hungry can one be over a mere thirty pieces of silver? The fact is, Matthew's confused story about thirty pieces of silver came from two sources: Zechariah for the number thirty pertaining to the pieces of silver, and Jeremiah for the ultimate fate of the thirty pieces of silver, namely the purchase of an acre of land. As the story went, Jeremiah bought land and placed the deed for his land in a pot, and because of that the gospel writers had Judas use his pieces of silver to purchase land called Potters Field. Fairly clumsy symbolism was that, I'm afraid. But the purchase of an acre of land does well symbolize *extremely petty attachment to the material world*. So we see that Judas was both greedy and petty. But if we look beyond Matthew's clumsy symbolism, back to an earlier source, namely Mark, we find no motive for Judas' actions at all! And that's because Mark was himself rather confusedly adapting still earlier traditions about Judas to his story."

Theophilus interrupted to say, "Uzziah, I do believe you're about to strip away *all* of the remaining Twelve Apostles as embellishments to the Jesus story."

"As the very number 'twelve' should have warned you all along! Twelve is the number of the of the Twelve Tribes of Israel and also the number of the zodiac. We'll deal with only one of the apostles for now: Judas who broke bread with Jesus to signal a betrayal. The reason that breaking bread with someone signaled a betrayal was that one of the psalms said, 'Even my bosom friend in whom I trusted, who ate of my bread, has acted against me.' John's gospel even had Jesus refer to this psalm. John had Jesus say very specifically, 'There is a text of scripture to be fulfilled: 'He who eats bread with me has turned against me.'' Now I must correct myself. We're going to deal with *two* of the apostles right now. That's because *two* of the apostles were named Judas. And one concept is all-important for you to appreciate now: *nomen est omen.*"

"So you do know some Latin!" Theophilus smiled. "Yes, a name is an omen. So what can the name 'Judas' mean? It means the Jewish people, doesn't it?"

"Exactly. Just as the name 'Jesus' means 'salvation.'"

"Are you now going to tell me that even Jesus' name was a fabrication?"

"Not at all. 'Jesus' is Jesus' real name. It's a very common name. Now then, we're talking about two apostles named Judas: Judas Iscariot and Judas Jacobi. The first one's name indicates a connection with the *sicarii,* the 'dagger-men,' which is to say the zealots, the men who terrorized Judea with anti-Roman violence at the point of a dagger. The Essenes who wove many of these tales despised the dagger-men, and they despised the dagger-men's founder, a man who was actually named Judas. *So those Essenes invented a villain called Judas Iscariot. Here was a fictional way to revile Judas, the true-to-history founder of the dagger-men, forevermore!* They could revile the dagger-men by placing this Judas, alias Judas Iscariot, in a memorable tale as the ultimate villain! The second apostle who was called Judas, namely Judas Jacobi, had a name that indicated that he was a son of Jacob. The prophet Jacob was the founder of the nation of Israel; Jacob was even surnamed Israel. So... See how this works. *Judas Jacobi is a symbolic name denoting those Jews who remained loyal to the traditions of Israel,* the Jews who were nourished at God's breast and were close to God's heart! In the scriptures, Judas Jacobi is also sometimes called Thaddaeus, meaning 'breast,' and Lebbaeus, meaning 'heart.' Thaddaeus-Lebbaeus-Judas, as we may call him, was certainly a complicatedly-named fellow. For he was also snidely known as Jude the Obscure. He was indeed obscure. He spoke only once in the gospels. On that one occasion he asked Jesus, 'How is it you will manifest yourself to us and not to the world?' Very well, my student, who was meant by '*us*'?"

"Those Jews who are true to the spirit of Israel! Those who live in the spirit of the good Judas Jacobi! Thaddaeus the breast man! Lebbaeus the heart man!"

"Very good!" commended Uzziah. "Yes, such people, the righteous people of Israel, are symbolized by Judas Jacobi. Judas Iscariot stands in contradistinction to the saintly Judas Jacobi. *Judas Iscariot represents all the Jews who rejected Jesus*! In sum, the name Judas Iscariot indicates all those Jews who were dagger-men, *sicarii.* Now note something important: *betrayal* was not the concept that was originally intended by this symbolic Judas Iscariot story. The Greek word *paradosis* allowed itself to be expanded and abused by mythmakers. *Paradosis* is, properly, a 'giving over.' Judas Iscariot represented that portion of the Jews that 'gave over' its Jesus, which is to say 'gave over its hopes for salvation,' to the priests. In other words, these Judas-folk left their salvation to the religious establishment and ignored their 'Lebbaeus,' their heart. As a further indication that this interpretation of Judas is true, another Judas has been skulking around the holy literature, but never made it into the best-known gospels. He is Judas Thomas, 'Judas the Twin,' a symbol of the physical self that threatens to destroy the spiritual self. Remember, Judas was not only greedy and materialistic, as symbolized by his using his blood money to buy an acre of land, but he even died by bursting open, so bloated was he with physicality!"

"Yes, Christian scripture presents two totally contradictory stories for Judas' death, which is certainly a strong indication that Judas was entirely mythical. *Acts* said that Judas' bowels burst, but *Matthew* said that Judas hanged himself."

"Quite correct. The two contradictory stories about Judas' death do indeed strongly suggest his purely mythical nature. Now, about that hanging: mythical Judas obediently followed an old mythic tradition of a False Self who tried to kill the True Self, but ended up hanging on a tree. The story of 'Jesus the True Self confronting Judas the False Self' is paralleled by the Egyptian story of Osiris confronting Seth, and also by the story of Dionysus confronting Pentheus. Throughout Jewish scripture there is perennially repeated the mythical duel of 'the rejected versus the anointed.' Cain versus Abel. Ishmael versus Isaac. Esau versus Jacob. Saul Versus David. And finally, Judas versus Jesus. Out with the old and in with the new! In these spiritual tales, the more dynamic and the more holy of the dueling pair is always the one who prevails!"

"Uzziah, I thank you. To me you're a light brighter than your land's incredible sun!"

Insisted Uzziah, "You'll thank me more in a moment, because our story knows not only two men named Judas, *but also two men named Jesus!*"

"Oh, I do already know all about this, Uzziah, believe it or not. Matthew mentioned a Jesus Barabbas. But for reasons of reverence, Jesus Barabbas was excised from all but a few versions of *Matthew,* and became simply Barabbas. The original tale set up a 'rejected-versus-anointed' pair. That pair was Jesus Barabbas versus Jesus Christ. 'Barabbas' means 'son of the father.' This character Barabbas existed only as a symbol-man, a symbol-man who demonstrated the hard-headedness and hard-heartedness of some of the Jews, the Jews who rejected the new salvation of Jesus, and clung stubbornly to the salvific habits of their forefathers. Legal experts have informed me that that notion of Pilate freeing a prisoner as a favor on a Jewish holiday is quite out of the question. Pilate freeing a convicted prisoner? No. Certainly not. Philo correctly described Pilate as 'inflexible, merciless, obstinate, murderous, cruel, ferocious.' But in Pilate's time the Jews really were indeed offered two choices. The first choice was the new salvation, the true salvation: Jesus Christ. The second choice was the salvation that had always contented their forefathers, in other words 'salvation-son-of-the-father,' which phrase would be 'Jesus Barabbas' in Aramaic. In the clever legend, the mob was offered a choice between the two men, and the mob made its choice. The mob howled 'Give us

Barabbas! Give us Barabbas!'"

Uzziah asked his student, "And do you know about the deeper ramifications of the Barabbas story?"

"Yes, indeed. The Barabbas episode revealed a Jesus who would serve as a human replacement for the holiday known as Yom Kippur. On Yom Kippur, the nation of Israel would conduct a ceremony with two identical goats. One goat would be *released into the wild* to carry off the sins of Israel. And the other goat would *have its blood shed* to atone for the sins of Israel. So note the elegant symbolism that replaced the old holiday of Yom Kippur with the new holiday of Jesus' Passion. Goat-Barabbas: he was released! Goat-Jesus: he was bloodied and killed! Jesus replaced Yom Kippur with an entirely new concept of salvation and an entirely new celebration!"

"It is clear that Jerusalem inspires you, Theophilus. Jerusalem inspires you."

"So, what exactly was the nature of this new salvation, Uzziah?"

"You'll soon see. You're nearing the climax of your search now, Theophilus, and for that I think it appropriate that we move on to Mount Zion."

# XI KORBAN... THE SACRIFICE

Somber Jewish teacher and eager gentile pupil sat atop Mount Zion, a bare hillock much like the other bare hillocks of Jerusalem, located at the southern end of what remained of the city. Uzziah spoke.

"So, this disappointingly unspectacular hill is the great Mount Zion. This hill is a source of much confusion. Probably the true Mount Zion is actually the Temple Mount itself, formerly known as Mount Moriah, which means 'Mount Light.' This ordinary-looking Mount Zion upon which we sit is accorded much honor. Why? Because a confusing phrase in the prophet Micah has prompted Jews to believe that Mount Zion is a mountain distinct from the Temple Mount. So now most Jews believe that this mountain upon which we stand is Mount Zion. Now look over to the east at the place where we were previously sitting, in the Garden of Gethsemane on the Mount of Olives. At that place there transpired Jesus' moment of truth. Jesus ascended the Mount of Olives at his moment of self-doubt to dedicate himself completely to God, in emulation of King David who made exactly the same ascent, up exactly the same mount. This was 'David-Jesus.' And on the Mount of Olives 'David-Jesus' had his moment of truth.' Jesus was tempted to abandon his mission. Luke originally wrote that Jesus sweated blood and was visited by a reassuring angel, but most editions have excised that unsavory passage of Jesus sweating blood and requiring outside assistance."

"Uzziah, we too have now reached a sort of moment of truth. I've now reached a sort of mountaintop of doubt myself. It seems as though everything you tell me is mere *embellishment* to the story of Jesus! When, in the name of Jupiter, if you'll excuse the pagan expression, do we come to the literal truth?"

"We'll come to the truth. But first must come a great deal more embellishment, I'm afraid. Mark stated that at Jesus' arrest in Gethsemane a certain young man escaped by running and leaving his loincloth in the soldiers' hands. The basis for this incident was a passage from Amos: 'He who is stout of heart among the mighty shall flee away naked on that day.' But the gospel writers other than Mark apparently saw nothing uplifting in the loincloth anecdote, so they simply left it out of their texts."

"Ah, look!" exclaimed Theophilus, who had little interest in the bizarre loincloth incident. "Jerusalem has people after all!"

A few dark figures stood by the Temple Mount, bowing and chanting in melancholy disharmony.

"This city is still the holiest place in all creation to the Jews," reminded Uzziah. "Jews still come to pray here, especially at the only impressive remains of the Temple: the Temple Mount's Western Wall, known as the *Kotel*. Now, Theophilus, I've revealed to you the layout of the Temple complex and pointed out where the Sanhedrin must have tried Jesus. There has been much confusion as to exactly *who* who tried Jesus, and when and where. Mark said simply 'priests,' and the other gospel writers added the names Annas and Caiaphas, but never really seemed very clear as to who was in charge of the proceedings. Caiaphas was the High Priest, while Annas was the former High Priest who still wielded a great deal of power. The earliest report of Jesus' trial, Mark's report, certainly didn't make the trial seem like much of a noteworthy event. Mark reported curtly that the priests held a consultation and decided to deliver Jesus to Pilate.

"Later editors adjudged this narrative of Mark's to be unsatisfyingly brief, and added a trial scene in which Jesus makes sweeping messianic claims for himself. Try to picture the man who stood before Pilate in the Praetorium on the Stone Pavement. He was the Man of Sorrows whom we hear so much about in Isaiah: 'Set among the transgressors, he bore the sins of many.' Mostly this Man of Sorrows remained strangely silent. And that was so because in *Isaiah* it was stated, 'Yet he opened not his mouth, like a lamb that is led to the slaughter.' The crowd wanted Barabbas, not Jesus, and gave Jesus only its scorn. And Jesus was flogged. For the psalms said, 'I gave my back to the smiters. I hid not my face from shame and spitting.' And the psalms said, 'I hear the whispering of many as they plot to take my life.' There he was. He was the *korban*. He was the sacrifice!"

Theophilus commented, "And it all happened right down there, where the three remaining stout towers mark the site of the palace of Herod which had been transformed into the Roman

Praetorium by Jesus' time."

"Yes, but Luke added another brief episode. He had Jesus taken to King Herod Antipas, since that fellow happened to be in town and was the ruler of Jesus' homeland, Galilee. Thus could be fulfilled the psalm that runs, 'The rulers take counsel together against the Lord and his anointed.' But it was Pilate who sentenced the Man of Sorrows, and then washed his hands of the guilt, for as another psalm says, 'I wash my hands in innocence and go about the altar, O Lord.'"

"I admire your memory for scriptural quotations, Uzziah, but they're all so general in nature. Would anyone really have had an interest in making up a story by stringing such quotes together, one after another?"

Uzziah replied, "The quotes are about to 'make a story,' as you put it, ever more tightly and conclusively. Look there. Look at one of the main places that we came here to see. You can just make out a skull-shaped rock whose location was formerly just outside the northern gate of Jerusalem."

"Calvary!"

"Yes. The Place of the Skull. The Place of the Skull is 'Golgotha' in Aramaic, and 'Calvary' in Latin. Golgotha was originally a quarry and later became a cemetery. It sat by a main road and a main entrance to Jerusalem. The Romans chose to perform their Jerusalem crucifixions at Golgotha for two reasons. Firstly, because if crucifixions were conducted in a cemetery they would be even more humiliating than otherwise. And secondly, because crucifixions by a main road would be even more public than otherwise."

Both men's faces darkened at this point. "I've seen a crucifixion," let out Theophilus softly. "Ghastly."

"'I've seen hundreds of them, and many of the victims were people I knew! But such is Roman law. Pilate sentenced the Man of Sorrows and ordered an appropriate placard made. The inscription read, 'Jesus the Nazarene, King of the Jews'. The abbreviation would be INRI to you Romans. That stood for *Iesus Nazarathaeus Rex Ioudaeorum.* But the inscription was written in Greek as well. And in Hebrew too. In Hebrew it was '*Yeshu Hanotri Wumelech Hayehudim.*' The abbreviation was YHWH!"

Theophilus gave a start. He shifted his gaze from the Place of the Skull and fixed it on his instructor. "Uzziah, I'm beginning to wonder..."

But Uzziah interrupted his student, his eyes ablaze, his voice a rumble. "The Jews objected to the inscription but Pilate refused to change it! 'A ruler's writing is not to be changed,' said the *Book of Esther*! It is written! God has written it! A Jew is born to be crucified as a Roman is born to crucify! 'They have pierced my hands and feet,' says the psalm! They crucified him there, and none of those dear to him were there with him, except for a few who stood far off! Why? Because the psalm says, 'My friends and companions stand aloof from my plague, and my kinsmen stand far off.' And the psalm says, 'They gave me poison for food and for my thirst they gave me vinegar to drink'! So the soldiers put a sponge on a spear and held up sour vinegar, *oxos,* for Jesus to drink!"

"Uzziah..."

"The sky darkened at noon and the earth trembled!" Uzziah looked as though he believed these calamities were happening at that very moment. "Thus was fulfilled the prophecy of Amos! This was the Man of Sorrows, sacrificed on the day of the sacrifice of the paschal lambs during Passover! Yet all knew that he was not despairing when he cried out from the cross, 'My God, my God, why have you forsaken me?' For he was quoting the first line of a psalm of hope, and that psalm also says, 'They divide my garments among them, *diemerisanto ta himatia mou,* and for my raiment they cast lots'! The dividing of the raiment symbolized the violating of the Seamless Robe that is the reality of the cosmos to "those who know." One of the soldiers who cast lots for Jesus' garment pierced Jesus' side with a spear, and he did so because the scriptures say, 'They shall look on him whom they have pierced'!"

"Uzziah..."

"You'll have your answer, Theophilus! The Man of Sorrows is about to expire! 'Father, into your hands I commend my spirit!' These were his last words, and once again they were words from the psalms! Jesus spoke seven times on the cross. Doubtless you know all about the holiness of the number seven! Jesus died so quickly that the soldiers had no opportunity to follow the usual custom and break his legs! And the psalm says, 'Many are the afflictions of the righteous, but the Lord delivers him out of them all. He keeps all his bones. Not one of them is broken'!"

"Uzziah... You've peeled away too many layers of the onion by now! That's a simple fact. That's a simple fact. At last comes the reckoning, and you must tell me what I think I'm going to hear and what I think I'm dreading to hear. The entire biography of Jesus seems to be embellishment upon embellishment. What is left of his biography at this point? You must tell me unambiguously. Are we now left without any Jesus at all?"

Uzziah contemplated the ground as though ashamed of what he might utter next. "You must see it..."

"Uzziah! Did this man Jesus ever really live!?"

"And if not? What's one Jewish wonderworker more or less?"

"You must tell me now!"

"Strange... Strange... The words don't come easily."

"Tell me!"

Uzziah turned away and scanned the most distant hills, straining to see the red desert and Qumran.

"... No. No such man ever lived..."

Theophilus, stunned, gazing at the utterly ordinary-looking ground of Mount Zion, murmured in repetition, "No such man ever lived."

Then for a significant amount of time Jerusalem was silent for the two men.

At length Uzziah intoned, "According to Luke, at the moment of Christ's death the entire sky darkened, and according to Matthew the earth trembled. These scenarios come from the prophet

Amos who describe a "darkness at noon" and described God causing the earth to tremble. And Matthew contended that that trembling opened tombs so that all over Jerusalem people saw the spirits of the dead walking around! You won't hear Christians mentioning that particular episode much! There, in those occurrences, *utterly incredible occurrences that are not recorded anywhere else but in the gospels*, one can see something perhaps better than anywhere else! One can see that there is no history in the story of Jesus! It has all been symbol-talk all along! It has always been, in its entirety… *myth*!"

The sky did darken and the earth did tremble for Theophilus He felt blood drain from his face and tears fill his eyes. This seemed to be the end of the trail, this heap of discarded onion peels. Why? Why such an ending? And why did he care so much? He had lost Jesus and felt aggrieved. But why?

"So the world is one marvel-working rabbi poorer," said Uzziah. "What does it matter?"

"Somehow it does matter. I don't know why."

"The proper place for the shedding of tears is down there by the base of the Temple Mount at the Western Wall. We call it the Wailing Wall. There I can shed my tears for my lost Israel, and you can shed your tears for your lost Jesus."

I did want him, Uzziah. I... I don't know why. I can't explain."

"We'll go down there to the wall. And there, indeed, you should wail. But you won't be wailing for long. You're actually going to *find* that which you think you lost, Theophilus. I'm going to explain to you why your search for Jesus has, in reality, *only just begun!"*

## XII BEN ADAM... THE SON OF MAN

The remaining foundation blocks of Herod's Temple Mount, the *Kotel* or Wailing Wall, were of cyclopean dimensions. Theophilus leaned against them and felt very small. And he was completely silent.

"What did you want from Jesus anyway?" Uzziah's question was blunt.

"Jesus was good. The world is such a swamp of evil and sadness. As one of the letters of John said: "*Ho kosmos holos en to ponera keitai,*" "The whole world lies entirely in the grip of evil." In that morass, Jesus was goodness shining through. Him and only him. And now he's gone."

"But is he? All that he ever said or did exists just the same as before, but on a higher plane than you imagined: the plane of the ideal rather than the real, as expounded by Plato. The profoundest secrets still await you. Your realization that Jesus was not a living human being marks only the beginning of your coming to understand Jesus."

"I'm impressed that you understand the essence of Plato, good friend."

"Jews are not blithering savages. You'll be amazed to learn how much of the best of Greek thought we Jews have absorbed. The Jesus myth is an amalgam of ideas from both thought worlds, the Jewish and the Greek. An amalgam, I might also point out, that also sits upon the basis of things Egyptian."

"I still can't bring myself to believe that Jesus was only a myth!"

Uzziah sighed. "Roman! Pitiable Roman with the mind of a lawyer or a soldier or an engineer! The fact that you can say '*only* a myth' demonstrates how little, how very little, you really comprehend!"

"No, I can't comprehend it! How can we be talking about a myth? I've spoken with people who knew Paul. And I've held a letter written by Pontius Pilate in my hands! And your own father said that he was baptized by John the Baptist!"

"And why not? Those were real people! Paul and Pontius Pilate and John the Baptist were completely real! As were certain others, including Paul's acquaintances, and Caiaphas the High Priest, and Herod and Herod Antipas, and James the Just, and of course the gospel writers Matthew, Mark, Luke, and John.""

"Real people? And yet they hobnob in stories with people who never existed?"

"Yes, and you shouldn't be so terribly surprised at that. Haven't you ever even looked carefully at your own Roman imperial

179

reliefs? And Greek reliefs? Gods mixed with mortals. Mortals mixed with gods."

Theophilus straightened up and raised his eyebrows in amazement. Yes, Uzziah was right: Romans and Greeks, too, liberally mixed their celebrities with beings of fable.

"This literary genre has been resoundingly popular for the last few centuries," continued Uzziah, "this mixing of historical personages with fictional personages. It's one element of Midrash, the interpretation and augmentation of Holy Scriptures by means of moralizing tales, sayings, parables, puns, genealogies, and so on. A typical tale which deftly illustrates the nature of Midrash is the tale of Judith. The tale of Judith was fabricated during the Maccabee rebellion as a means of stirring patriotic fervor, but it *pretended* to take place during the reign of a real king named Nebuchadnezzar. Nebuchadnezzar was included in the story purely as a code-character standing for the Maccabees' enemy, Antiochus. In the story, Judith seduced Nebuchadnezzar's general Holofernes in order to gain an opportunity to behead him, thus saving the Jewish people. Judith, as the name 'Judith' makes *very* clear, was a personification of the Jewish people. Quite similarly, Esther was a fictional Jewish heroine who mingled with genuine historical figures, notably the Persian king Xerxes. And there have been many other examples. Many, many others, particularly in the late scriptural books that culminated with the important prophet Daniel. He was a *fictional* figure who challenged the *historical* figure Nebuchadnezzar. So accept it. The story that mixes real people with unreal people is an established literary form, and a useful one. Who knows? You may appear in one such story yourself someday!"

"Well, I can't say that I don't accept it. I do accept it. But it all makes Jesus seem so trivial."

Uzziah banged his fist on a tumbled Herodian building stone with a forcefulness that took Theophilus aback. "No! No! Not trivial! Anything but trivial! Theophilus, you're truly a child in these matters!"

"Everything seems to be up for grabs, Uzziah."

"No, that's not the case at all! Listen to me more carefully this time, and I'll explain to you the extreme value of figures of myth. Certain prophets were not men but myth-men, myth-men who embodied *an entire era and that era's lesson!* 'Elijah' for instance meant 'Only Yahweh is my God.' His era was preoccupied with throwing down the graven images and worshipping solely Yahweh. Daniel was a product of a much later time, when the Jews were faced with the tribulations of living under foreign rulers. His name meant 'Only God is my judge.' The fictional character Daniel confronted real-life villains such as Nebuchadnezzar, just as the fictional character Jesus confronted real-life villains such as Herod and Pilate."

"What of Moses?"

"Moses was an Egyptian. You'll have to go to Egypt to comprehend Moses. Really, you'll have to go to Egypt to comprehend just about anything deeply, with your wholly Greekified mind. But I can tell you of Daniel. He was created in the time of the arch-villain Antiochus in order to hearten the Jews against that tyrant. In his stories, Daniel battled the tyrants of an already long bygone era, real characters such as Nebuchadnezzar, and prevailed against them. Just as the Jewish people went on to prevail against Antiochus and the Greeks. The Daniel tales were an inspiration that that era cried out for. The Daniel tales and the Judith tales, and other such stories, helped my people to marshal their courage and drive out the Greeks."

Uzziah had a distant look. He stared at his people's lost Temple and his mouth opened, but he could not speak. Theophilus waited a long time before determining to ask his friend if he were all right, but then suddenly Uzziah spoke again, very softly.

"Then came another adversary, even more powerful than the Greeks. The Romans. The latest of the *Kittim*. The most powerful of the *Kittim*. Long, long before the dreadful times that I myself experienced as a boy the dreadful inevitability of those times was set in motion. In Augustus' time his general Varus crucified two thousand rebellious Jews along those glorious new Roman roads. Varus found God's retribution deep in the wilds of Germany. A barbarian ambush deep in the endless German forest annihilated him and his three legions. *Three* legions! It was Rome's greatest defeat, a debacle so massive that the disappeared legions were never reactivated."

"I know all about Varus' end. He was responsible for the worst defeat in the history of Rome. I didn't know about his gruesome activities in Judea. I'm sorry."

"Thousands of crucifixes decorating a country are a memorable sight, I can assure you. The sight is bound to awaken a yearning for a savior, and to have an influence on the perceived nature of that savior. And so, partly because of the trauma of those mass crucifixions by the Romans, there arose the tale of a *crucified* savior! Yes, specifically a *crucified* savior. Stories about this crucified savior were already circulating. They coalesced at that time. That's when they began to take on solid form."

Theophilus recalled, "I've been told that the official imperial *evangelia* declaring Augustus to be a savior prompted embellishments to the Jesus story as counter-propaganda. That was the beginning of the Christian *evangelia,* in other words the gospels, wasn't it?"

"That's true, but I caution you not to let the presence of such embellishments mislead you into regarding Jesus as a casual and trivial human invention. You'll find his origin goes much deeper. Much deeper. Now then... Early Jesus was a hazy figure, a reciter of sayings and parables. Read early texts such as the *Wellspring of Life* or the *Gospel of Thomas* to confirm that. Then Mark came along."

At this point Uzziah produced a piece of parchment. He displayed it to Theophilus and described its contents.

"I compiled this little list a while back, knowing that it would be useful to show it to you at a certain point. I know how much you've liked such little lists. You see, Jesus was a figure of maximum haziness till Mark wrote that figure's first biography, small and simple but somehow deeply compelling As you've known, in a way, since you first began your studies, it all began with Mark. And with this little list I want to make the point that a bit of research shows that Mark was writing fiction, not history. Here I've compiled a list of episodes in the *Book of Mark* that together demonstrate that Mark was writing fiction, not history. *Because Mark was writing from the point of view of an omniscient narrator! Not an historian! He wrote as an omniscient narrator, as one would write a novel!* He wrote about so many things that a biographer or historian could not have known. He was a novelist. Do have a look."

Theophilus quickly read the list of episodes from *Mark* that demonstrated that Mark wrote from the point of view of an omniscient narrator.

| | |
|---|---|
| **I** | Of Jesus going into the wilderness: "He got up to a deserted place and prayed." |
| **II** | Some of the scribes were questioning in their hearts, "Why does Jesus speak this way?" |
| **III** | "A certain woman touched his garment and her bleeding immediately dried up." |
| **IV** | "When the Syro-Phoenician woman went home she found the child was lying in bed and the demon had gone." |
| **V** | A private conversation between the priests and scribes plotting to kill Jesus. "Not during the festival, or there may be a riot among the people." |
| **VI** | Judas's conversations with the priests. And with the guards who were sent to arrest Jesus, concerning the |

signal kiss.

**VII**    Mark knew the prayer that Jesus prayed alone at Gethsemane, when all of the possible witnesses, the apostles, were asleep.

**VIII**    Even though the apostles had fled and the women watched the Crucifixion from a distance, Mark knew that the Centurion said, "Truly this was the son of God."

**IX**    Mark said Joseph of Arimathea went "boldly" to Pontius Pilate to ask for the body of Jesus. Even more strangely, Mark knew the words exchanged between Pilate and his centurion.

**X**    Mark knew the words of the priests to each other mocking Jesus: "He saved others, yet he cannot save himself."

"Interesting," assessed Theophilus. "This list will bear some thought. Some study. I suppose that you have some more to tell me about Mark?"

"Yes. You can discern *exactly* when Mark did his writing. He wrote that the apocalypse predicted by the prophet Daniel would occur when 'desolating sacrilege (let the reader understand) stands in the holy place.' You see, Mark was describing, fearfully and in a disguised manner, the desecration of the Temple in Jerusalem that was scheduled to occur with the arrival of a statue of Caligula inside the Temple. That desecration was expected to happen at any moment during the reign of Caligula. To a faithful Jew that dreaded event could only mark the end of the world."

"What was this apocalyptic prophecy of Daniel?" asked

Theophilus.

"Daniel's so-called 'prophecies' mostly consisted of the authors' putting into Daniel's mouth 'predictions' of what was already happening in their own time. But Daniel's apocalyptic prophecy is different, and it's vital to your own understanding, in that it's *the one and only description of the human afterlife in all the Jewish scriptures*. Here it is: 'And there shall be a time of trouble such as there has never been... but at that time your people shall be delivered, every one whose name shall be found written in the book. And many of those who sleep in the dust of the earth shall awake, some to everlasting life, and some to shame and everlasting contempt. And those who are wise shall shine like the brightness of the firmament... like the stars for ever and ever. But you, Daniel, shut up the words, and seal the book, until the time of the end. Many shall run to and fro, and knowledge shall increase.'"

Uzziah's thunderous recitation from the *Book of Daniel* had won him an audience: those pious Jews who had been wailing at their wall. Their attentiveness caused Theophilus to make his next statement in hushed tones.

"That's certainly no clearer a description of the afterlife than any of the others I've heard. But the promise of an afterlife is Jesus' central theme and the basis of most people's interest in him. And that's exactly where we left off our discussion of him. We left him crucified but not yet risen."

"Yes. Jesus died, and wealthy Joseph of Arimathea donated a tomb for his use. For Isaiah declared, 'And they made his grave with the wicked and with a rich man in his death.' But Hosea had written, 'Come let us return to the Lord... After two days he will revive us. On the third day he will raise us up.' Moreover, this fictional character Joseph of Arimathea was a good example of how the gospels drew from both Greek motifs and Jewish motifs. He was a combination of King Priam begging for the body of his son Hector in the Iliad, and of the patriarch Joseph asking the Pharaoh's permission to bury his father Jacob in a cave-tomb."

"So the game goes on, and all I can expect is more stringing-along of old quotes and old stories."

Uzziah's voice was thunderous once more. "This is no game! You have no right to say that, you who are barely at the beginnings of true understanding!"

"I'm sorry, but I'm disappointed to find Jesus to be no more than the tale-bearers' fabrication, a character around whom to spin fables that promise some sort of salvation."

Uzziah appeared genuinely saddened by the waywardness of his pupil. "Theophilus, our studies together must end here. Go to Caesarea and I'll have your belongings sent to you there. Go back to living the blind and carefree life of a Roman. Caesarea is the place for that. It is Rome's gleaming marble intrusion in our holy land. Then, if you still are determined that you want something more in your life, if you are quite sure that you want your eyes opened and think you can bear the flooding-in of the light, then board a ship for Egypt and you'll be there in three days. And in Egypt you must look for the Dweller in the Crypt."

"Is that Jesus?"

"No."

"I fully intend to go to Egypt, but am I to be chasing ghosts and fables all over again?"

Uzziah smiled gently. "No. Not this time. The Dweller in the Crypt is a very, very old man, an acquaintance of my father. He will tell you what you need to know. How much you will need to know will depend on you."

"But surely there's a great deal more that you yourself can tell me before I go, Uzziah."

"I honestly feel your further instruction is beyond me."

"But why?"

"You really have no conception of the nature of the path you're treading, Theophilus. You think that a silly pack of storytellers created Jesus. True, they've often abused Jesus, as much as Pilate's soldiers did, but they didn't create him. He's God's creation. He is the Son of God."

"I don't understand that, Uzziah. Please explain what I'm failing to see."

"I feel incapable of helping you."

"Please, Uzziah, please."

Uzziah sighed deeply, rose, and led Theophilus slowly to a spot from which they could see the Place of the Skull. He proclaimed gravely, "There they crucified Jesus. Or so the tale-bearers tell us. You know better now, or think you do, but picture the scene nonetheless. Picture him spread out, nailed, bleeding, crying out in pain. You've seen pain, Theophilus. To live in the world is to know pain. To live is to hang spread-eagled on the cross, Theophilus, painfully nailed to four dimensions, the four dimensions of material existence. Can you see the terrible and wonderful truth now, Theophilus? Can you see the awesome truth? Jesus was not a man!"

"But I'm already aware that Jesus was not a man."

"Open your eyes now, in God's name! Jesus was not a man!... *He.... is.... man!*"

Theophilus' quizzical expression won him an elucidation.

"Jesus was born of the Virgin. The Earth Mother was a virgin, Virgo, Virgo who is material reality itself, ready to receive and give birth. She gave birth to the Son of God. The Son of God must hang on the Tree of Life in agony, but the agony must in turn culminate in a rising into the greatest glory. 'For the Father loves the Son and gave everything into his hands,' says the gospel of John. Do you understand me at long last, in heaven's name!? The father loves his son and gave *everything* into his hands! He is to rule a kingdom of unimaginable splendor! 'For God so loved the world that he gave his only begotten son, so that whosoever believes in him may not perish but will have eternal life'! Jesus is resurrected from the tomb which is the material world. When he comes into his glory he will be the Son of Man, and he is at the same time, and for all time, God's beloved and only begotten son! The Son of God... Born of the Virgin to be crucified and die... To rise again in everlasting glory, the Son of Man arisen to rule his Kingdom! My God, am I conveying anything to you at all!?"

He was. The hair on the back of Theophilus' neck was standing and a tingle ran up and down his spine.

*"I believe I see it! I believe I see it! Jesus is all of us in aggregate! We'll rise! We'll leave this grave!... This vale of tears!..."*

Uzziah closed his eyes and nodded. "And we'll be resurrected in glory. All those of us who live our lives 'in Christ' will have a share in that glorious Kingdom. We live 'in Christ' and Christ lives in us. The mysterious words of Paul are a mystery no longer. Go to Egypt, Theophilus. I can unravel the mystery no further for you. It's sealed with seven seals."

"But I see something now. Pilate said of Jesus, *'Ecce homo,'* 'Here is man.' John's strange trial scene presenting Pilate and Jesus as a pair of dueling philosophers had much hidden depth indeed. Jesus was Ben Adam, which meant both 'man' and 'Son of Man.' *Jesus-hood is humanity's very destiny!"*

"It is so."

"Come with me to Egypt, Uzziah."

"My place is here. To wail over lost Zion. I know not how long that will need to be done. But I have faith that you'll find your Jesus, the last and greatest of the myth-men, the culmination and the summation. The alpha and the omega."

"I can never thank you enough. Uzziah, I will indeed go to Caesarea, and from there I will indeed go to Egypt. But I have a feeling that your yearning is as great as mine. You're yearning to tell me more before you're through with me. You have more to tell me right here in Judea. Don't you? Be honest!"

"Yes. You're right. It is so. More needs to be said. My angel tells me now, inwardly, that I have a responsibility to tell you certain additional things before our time together is through. Let's walk now up to Golgotha, each one helping to carry the other's cross, as it were."

"Yes. To Golgotha. And you know, Uzziah, I just remembered something, something that shines in light, and helps me realize the truth about Jesus being a parable."

"And what is that?"

I realize now that my winding and difficult path to the truth of Jesus was *as it had to be*. After all, Matthew said about Jesus, "He spoke to them in parables. *And other than in parables he addressed them not*"!

# XIII GOLGOTHA… THE SKULL

Golgotha was a skull-shaped hill situated in a quarry just outside where the walls of Jerusalem had stood. It was 'the place of the skull,' so to the Romans its name was Calvary. This spot had been the obvious venue for centuries of Jerusalem's executions, owing to its much-trafficked location just outside a city gate.

Uzziah uttered a prayer appropriate for this unspectacular-looking place Golgotha where the two men now stood, then spoke to Theophilus in a manner that was new.

"Jesus is *man*. And to come to realize this is to reach *manhood*. No more boys' games, as far as spiritual outlook is concerned. No more the chattering of ill-informed philosophers. You are now making the approach to true wisdom. As Paul said, 'When I was a child I thought like a child and behaved like a child, when I became a man I put aside childish things.' From now on, don't search your memory for the various postulates of dead philosophies. Instead, *let wisdom speak to you freshly and directly*. Such wisdom that speaks to you freshly and directly has come to be called Gnosis. So... This place Golgotha is the climax-place of Jesus. This is the place of the Passion, the place of human suffering and resurrection. So tell me now, you who seek Gnosis, where does all suffering occur?"

A baffled Theophilus did in fact search his memory for various philosophical postulates, despite Uzziah's warning. The resulting mumbled answer proved unsatisfactory to Uzziah, so Uzziah repeated,

"Where does all suffering occur, Theophilus?"

Theophilus muttered a few banalities and inconsequentialities that were even worse-received than before.

"Again. Where does all suffering occur, Theophilus?"

Theophilus quieted down his mind some, and made a more serene answer on his third attempt, but by no means a more sensible one.

Where does all suffering occur, Theophilus?"

Theophilus breathed deeply and made a determination to concentrate solely on the question and the answer, dismissing all externalities. Then suddenly, once he had reached a state of inner silence, Theophilus realized that the answer was not to be found in memory or in speculation, but in communing with the here and now. That accomplished, he realized that the answer had been staring him in the face all along. Then to his amazement the answer came to him as sure and swift as an arrow shot. He exclaimed, "All suffering occurs *in the skull*!"

Uzziah nodded approvingly. "Yes indeed, in the skull. All

suffering takes place in Calvary, or Golgotha, in other words *in the skull!* All suffering takes place purely *inside the human head!* This is the only locale where the Passion can ever take place! This is the only place where Jesus could have been crucified! This is Jesus' Passion! And *your* Passion! And *all* human Passion! The head is the only possible site of both your suffering and your resurrection! This is the seat of suffering crowned by *a crown of thorns*, in other words *crowned by a multitude of distresses and pains!*"

"I am in awe," declared Theophilus. "I can visualize this holy tableau, the Passion on Golgotha, that you're telling me about, and I can feel its prodigious wisdom. To live in the material world is to be spread-eagled helpless and suffering in the four dimensions, like the dimensions of a cross, wearing a *false crown!* A crown of anguish that is a *crown of thorns!*"

"See the tableau of the Passion even more clearly now, before you, in your mind's eye," instructed Uzziah. "Crucified on either side of Jesus on Golgotha there were two thieves. They were two highly symbolic thieves. I remember how at one point you did so well at understanding the Gemini, *the twins who symbolize twin aspects of mankind: the material and the divine.* You realized that the 'sons of thunder' apostles, the brothers James and John, were just like the Gemini twins in symbolizing the material on one side and the divine on the other. All over the Empire the Gemini are depicted as two torch-bearers, being one who holds his torch up and another who holds his torch down. The scenario of Jesus flanked by *two thieves* equates to those *two torch-bearers*, one who holds his torch up and the other who holds his torch down. Not obvious now? To only *one* of those two thieves did Jesus address the assurance that he would be, *timelessly,* with Jesus in paradise!"

Now Theophilus, standing on "the place of the skull," nodded his own skull up and down, and veritably felt it burst with a surfeit of elements of the wisdom that he had traveled so far to attain. He declared, "I am overwhelmed. And though this spot is almost as bare of foliage as the desert which you told me is the font of Jewish wisdom, I can feel now the message of the cross. I can feel now what I should have sensed all along: that at the center of this Passion tale of Jesus stands the ancient sacred symbol the Tree of Life! The Tree of Life is part of the symbolism of the cross!"

"Correct. In virtually any culture you will find a god-man who represents the human saga itself. And in many cases that god-man will attain wisdom by *hanging suspended and suffering on the Tree of Life.* The list of such god-men goes on and on. Odin. Bacchus. Dionysus. Attis. Adonis. Marsyas. Jesus. You no longer need to be confused by something that seems confusing in the scriptures. You no longer have to be confused by the question as to whether Jesus was crucified on a cross, which is the usual image, or was hung on a tree as described by Paul and the *Book of Acts.* Symbolism knows much flexibility. A god-man suffers for us all, not because he is a hero so wonderful and brave, but because he is a symbol for us all, *a symbol of the human predicament.* In part, the tale of Jesus' crucifixion existed in the ancient spirit of ritual scapegoating. In fact, in the gospels the villain Caiaphas gravely announced that one man should die for the good of all. So it was not a matter of a normal political or law-enforcement execution at all. No. Josephus mentioned six purported messiahs of Jesus' era who were executed, but who cares? Jesus was not to be mentioned in any historic writings; he existed at a different level. Unfortunately, later editors with a grudge against the Jews added to Caiaphas's important statement about scapegoating a terrible reply from the crowd: 'His blood be on us and on our children.' That dreadful interpolation was a sign of the beginnings of a complete loss of the original meaning of the crucifixion tale, and the interpolation also showed the beginnings of Christian anti-Jewish animosity."

Theophilus mused, "The Christ Passion tale is the ultimate tale, isn't it? It carries within it the possibilities of infinite inspiration, as well as, unfortunately, the possibilities of infinite misinterpretation."

"That is indeed the case, sagacious pupil, that is indeed the case. And that being the case, always remember to pay attention to the soul-teaching impact of the tale rather than its supposed factual and historical sequence of events. Always the Christ Passion tale will bear within it so many internal inconsistencies and discrepancies that the wise will be able to ascertain that it *cannot be taken literally,* and that it is purely legendary. The inconsistencies are everywhere. Just one example is Jesus' trial before the Sanhedrin. Mark and Matthew said Jesus was tried and sentenced by the Sanhedrin. Luke said Jesus was tried by the Sanhedrin but not sentenced by it. And John did not have Jesus appear before the

Sanhedrin at all."

"Well, Uzziah, I suppose that brings us neatly to the component of the Jesus tale that is the most important of all, but which also contains the most inconsistencies of all: the resurrection."

"Yes," agreed the guide. "That episode is a farrago of inconsistent fables that no one, from a genius to a madman, could ever successfully sort out. No one can ever turn it into anything resembling genuine history."

Theophilus suggested, "May I review the episode of the resurrection tales a bit now, just to get it all straight in my own mind? Now, then. Who was the first person to go to Jesus' tomb? Was it Mary Magdalene by herself? So said John. Or was it Mary Magdalene with another Mary? So said Matthew. Or was it Mary Magdalene along with another Mary, plus Salome? So said Mark. Or was it Mary Magdalene, Mary, Joanna, and a number of other women? So said Luke. Was the stone already rolled away when they arrived at the tomb? So said Mark, Luke and John. Or was that explicitly not the case? So said Matthew. Whom did they see there? A man? So said Mark. An angel? So said Matthew. Or two men? So said Luke. What did the mysterious human or angel at the tomb tell the women to do? Did he tell them to tell the disciples that Jesus would meet them in Galilee. So said Mark and Matthew. Or did he tell them to remember what Jesus had told them earlier when *he* had been in Galilee? So said Luke. Did the women then tell the disciples what they had been told to tell them, as Matthew and Luke maintained, or not, as in *Mark* where the narrative was abruptly cut off. Did the disciples see Jesus? So said Matthew, Luke and John. Or did they not see Jesus, as in *Mark* where the narrative was cut off? And where did they see him? Only in Galilee, as stated by Matthew, or only in Jerusalem, as stated by Luke? A total jumble of confusion! And, as you know even better than I, Uzziah, there's much, much more to the episode than the mess that I just related now!"

The purportedly very grave matter of Jesus' resurrection, when presented in the vein in which Theophilus had presented it, actually made Uzziah laugh a little.

"Yes. Everyone and his brother had a hand in adding something to the Jesus resurrection tales. Most additions were made in order to make some fondly-held theological point. In their original form, the gospel stories presented the resurrected Jesus as a completely ghostly figure. John's gospel has Mary Magdalene unable to recognize Jesus, mistaking him for the gardener! And this for-some-reason-unrecognizable Jesus ordered her not to touch him. And two disciples on the road to Emmaus also encountered the for-some-reason-unrecognizable Jesus. Then he vanished! The thing was, both of those early resurrection stories seemed too much like ghost stories. And so, later mythmakers set out to present the resurrected Jesus as a recognizable solid human. Accordingly, in those later myths Jesus ate broiled fish in front of the disciples to prove his physical existence! And this new sort of resurrected Jesus was so unlike the old sort, the one who had ordered Mary Magdalene *not to touch him,* that he ordered Doubting Thomas *to touch him,* to prove how real he was!"

Uzziah led Theophilus to another section of the Golgotha quarry and announced, "Yes, we've now come to the vast subject of the resurrection. Come. There's something I want to show you."

And he showed Theophilus that in this barren vicinity there did stand a few proud and gallant trees, though small ones. He touched them with surprising affection, then prayed to them with zeal. Then he explained.

Trees are conduits to God. There are two types of tree before you: *elah*, which means terebinth, and *alon* or *elon*, which means oak. Both of those names connote loftiness in our language, and you can readily hear how close those names are to some of our local names for God: El, Elohim, Ali, Allah. Now allow yourself to feel an even deeper understanding and reverence for the holy crucifixion tableau, Theophilus. The Tree of Life is where *we all hang*, suspended and in pain and seemingly helpless, as the necessary prelude to our divine resurrection which *we all* will undergo. So it is with our *True Self,* which is our *Jesus.* And so it is with our *False Self,* which is our betrayer *Judas,* who, very meaningfully, was hanged on a tree as well. You might as well picture the two of them, Jesus and Judas, as hanging on the Tree of Life in the same vicinity. Pick a spot and imagine Judas hanging himself there, if it helps you to construct a compelling tableau. He was buried in Potters' Field, a very old and very rich symbol-name for this material world where we shape heavenly destiny *by working in the earthly filth.* There's so much more to say about heavenly resurrection. *After all this is the 'divine salvation' that is seen in the very meaning of the name 'Jesus'!* This is the holy name that you have been questing after. *This is the man that you have been looking for!*"

"And I've just found something over here!" exclaimed Theophilus. He had found a crude inscription that someone had made on a slab. When he wiped the slab clean the two men could see that the inscription read, "*TOPOS KRANIOU PARADEISOS GEGNON,*" "Paradise is born at the place of the skull."

Theophilus heard his own voice resonate in the former quarry called the Place of the Skull. "We are well guided."

"Yes. That is extremely well said. There is so much more to say about resurrection. Now I have some more ideas that will surprise you. We will discuss them presently as we watch the Son of Man *rise*. Perhaps we will do so all night."

# XIV ADAM KADMON... THE COSMIC MAN

Night was falling. Uzziah led Theophilus up a hill with a sweeping view of the ruins of Jerusalem to the east, and announced that they would camp out here and watch the Son of Man rise to the heavens, in resurrection.

"You are serious about this?" inquired the bewildered Roman.

"Very much so. The Lord provides us with infinite instructive spectacle. The greatest story ever told, the Christ story, is one such spectacle. We will now watch another spectacle. Night will fall now, gradually. While we wait for the spectacle I will satisfy some of your burning curiosity, I'm sure, and I'll finally solve for you the mystery of why Jesus kept calling himself the Son of Man."

"Ah, yes! Finally, indeed!"

"Son of Man, which Jesus continually called himself in Greek, '*ho houios tou anthropou,*' is an overly literal and quite poor translation of the Hebrew: *Bar Nasha. Bar Nasha* is mentioned many times in Jewish scripture, and Jesus calls himself the Son of Man many times in Christian scripture. What does Jesus really call himself, when he calls himself the Son of Man? Perhaps the best translation would be 'the human archetype.' But I like to use the term 'Cosmic Man.' The Cosmic Man is *the pattern of human destiny*. Christ died for all of us because *he is all of us!* He is the latest and most powerful of the myth-men. He is Cosmic Man. Myth-men have, since time immemorial, depicted for us, with their lives, the essence of humanity. Now the world has Jesus, whose name means 'God's salvation.' Far to the east in India they have the instructive life of the one whom they call 'the Awakened One.' Here in the west, lately there has been Mithras, 'the joiner,' who may thrive as others of his legendary ilk have thrived, or may fade as others of his legendary ilk have faded. And, of course, for many centuries there has been 'Pharaoh,' 'the Royal Man,' the peculiarly Egyptian mode of looking at the ideal man. All of these have been ideals of what man can become. All of them are Cosmic Man."

"I like the concept of Cosmic Man. And I like that pithy phrase that the evangelist John had Jesus utter: 'I have overcome the cosmos.'"

"Well recalled. That's very much the right phrase at the right time," commended Uzziah. "And undoubtedly you know the even pithier Greek phrase: SOMA-SEMA. How potent is the simple truth, SOMA-SEMA. 'The body is a tomb.' Probably Mark had it right in the first place when he ended his simple tale of Jesus in the abrupt and simple way that he did. He simply had Jesus *be absent from his tomb…* and that was that! Later editors of Mark who thought they could do a better job of high symbolism added various alternate endings to his gospel, and the later gospel writers went wild with all kinds of embellishments to the resurrection story. But perhaps the original tale, the one told by Mark, was the best. *Jesus was not really present in his tomb… and that was that!"*

"I understand the import of that. Yes, I understand the clean simplicity of Mark's original ending to the tale of the savior Jesus. Jesus was the universal savior because he demonstrated that *the tomb is empty*, which is to say that *the body is an illusion* and the material world is an illusion! SOMA-SEMA!"

"Precisely. I suppose that other attempts at grand symbolism were amusing to dabble in. Peter, representing befuddled materialistic mankind (you'll recall that he denied Jesus to the tune of the crowing cock that stands for self-centeredness), was able to grasp only the *clothing* of the deceased Jesus! That vignette made the point that Peter was able to grasp only *the material and the superficial*. Three Marys were in attendance at the resurrection of Jesus. That vignette took place in honor of the role of the Earth Mother triad in resurrection, something you don't know much about yet. The resurrected Jesus helped the apostles catch a rich bounty of fish in the Sea of Galilee. That was rather a trite use of the powers of the supreme savior, but it was a memorable tableau showing that the supreme savior's essence is *abundance without measure*. Well, there exist so many more such stories. As John weakly ended his gospel, almost spoiling its whole effect: 'But there are also many other things which Jesus did; were every one of them to be written, I suppose that the world itself could not contain the books that would be written.'"

"Well of course," commented Theophilus. "Of course no amount of books could contain all of Jesus' deeds, since Jesus is all of human endeavor. Jesus has overcome the cosmos! Now it's getting dark, Uzziah. We have that spectacle that's always so delightful of watching the stars peek through the veil of heaven one by one. I assume that we're here to observe the cosmos. I assume that it's in the sky that we're going to witness the ascent of Cosmic Man that you mentioned."

"Certainly. We'll be surrounded by stars, we'll swim in stars. What better way to remind ourselves that all is united? We are our savior, and our savior is us! *The famous seamless cloak of Jesus represents the pristine oneness of human existence*! But ignorant souls in their blindness ('Father, forgive them, for they don't know what they're doing!') believe in randomness and in prevailing at others' expense. *So like the Roman soldiers, such benighted people cast lots for the pieces of Jesus' cloak that had they had oafishly ripped apart*!"

"And of course you're fond of the fact that those ripping oafs and gambling oafs were Romans."

Uzziah laughed and continued. "I'll speak of a far more significant ripping right now. At the moment of Jesus' death, so runs the tale, the great veil of the Temple was ripped asunder. Josephus wrote that that Temple veil was a tremendous panorama of the heavens, an 80-foot-high Babylonian tapestry that depicted the cosmos. Sophia, which is to say 'wisdom,' was a mystery-woman in a veil who was sometimes said to be the wife of Jesus. She was also said to be a *veil* that kept man from glimpsing the heavenly things above."

Theophilus watched the stars appear as night fell. He fell asleep, and awoke, and fell asleep again, and awoke again. Thus: the veil closed, the veil lifted, the veil closed, the veil lifted. For him, this night's stargazing mixed with visions and dreams. He saw the constellation Orion rise over the Mount of Olives, the very place where Jesus supposedly ascended to heaven forty days after his resurrection. And the revelation dawned on him that the two events were one: the resurrection was a "ceasing-to-be-human," and the ascension that inevitably followed the resurrection was a "beginning-to-be-divine." Jesus-Orion was Cosmic Man, the human potentiality for celestial ascent. Jesus-Orion was Adam Kadmon, the aggregate of all human souls. Three-star Orion was the world's perpetual display of "the magic of threes." Jesus was born as a creature who was predestined for Orion-ascent; his birth was greeted by three Magi according to Matthew, but Luke changed this threesome into three shepherds.

The Cosmic Man, in his guise as the constellation Orion, was in ascent. This Cosmic Man was spectacular. This particular Cosmic Man was equivalent to the Alpha-Omega who appeared to the stunned apocalyptic writer John at the beginning of his *Revelation*. This apocalyptic being, this Lord, or angel, or Cosmic Man, or Jesus who opened the magical events in *Revelation*, was made up of seven stars just like Orion, and held seven stars in his right hand. For indeed the seven *planets* would periodically pass through the upraised right hand of Orion. And this Cosmic Man whom John introduced in *Revelation* wore a belt of gold, a belt being the defining characteristic of Orion. Thus began John's lists of many "sevens" in *Revelation*, the climacteric of the *biblia*.

"Maybe I've been a bore for several days running now," remarked Uzziah with a grin. "I talk, and talk, and talk. Maybe I say too much. And maybe I shouldn't spoil the moment now, this moment that is so grand and cosmic. But on the other hand you may profit from a few things that I can tell you about ascension. In Christian scripture, Jesus' ascension is so anti-climactic that it can rightly be called uninteresting. Only Luke has anything to say about it at all, and he confusingly describes Jesus' ascension one way in his *Gospel of Luke* and another way in his own *Acts of the Apostles*. In some versions of the text, even Luke's terribly dull phrase 'And Jesus was carried up to heaven' is missing, replaced by the even more tepid 'Jesus parted from them.' Luke based his anti-climactic ascension of Jesus partly on Elijah's ascension and partly on Josephus's description of Moses' ascension. Astoundingly, Luke placed the ascension on Passion evening in his gospel, but placed it 40 days later than the Passion in his *Acts*."

"More than being uninteresting," evaluated Theophilus, "the bland and unsatisfactory nature of the Jesus ascension episode is like a huge gaping hole in the Jesus myth which is otherwise so gripping from beginning to end. From time immemorial mythmakers and philosophers have discussed ascension, exaltation, apotheosis, a 'being caught up into heaven,' and so on, and have picked apart the differences between these concepts ad infinitum. I have a long. lifetime ahead of me to figure out these matters, and I'll leave those matters to that long lifetime. For now, I'm not at all uninterested, but I'm very, very sleepy. Deliciously sleepy. And I intend to lie back and let divine Hypnos, the Lord of Sleep, take me where he will. And I thank him in advance for resting and replenishing my mental faculties. Good night!"

"Good night, O ever-more-learned Theophilus! I'll send you off to the land of slumber with this phrase in your mind. Do you remember how Luke began his *Acts of the Apostles*? He began it by referring back to something from his gospel. His exact words were, 'The first account I composed, Theophilus, about all that Jesus began to do and teach *until the day when he was taken up*'!"

# XV BETHLEHEM... THE SUSTENANCE

The next day, Jewish mentor and Roman student walked south to Bethlehem. Uzziah related how this was the very road upon which there took place the first crucifixions ever seen in Judea. In that episode two centuries before, the Jewish Maccabean-Hasmonean king Alexander Jannaeus crucified Pharisees upon many of the road's lovely olive trees. He crucified them in low and gnarled positions in order to humiliate them. Theophilus took note that Uzziah did not hesitate to emphasize that these, the first crucifixions in Judea, had been ordered a Jew, not by a Roman. His tone was rueful, not judgmental. The man seemed to be softening. Theophilus had a feeling that Uzziah had so easily agreed to engage in this Judean journey and these Jewish lessons because, deep down, he craved the lessons as much as did his pupil.

Atop a hill offering a panorama of the tiny village of Bethlehem and its placid fields the men paused to take their meal. Uzziah garnished several flat, round pieces of bread with spicy toppings, as was customary for a Judean meal. And he blessed his meal, as was usual too. However his discourse indicated that this particular meal would be something other than usual.

"It's fitting that we eat our bread here where we can enjoy a view of Bethlehem. Because 'Bethlehem' means 'house of bread.' And since in this part of the world bread is practically synonymous with food, what 'Bethlehem' really means is 'house of sustenance.' Bethlehem is indeed a place much associated with actual bread, because it sits in a rich grain-growing area. You can see that right now, by the look of those fields. Past those fields there lie various other areas that offer nothing but crags and arid nothingness.

"Bethlehem is a very ancient and sacred place. At certain places in the world people can feel the flow of the very power that sustains the world. Or at least *they used to be able* to feel that power. Unfortunately, for the 'fallen' and depraved people of our wicked times, the ability to feel the loving and sustaining power of the earth has become something quite rare. Mostly nowadays, that exquisite feeling is only a memory that is preserved in legends. This place Bethlehem was an origin-place, a wellspring of bodily sustenance and of material existence itself. Mythmakers made this town the birthplace of Jesus in order to connect him with David, it is true. But there was much more to Bethlehem than just David. In part, mythmakers made this town the birthplace of Jesus because of a prophecy of Micah. The prophecy ran: 'Bethlehem, small as you are, out of you shall come a ruler of Israel.' And there was still more. This little town of Bethlehem was the town of David because David, literally 'the gift,' was symbolic of the gift of life itself. Here the young David lived with his sheep who represented naturalness and guilelessness and passivity."

Theophilus asked, "Is that why Luke placed shepherds here to greet the birth of Jesus?"

"Yes, and Luke emphasized that they were *nighttime* shepherds. Nighttime shepherds? That is something that can make sense only symbolically. These were clearly very special shepherds, shepherds who were making a Christological statement with their presence. Nighttime shepherds were something that actually did exist. Nighttime shepherds were shepherds who were entrusted by the Temple to tend special Temple sheep who were destined for *sacrifice*!"

"That's both somewhat charming and somewhat horrifying. Even at his birth Jesus was surrounded by special shepherds because he was a sheep destined for sacrifice!"

"Yes." Uzziah went on. "So here lived David with his sheep and his music. Bethlehem was all about the natural and harmonious life. The world is full of demonstrative myth and sly myth. Take a look at that hill over there. That hill in the distance which is a sort of mockery of everything that Bethlehem stands for. That neat conical hill topped by those palatial white walls and towers, reached by 200 gleaming white steps, is the Herodium. It is just one of Herod's many palaces. Herod employed violence and cruelty so that he could afford to fill his world with private pleasure-palaces, complete with baths, theaters, and, I'm sorry to say, synagogues. This particular one of Herod's palaces near Bethlehem, this

Herodium, is especially illustrative of life that is *not* lived in a spirit of love and harmony!"

"Yes, it's all rather neat, symbolically," agreed Theophilus. "Holy Bethlehem on side, and greedy Herod's pleasure palace on the other."

"David was the son of Jesse, in other words the son of 'pure being.' Feel the power of that pure being. Jesse! Feel that! If it helps, feel it as the Latin word for pure being: *esse! Esse! Esse!*"

Theophilus had already begun to feel an otherworldly allure in this place, and said so.

"I sensed a special pull in this place when we first passed by it before we reached Jerusalem. At that time I most definitely didn't want to pass Bethlehem by. It was as though the place were speaking to me with some sort of purity. One might say some sort of *esse!*"

"That's not too surprising. You made a journey from your home to this distant land of Judea for the singular reason that you developed within yourself a longing for the spirit. In our troubled world, that longing is a paramount fact of life. But in most people that paramount fact of life remains covered over by all sorts of nonsense. So why is the Jesus legend so very magical? It is because the Jesus legend speaks directly to that longing! That is the reason why *everything* connected to Jesus is so powerful! And that Jesus legend begins right here in Bethlehem! This 'place of sustenance' that was home to the 'gift-of-life' figure named David is a place that speaks of the gift of life. Three Persian Magi, sometimes mistranslated as Three Kings or Three Wise Men, came here bearing *gifts.* Those gifts symbolized God's three gifts that are the three components making up a human being: body, mind, and spirit. The threefold gift of life! In the Jesus tale the Three Magi came from the east, but quite paradoxically they were guided by a star in the east. Myth speaks in such ways, strange and paradoxical ways. Just bear in mind that 'east' symbolizes the inner, the spiritual, the original. Around the time that Jesus was supposed to have been born, certain conjunctions of planets were extremely impressive and may have served as an inspiration for the famous 'star in the east.' However, at base the star in the east was purely symbolic."

Recalled Theophilus, "King Herod hosted the Three Magi, but his intention was to use them to find the baby Jesus so that he could kill him. The Three Magi completely distrusted Herod, as anybody but a halfwit would have, so they didn't return to him as they had promised they would. I believe that I can see now how Herod was a real person, but was also a larger-than-life personage who was just begging to be incorporated into the Jesus myth. In Greek, 'Herod' connotes 'heroic,' but also connotes all that is self-centered and egotistical. Herod is a symbol of what happens to a human being when *a human being is completely ruled by selfishness.* Right now we're looking at a ruined and abandoned Herodium that speaks of exactly that. A character like Herod hosts the components called body and mind and spirit, and yet doesn't really host them. He just wants to use those components for evil selfish purposes. He can't be trusted. Jesus was shown as representing *the opposite,* right from the start. He represents the salvific aspect of man. Therefore a repulsive character like Herod tries to nip in the bud, so to speak, the existence of Jesus. He'll do anything, cause any pain, wreak any destruction, to nip in the bud the existence of Jesus. I used to be so confused by the gospel story of Herod slaughtering all the newborns in order to kill Jesus, something that, historically speaking, couldn't possibly have happened. That foul fable was put together from several sources in the Septuagint. But the important thing, now, is that I see how that hyperbolic bit of dramatic myth *speaks directly to the soul*!"

Uzziah nodded. "Well said. Very well said. When you really look around, the right signs are everywhere. It may be that you're slowly learning to let things speak directly to your soul. Here we are in the place of David, he who was 'the gift of life,' and the son of Jesse who was 'pure being,' he who lived among the pure white sheep and played the psalm-harmonies of life upon his lyre. Picture Three Magi coming from a mysterious place and bearing gifts. Let the magic be! Magi, you see, were followers of Mithras, 'the joiner,' whose birthday was celebrated in late December. Mithras' birth was witnessed by three shepherds. Look at the threes. Three shepherds. Three Magi. Three gifts. Magic tends to come in threes. Let the magic be!"

At that moment a bright falling star streamed across the deep blue sky of the Bethlehem panorama. The coincidence of seeing a star like the star that lured the Magi overwhelmed the men. Uzziah fell to his knees and recited a long prayer that resounded with unfathomably deep Hebraic echoes. Theophilus' jaw had dropped, and it remained dropped. He was dumbstruck by the sudden realization that his universe was nothing like what he had believed it to be. He shuddered, and knew no prayer profound enough to express what he was feeling.

Uzziah returned to the world of the mundane but his voice was still sonorously Hebraic.

"The 'Third' has come! Magic happens in threes! You and I and the star in the east together make *a threesome*! We are three! Let the magic be! Your blanched face shows that you've been struck by the wonder of the magical star that we've just witnessed, Theophilus! Here in the village of God's gifts you've witnessed one of God's gifts! We are brought back to the beginning, to the 'house of sustenance'! What we have just seen is the most potent of symbols! A star falling to earth symbolizes human origins! *For a human being is a celestial light that has fallen to the earthly plane!* That is why a celestial light represented the birth of *the human called Jesus, who was all of us humans!* Such is our human tale! *We are, each of us, a star that falls to earth and is born in a cave among beasts!* Such is a human being! Such is Jesus! Birth in a cave: that is a symbolic illustration of *what life on earth is*! One can find the same image in Pythagoras, Plato, Empedocles and many other authors. Now let's descend to our 'cave' of today, the cave that is celebrated as the birthplace of Jesus, and make the most of the place."

"Awe-inspiring is the word for it!" intoned Theophilus.

"So just imagine how inspired were certain mythmakers of

old who contemplated these magical environs *at night*! They would have seen the three bright stars of Orion, also known as the Three Kings, point to where the brightest of stars, Sirius, comes up over the horizon, and is, in other words, 'born,' in conjunction with the constellation Virgo! And they would have contemplated, and added to their mythmaking, the nearby constellation of Cepheus, with its stars Errai and Alfirk, meaning 'shepherd' and 'flock'!"

On the way down to the little town that was called the 'house of sustenance' Uzziah returned to the topic of sustenance.

"Perhaps you have just eaten the most satisfying meal you will ever eat, Theophilus. Jesus said, 'Man does not live by bread alone.' Sacred places like Bethlehem were ordinarily dedicated to the grain god, the 'great sustainer,' and they were places full of ceremonies that were meant to assure good harvests and prosperity. But they were always, simultaneously, places of *spiritual* sustenance! Jesus said both 'I am the bread of life' and 'I am the true vine.' Since time immemorial people consumed both bread and wine to commune with 'the god-man,' be he Osiris or Adonis or Dionysus or Jesus. And now I'll quote one of your own people, Cicero, to you. Cicero said, 'Is anyone so mad as to believe that the food he eats is actually a god?' Well, I should hope not! To consume *bread* and *wine* in the name of the god-man is to partake of both the sustenance of the *material world,* alias bread, and to simultaneously partake of the sustenance of the *spiritual world,* alias spirit! Because 'Man does not live by bread alone'! Bethlehem is so ordinary yet so extraordinary!"

The men approached the ancient holy grotto whose presence assured that Bethlehem was much more than the nondescript dust-colored hamlet that it appeared to be. This grotto was called the Grotto of Adonis. A pleasant grove sheltered the grotto, and the windswept leaves of the grotto's trees whispered welcome. The grotto was large enough to hold numerous offerings, for many worshippers did come. The grotto was, however, not large enough to accommodate much human activity. Cramped and simple though it was, some people regarded it as the purported birthplace of Jesus. Theophilus felt drawn to this simple shrine in the same inexplicable way that he had previously felt drawn to Bethlehem itself. The men stood for a long time in silent devotion. First there was silence. Then there was a flood of images in keeping with the attribute of this site; it was a place of many tales.

Theophilus experienced this holy site as though in a dream state, as though in a blur. Some information came from his companion. Some information came from his memory. Some information came from voices that might have been the voices of fellow-visitors or might have been the voices of grove-spirits or angels. They all whirred and burbled as one, because this was a place imbued with a magnificent message of oneness.

He spoke to himself.

"This was 'Jesse': pure 'being.' This was 'David': 'life, the gift of God.' This was the 'house of sustenance,' the origin of material and bodily existence. There are many other 'house of sustenance' spots around the world, but this is one of the most powerful. Here the universal tale is especially powerful. Here one can well imagine the Three Magi bringing forth the three gifts that spell life: body, mind and spirit.

Outside the grotto, Uzziah discoursed.

"One of the gifts of the Magi was said to be myrrh, which you and I talked about in the Arabian desert. As far as most worshippers here are concerned, this grotto has always been the birthplace of the god Adonis. Adonis was so very Christ-like. He was Adonai, meaning 'the Lord.' Adonis was God, but he was also Primal Man. The sonorous name 'Adonis' has always said so very much, in slightly varied forms. 'Adam' to Jews. 'Atum' to Egyptians. And even 'Atom' to Greeks who frequented certain Mysteries. Adonis was reputed to have been born in this grotto to his mother, the Virgin Myrrha. So there you see whence came the myrrh in the Christian story! Adonis' mother was that 'gift of the Magi' known as myrrh, and she was also the Virgin Myrrha, and she was also the Virgin Mary, just with a slightly different pronunciation. Here, now, you see who the Virgin Mary was. The Virgin Mary was 'Mother Earth giving birth to humanity.' And, in this cave of profoundest magic, she was simultaneously 'Mother Earth giving birth to *God!*"

Uzziah's words confirmed what Theophilus was beginning to know inwardly: that this tale of the birth of Jesus was both the most basic of tales and the most wondrous of tales. For it was the tale of both man and God. A star appeared in the heavens, and then a birth occurred in a cave. God had become man! God had become man! God had become man! In Antioch, the Mysteries of Adonis were customarily celebrated with cries of, "The Star of Salvation has dawned in the East!" And Matthew, who was a man of Antioch, said as much when he spun the Nativity tale that would captivate the world.

But, thought Theophilus, there were many old tales that Matthew twisted and distorted as he spun tales of his own. Very crucial was the fact that Adonis not only was born in this cave in Bethlehem, but also *died* here. The resurrecting Jesus, on the other hand, was assigned a different cave for his death-tale, a cave in Jerusalem. In the pristine original tale of the god-man, this Cave of Adonis, this cave of deepest splendor, represented both the transit *into* the material world and the transit *out of* the material world. This circumstance was retained in the Jesus tale only in that myrrh appeared twice: both at Jesus' birth and at his death. For Jesus was born to the Virgin Myrrha, and at his death Jesus drank myrrh on the cross. And myrrh was doubly present at the Passion because it composed Jesus' crown of thorns.

Theophilus mulled all of this over as he now donned a crown of myrrh, as was customary for pilgrims here in Bethlehem. Never before had he felt so crowned with success in his quest for Jesus.

Theophilus felt that this little pilgrimage to Bethlehem was a coming-close to an actual touching of the reality of Jesus. This was an experience of the Cosmic Cave. All over the world there were tales of Mary the Earth Mother who incarnated souls and dis-incarnated souls. No wonder there persisted stories of Jesus' mother

Mary being a seamstress. No wonder Mary Magdalene was the first witness to the resurrection. And there was so much more in this glittering legend. For Uzziah pointed out that often the traditions from around the world referred to the Cosmic Cave as being an inn! That reference existed to emphasize the notion that the material world is only a temporary lodging. And the presence of animals gathered around a glowing manger, which was Luke's image, invigorated the symbolic message that the divine had suddenly appeared *in the material world of many sentient beings...* and was sustenance.

Uzziah explained how Luke was well aware of the correct Greek word for inn, *pandocheion,* since he used the word in his story of how a Good Samaritan carried a distressed traveler to an inn and left two denarii with the innkeeper for the man's upkeep. (Those two denarii were the only genuine price mentioned in the gospels; Luke seemed to be a man very aware of money.) So Luke knew all about the concept of a *pandocheion,* but in his Bethlehem story he stated that the Holy Family stayed not in a *pandocheion* but in a *kataluma.* A *kataluma* was a lower chamber where livestock lived. Animals' presence and a manger's presence were necessary for this tale. For the Jesus Nativity tale decreed that the divine had suddenly appeared in the material world... and was sustenance.

And lastly there was one rather silent witness to the miracle-tableau of Jesus' birth, a man called Joseph. Joseph, endowed with a name meaning "he increases," was Father Nature, very logically present in a pairing with the Virgin Mary who was Mother Nature.

Being Father Nature, Joseph was also the Demiurge and the Spinner of Dreams. He dreamed an important dream in the gospels, just as the original Joseph dreamed an important dream in the Torah. And the myth figure Joseph was often called "the Craftsman"! No wonder that much of the world now regarded Jesus' stepfather as a carpenter! According to Gnostics, the material world was the False Home, and various mythic threads entangled this Joseph character inside of stories about the False Home and condemned him as the False Father. Subtly, the gospel writers who related tales of Jesus' birth introduced Joseph into their tales as a sort of False Father, since he had not impregnated May. But like every other mythic thread, this False Father too had his value. After all, Jesus was resurrected in a cave that was provided by a certain Joseph of Arimathea. This was "Joseph the builder," a figure who was merely another mythic manifestation of this same Joseph who so usefully bounded about inside the various myths.

And there was much more, still, to the sacred tableau. The two pilgrims stood in place to experience the magic for a very long time. And many others also gathered around, and gazed in awe... and always would.

# XVI BETHANY... THE LUSCIOUSNESS OF LIFE

Uzziah led Theophilus a few miles onward, to what would be the last stop in their shared tour of this the Holy Land. He explained that he could not stay away from his home in Tiberias much longer, so this place called Bethany would be the place where they would part.

He announced, "Yes, this is the last of it. I will now show you Bethany. Here I will leave you, and let's hope that in our parting you will become as one miraculously *brought to life*. Do you know to which chapter in the life of Jesus I now refer?"

Theophilus replied, "Yes. We are in Bethany. Bethany is the town of Lazarus."

"Yes. Bethany is probably fated to be remembered solely for the incident of Jesus raising Lazarus from the dead. But Bethany is really so much more. As with Bethlehem and its bread, let's make Bethany forever memorable by enacting a scene of actual culinary absorption. Please eat some of these."

He handed Theophilus some fresh figs, sliced to reveal their bright red juicy insides. As Theophilus enjoyed this most delicious of foods, Uzziah laughingly observed, "They're known to be almost sinfully savory, and are even shunned in some quarters because of their delightful appeal to the senses. What do they look like to you, the insides of these figs?"

Theophilus did not pause in his feast. "Yes. I'm well aware. They look like female genitalia."

"Yes, I can see that the point is well made and that you enjoy your figs. Remember well the savor, and remember well what I tell you now. That way, in the future you will be able to avoid a whirl of confusion that has plagued many people. We're in Bethany now, and as you can see it's a village that looks just like all the other villages in the environs of Jerusalem. Whatever was special here in ages past is lost on us jaded people of the current debauched and foolish era. This particular Bethany is just one of several places called Bethany. 'Bethany' means 'house of figs.' 'Bethphage' also means 'house of figs.' And there are many places called Bethphage. A nearby Bethphage was the last town that Jesus passed through before his fateful entry into Jerusalem. In days of old, these places called Bethany or Bethphage were all dedicated to the worship of the gods of fertility. Nowadays whatever little they have retained of their importance is just a distant echo of more enlightened times. Thus, towns named Bethany and Bethphage were incorporated in various confusing ways into the legends that were fabricated about Jesus."

"It is so. It is so. I always found the various Jesus tales

concerning Bethany to be especially confusing."

Uzziah nodded. "Yes, it's a real muddle. To Mark, Bethany was simply the place where an unnamed woman anointed Jesus' head with oil. When John set the stage for Jesus in Bethany with a jumbled combination of stories, he took Mark's simple story and confused it with Luke's story of another unnamed woman, a sinful woman, who wiped Jesus' feet with her hair and anointed his feet with myrrh. To Luke, Mary and Martha were sisters who welcomed Jesus to their home in an unnamed village. This homey Mary of Luke's s story sat raptly at Jesus' feet. So John transformed that Mary into the woman who anointed Jesus' feet, a woman who was already misidentified with Mark's 'woman of Bethany' who anointed Jesus' head! Are you confused?"

"I most certainly am. My own head, though not anointed with oil, gets liquidly at this point! It's swimming in confusion!"

"Yes, these mixed-up stories do get a bit dizzying. Bethany has been considered a place so holy that Jesus just *had to* do great things there, so Bethany is the setting for a whole series of gospel stories that could keep a discussion going for weeks. But I'll get right to the main point. There was a catalyst that prompted John to bring in a whole a lot of stories to make one grand Bethany story. That catalyst was *Egyptian myth*. The sanctity of Bethany goes all the way back to the time when this area was a province of pharaonic Egypt, and Bethany was called by its older name, Beth-Annu.

Theophilus slapped his hands together. "At last! Jesus mysticism and Egyptian mysticism certainly seem to belong together!"

"True enough. So we come to the magnificent and unforgettable deed: Jesus' raising of Lazarus from the dead. The name Lazarus is a modernization and Latinization of the ancient name Eleazar. And when traced to even more distant times, the name Eleazar reveals itself to be a two-word phrase stating, 'El-Eazar,' which means 'the god Eazar.' So we're down to the ancient god Eazar as the origin of the myth figure Lazarus. This god Eazar is better known as Asher, who is familiar to us us an old fertility god, and as the patron of the Israelite tribe of Asher. Now for the key point. The key point is that this fertility god Eazar is the Israelite version of Egypt's all-important fertility god *Osiris*, whose name should actually pronounced as Ausar. Ausar was the god of fertility, resurrection and death, and he was worshipped in several places bearing the names Bethany and Bethphage. So here in Bethany, Ausar gradually became Eazar, who gradually became El-Eazar, who gradually became Eleazar, who eventually became Latinized as *Lazarus*!"

"Aha!" exclaimed Theophilus delightedly. "Some hazy points have now been cleared up marvelously! To the gospel writer John, Lazarus was the acclaimed personage who was brought back to life by Jesus. But to the gospel writer Luke, Lazarus was merely a terribly incomprehensible fellow who was stuck in the underworld. In actuality, both of these 'Lazari' were manifestations of *the old god of the resurrectional underworld Osiris*, manifestations who were adapted into Christian legends to make points about Jesus' complete power over life and death!"

"Precisely! This Osiris-sacred-place called Beth-Annu has recently been transforming into a Jesus-sacred-place called Bethany. Many of the statements uttered in the gospels in Bethany correspond very closely with ancient Osiris prayers that were uttered in Beth-Annu. Moreover, Osiris had two sisters, Isis and Nephthys; and the gospel writer John conveniently converted them into Lazarus's two sisters, Mary and Martha. Isis and Nephthys were known as 'the beloveds,' which translates in Greco-Egyptian as the Mertae. These sisters who were called the Mertae were, yes you've guessed it, converted into the sisters called Martha and Mary!"

Theophilus pleaded, "Can we pause now for just a moment? I've been inundated with so much information lately, I need to pause a bit to absorb this latest material, which is completely new to me. Bethany was an Egyptian sacred spot called Beth-Annu. It was devoted to the resurrection god Osiris, whose name was actually pronounced as Ausar, or Asher, who eventually became Eazer, and then El-Eeazer, and then Eleazer, and then Lazarus. Osiris had two sisters who were called 'the beloveds' or the Mertae, and they were the inspiration for Lazarus's two sisters Martha and Mary. All of the gospel stories that were set in Bethany, or involving Marys, are still awfully confusing, but at least one can begin to make sense out of them, knowing the Egyptian background!"

"Yes. Still confusing, but at least decipherable. Now then, there's the earliest Christian story about Lazarus, namely Mark's story. The exciting well-known Lazarus story by John, which should be Jesus' ultimate miracle, falls completely flat when one finds out what it was originally all about. For Mark's more humble story was the earlier Lazarus story by far. In Mark's story, Lazarus was actually *alive* in his tomb, and was released by Jesus on the third day. This episode was a re-enactment of an Essene initiation, full of deep symbolism but devoid of any appeal to non-Essenes, and devoid of any resurrection of the dead. This episode in its original unexciting and confusing form was *excised* from the *Gospel of Mark*. Ignatius of Antioch took the lead in excising material of that sort, material that made Jesus seem insufficiently heroic and excessively symbolic."

Theophilus made a face. "Oh, yes, *him*! Ignatius!"

Uzziah continued.

"Yes, him. Him and others of his ilk. They're butchering the Jesus legends left and right. But they are not the only ones responsible for making Jesus a figure of tremendous confusion. The fact is, the original Jesus tales were full of obscure esoteric references that could make sense only to a few highly informed people. There exists a *Secret Gospel of Mark* that mentions that initiates wore only a linen loincloth and were considered to be reborn. That linen loincloth could mean nothing to you, but it is well known to me. It is the white linen loincloth symbolic of the purification of the lower drives. It signifies initiation into the secret brotherhood of masons, masons like Jesus. In Mark's standard non-secret gospel, the well-known *Gospel of Mark*, Mark recorded how an unidentified young man wearing only a linen cloth was seized at

Gethsemane but slipped out of the linen cloth and ran away naked. Let future generations wonder at this symbolic nakedness, this somewhat obscure symbolism! Nakedness incorporates the symbolism of being born anew!"

"Much does indeed become clearer all at once, if one takes the right approach. I always wondered about the inane suggestion of the apostle Thomas in reference to Lazarus: 'Let us go and die with him.' The suggestion is less of an oddity if Lazarus is recognized to be a mystical god of resurrection, rather than just a deceased friend of Jesus. It's all not to be taken literally. It's all not to be taken literally, no indeed. Bear in mind the following. In the gospels, Jesus raised from the dead three people. Always there is the magic of threes! He raised from the dead the daughter of Jairus, whose name meant "he will awaken." And he raised from the dead the son of a widow. But the raising of Lazarus was the supreme raising, because Lazarus was the ancient god Osiris who prevailed over life and death!

"Much, much more of the mythic material will become clear to you in due course. It need not all happen all at once. Lazarus had sisters named Mary and Martha who were aspects of the Virgin Mary, the Earth Mother, whom we discussed a bit in Bethlehem. Much more valuable information about them will come your way in due course. For now I'd like you to do one simple thing. Just remain quiet for a little while and look into you heart to see what you feel about Bethany."

Theophilus did as instructed. At length he told his instructor,

"There's both joy and sadness, mixed. There's a specialness. I feel that Bethany was a very special place in the legend of Jesus. It seems to me that Bethany was the place where… how shall I put it… the place where Jesus felt most at home!"

"That comes close to what I was aiming for. The point I was aiming for is this. This is the bittersweet place, this Bethany. This is truly the 'place of life.' Figs are the most delicious things imaginable. But fig leaves in the wind are notable for the way they moan, and there are certain times when fig trees are fit to be cursed, as we've previously discussed. Jesus enjoyed the company of some of his best friends while he was here in Bethany. But this place also engendered one of the shortest sentences in all the scriptures. That sentence was, 'Jesus wept.' Here is the point I wish to make now, dear friend. Bethany is the epitome of life, as opposed to non-life. Because aside from the mysterious unidentified 'apostle whom Jesus loved,' the only people whom the gospels identified as people that Jesus *loved* were Lazarus and his sisters Mary and Martha!"

"It's been quite a journey, Uzziah. We've discussed disputes, accusations, beheadings, crucifixions, hypocrisies, desert starvation, family abandonment, name-calling, demons, denial, betrayal, slaughters, and I don't know at this point if I've left anything out. And often it has occurred to me: where is the *love* that should have been the whole point of the Jesus message all along, if there is to be any point at all?"

"You'll have that and a lot else to think about as you make your way alone to Caesarea and to Egypt. As I've told you, I have my own loved ones to return to now. You, my friend, have ties of your own. I've been informed that waiting for you in Caesarea there are both letters and people waiting for you."

Through a dropped jaw Theophilus asked, "How on earth can you know that?"

"As you've been told before, word quickly gets around in this small but special nation called Judea. Now then, I want our goodbye, yours and mine, to be short but memorable, taking no more time than it takes me to rearrange our belongings here by the roadside to get you ready to proceed on your own."

"I don't like long goodbyes either. Let's make it quick. And tell me, how will our goodbye be memorable?"

Uzziah needed some silent time to put the belongings in order. Then he gave a few instructions about the road to Caesarea, which were trivial, and then proceeded to the memorable.

"It's a mitzvah, a blessing, to part ways with words on the subject of love. It isn't hard for me to think of what to say right now, because these parting words originated in my own favorite scripture, the *Book of Daniel*. Matthew adapted these words to portray Jesus as he was departing from his disciples, *but this time without any surprise-return in bodily form!* Matthew's Jesus said to his disciples at this juncture, *'Ego meth humon eimi pasas tas hemeras, heos tes sunteleios,'* 'I am with you always to the end of time.' And such is the best ending to any gospel, and to any personal story as well!"

There was an embrace, which Theophilus appreciated, and then a mutual kissing of cheeks, which was something Theophilus had long had difficulty getting accustomed to while traveling in the East. Then Uzziah went his own way. Theophilus resolved to concentrate hard, and to think of almost nothing but *agape,* universal love, on all of his dusty way to a famous city that was hardly known for that. Caesarea.

# XVII CAESAREA...THE INTERLOPER

Caesarea. The stadium. The amphitheater. The marble-pillared temples. The finely paved streets. The long colonnades and the rows and rows of arches. The impressive aqueduct that brought in the city's essential fresh water from afar. Most notable of all in Caesarea was the artificial harbor, the first such wonder that was ever constructed. The Romans had cleverly fashioned this artificial harbor when they discovered that concrete would harden underwater if it were made with ash instead of sand. Theophilus admiringly regarded the breakwater, the lighthouse, the docks, and the giant warehouses that made Caesarea the most thriving city in Judea, with a quite substantial population of 50,000. In Caesarea, all was in place to announce that a mini-Rome had been constructed in Judea, and that the Roman conquerors of Judea were in place to stay. Such construction was the normal procedure in every Roman province, but in tempestuous Judea it had been all the more important to construct a mighty "city of the Caesars" to demonstrate, in solid brick and stone, who was in permanent control. The city was

231

secondarily known as Caesarea Maritima, which made it sound especially beautiful, which in fact it was.

Pontius Pilate had resided here in Caesarea in his Praetorium, which had previously been one of Herod's many palaces. This luxurious edifice sat next to the hippodrome, the racetrack, which was the city's largest edifice of all. Pontius Pilate had been utterly discredited by the coarse course of his career, but he had nonetheless been one of the upholders of Roman power, and would, therefore, certainly not be entirely erased by Rome. Theophilus smiled to see the name PONTIUS PILATUS engraved in stone, in honor of a man who was dishonorable, but who was nonetheless the most famous person ever to have inhabited this city.

"Ah, no," thought Theophilus. On second thought, more famous than Pontius Pilate was Paul, who seemed to have lived most everywhere, and who had lived here in Caesarea for two years. He had lived here as a prisoner. "Our paths cross yet again, this time for the last time, I think," pondered Theophilus, apropos of Paul. In a pro-Roman passage that was typical for Luke, Luke described how Paul was almost killed by persecutors in Jerusalem, but was then escorted by hundreds of Roman troops to Caesarea, to begin two years of house-arrest residence there in the Praetorium. One of the first things that Theophilus did in Caesarea was to sit by the Praetorium and gaze out to sea as Paul must have done, to become acquainted with one more aspect of the biography of that strange and multi-faceted man.

After settling in at his lodgings Theophilus embarked on a

series of inquiries concerning Paul's sojourn in Caesarea. Theophilus's next destination, Egypt, was one of the few important eastern lands never visited by Paul, so this investigation felt to Theophilus like the last of anything that he would do in connection with Paul. Moreover, Caesarea represented a prelude to the physical *finis* of Paul; from here the man was destined to be shipped off to Rome and execution.

As with his imprisonment in Rome, Paul's two years in Caesarea were hardly an imprisonment at all. Theophilus was able to inspect Paul's lodgings in the Praetorium, a site of major luxury, and he immediately saw that Paul's lodgings in Caesarea were actually better than his own, at an inn. Moreover, as was related in the *Book of Acts,* the Roman governor Felix ordered that Paul "be given some freedom, while his friends were permitted to see to his needs." *Acts* further related that Felix was well acquainted with Paul's movement, which was known as "the Way," and that Paul's accusers accused him of being a leader of "the Nazarenes." That mention of Nazarenes certainly stood out, for it was the only mention of Nazarenes in Christian scripture. Try as he might, Theophilus was never able to find any testimony or documentation on "the Way" or "Nazarenes" in Caesarea. He concluded that the usage of those terms must have faded fast, once the word "Christian" started to gain currency.

Theophilus's investigations confirmed for him that Luke's *Book of Acts* narrative about Paul's sojourn in Caesarea was accurate. Though many described Felix as "a man driven mad by a province that was going mad" Felix was quite benign in his treatment of Paul. Felix often spoke with Paul about his faith, and so did his young Jewish wife Drusilla. At this time Paul decided that his closest collaborator, young Timothy, could be of no more use to him in Caesarea, and sent him to live in Ephesus, the mighty metropolis where Timothy seemed likely be the most effective in spreading the Pauline message. Felix's successor as governor, Festus, was even more gentle in his treatment of Paul than was Felix. Paul's neither-here-nor-there mild detainment could well have lasted indefinitely, but after two years Paul decided to make a legal appeal to the emperor and thus break the legal impasse. Such an appeal was Paul's right, since his status as a citizen of Tarsus also made him a Roman citizen. The appeal meant that Paul would be sent to Rome. Festus was happy to fill out the paperwork.

This episode of Paul in Caesarea made all the more certain a conclusion that Theophilus had come to long ago. This conclusion was that to a remarkable degree Paul worked hand-in-hand with the Roman authorities. Theophilus wondered if he would ever be able to figure out the "why's and wherefores" underlying that fact.

Next Theophilus investigated another curious incident set in Caesarea that Luke described in his *Book of Acts*. Luke discussed the short reign, as governor of Judea, of Emperor Claudius's close friend Herod Agrippa, who was a grandson of the infamous King Herod of gospel notoriety. The "Agrippa" appellation unmistakably tied this man to Emperor Augustus' entourage, since Agrippa was Augustus' best friend. Luke claimed that Herod Agrippa curried favor with the Jews purely by persecuting Christians. And Luke claimed that Herod Agrippa imprisoned the apostle Peter and executed the apostle James by the sword, with that execution being the first recorded martyrdom to befall one of the Twelve Apostles. Then one day in Caesarea, governor Herod Agrippa presided over games in honor of his friend Emperor Claudius. He appeared before the crowd arrayed in fine dazzling silvery raiment, raiment that gleamed so wondrously that the crowd exclaimed that he must be not a man, but a god. For this sartorial hubris, God commanded an angel to strike down Herod Agrippa, so that that short-lived governor of Judea died in an utterly miserable state, eaten by worms.

Theophilus's inquiries quickly showed him that none of this story by Luke was true. Herod Agrippa was actually a clement and capable ruler, like his friend Emperor Claudius. And for a few years Herod Agrippa demonstrated that that troublesome province Judea could actually be ruled well, and could actually experience peace. In actuality, all that had been unusual about this man's death was said to be the appearance of an owl as an omen that preceded that death. The consensus was that Herod Agrippa calmly recognized and accepted the owl-omen, and died gracefully. He was not eaten by worms; that tale was made up to equate him with his hated grandfather King Herod, who was well known to have been eaten by worms. Careful investigation of the Herod Agrippa episode confirmed Theophilus in what he had concluded long ago: The *Book of Acts* was most definitely not trustworthy history; it was more like an immense propaganda graffiti wall on which various authors could scribble favorite propaganda points. Some rather fanatical Christian, perhaps Luke and perhaps not, had written the Herod Agrippa worm episode purely to emphasize how despicable were authorities who showed any signs of favoritism towards Jews and against Christians. The *Book of Acts* was one long record of a vicious Jewish-Christian split.

Like all Roman governors of Judea, Pontius Pilate had used this bastion of Roman might, Caesarea, as his administrative headquarters, and had ventured into troublesome Jerusalem only occasionally. There were many ways to worm oneself into history, thought Theophilus wryly, who had worms on his mind after investigating the controversial death of Herod Agrippa. Pontius Pilate was destined to be remembered only for one fictional foray into Jerusalem. This short but portentous tale destined him to be employed forevermore as a literary device to portray Roman villainy.

The real Pontius Pilate had perhaps been even simpler than that. Theophilus recalled how as part of his earliest lessons on Christianity he took in the fact that the name "Pilate," "spear carrier," denoted a Roman citizen of lowly origins. During his term as procurator of Judea, Pilate had been out to enrich himself as quickly as possible, and to him all other considerations had been decidedly secondary. His rapacious record made it almost unthinkable that he was anything like the reflective philosopher that was conjured up in the *Gospel of John*, written many decades after the life of Pilate.

Curiously, the name "Pontius" denoted the sea. Caesarea was a seaport with a gentle climate and gentle pleasing, endless waves, a city which offered the perfect setting for a man as enamored of luxury as Pontius Pilate. Perhaps in this city Pilate was a bit more mellow than he was whenever he sojourned in troublesome Jerusalem. On one occasion, mobs of Jews walked the 65 miles from Jerusalem to Pilate's palace in Caesarea to implore Pilate to remove the idolatrous legion standards that he had installed in the Temple. And on that occasion the famously tyrannical governor of Christian lore actually did relent and do the right thing.

Now back in the world of the Romans, Theophilus had much mundane business to attend to, above all arranging his finances for further travel. As had happened several times before, there took place queer multiple reappearances of the amount "30 pieces of silver" in his dealings. He filed away this odd reoccurring coincidence in his memory. He gathered up letters that were waiting for him. He read the briefest one first. This briefest letter was from his former slave Titus, brief partly because the illiterate Titus had needed to pay a letter-writer to compose this letter. Titus was making a good, if simple, life for himself in Corinth: simple business, simple wife, simple concerns. He was a reminder of that broad spectrum of Christians who thought in terms of belief rather than investigation. There were letters from relatives in Venetia. Theophilus passed these up in order to first read a letter whose presence in his pile greatly surprised him. This letter was from one of the busiest men in Rome, the celebrated author and statesman

Pliny.

I send you greetings from all of your well-wishers in Rome. And I include among those well-wishers not only our good friend Hadrian but Emperor Trajan himself as well. They have enjoyed your letters immensely, as I have myself, having been privileged to look at them. Trajan and Hadrian regret that pressing matters of state rob them of the time that would be required to send you the sort of answer you deserve; but I, irrepressible letter-writer that I am, have been pressed into service to offer you at least the inadequate reply that you now hold in your hands. Forgive me this letter's brevity, but you must understand we have little notion of where you might be, or of whether you will receive this missive at all.

"The die is cast," as once announced Great Caesar. Trajan will lead the legions into battle against the tribes north of the Danube, in Dacia. As you'll have no difficulty in imagining, Trajan is therefore as preoccupied right now as a man can possibly be. Hadrian, on the other hand, does promise to try to write to you as soon as possible. Personally, I believe the explanation for his delay in writing is that your poetry is so good that he is hesitant to compete! I feel sorry for Hadrian right now. His sincere belief is that the Empire must settle into defensible borders in order to proceed to matters that are more important than endless combat. Yet what border is more "defensible" than the Danube? Unfortunately, barbarian raids from across the Danube have made the conquest of those tribes across the Danube, the tribes of Dacia, unavoidable. For many decades the Empire seems to have been obliged to grow in order to survive, without any end to that process in sight. A final reckoning with the Persians will surely be next, as Trajan talks of it constantly.

All of us were deeply saddened by the news of the death of Cato. While remembering him here, we thought of something which you surely have already thought of yourself: that dedicating your book to him would be most appropriate. Lucius Livinius Piso also passed away recently. He seemed to have become a fan of yours, believe it or not, somehow having come to the conclusion that you were setting out to retrace Paul's steps in order to undo Paul's work.

The fact is, you have a following among the "library loiterers" here in Rome's library comparable to that of established authors! We await your book as anxiously as we await Plutarch's multi-biography epic that we have gotten wind of. What has the whole town talking, however, is Tacitus' next project. Taking advantage of the current unprecedented freedom of expression extant in Rome, Tacitus intends to wrestle with the unsurpassably fascinating historical topic of Rome's past emperors. We can trust Tacitus not to pull his punches, each punch being a studied blow for the blessed cause of good government in Rome's future.

And, lastly, thoughts of the future bring me to thoughts of the young. Marcellina is among those who inquire about you often. As a favor to me, and not at all a disservice to yourself, why not answer this letter by writing not to me, but to her?

Your research is too intriguing and too significant to insult with a casual commentary here. I'll only make you cognizant that your Delphic oracle reply has become known here in Rome, and has been keeping many heads busy. "Socrates in his wisdom said 'Know yourself.' But Jesus is the wisdom. He is the self. He is the knowing." May you be much closer to an answer to this riddle than we are! And may you return to us with that answer soon!

It felt so good to learn about the doings of his acquaintances, and to learn that they were thinking of him, that he was ravenous for more. The next letter was from Old Zadok.

I greet you with warm best wishes, young Theophilus. By now you have been exposed to much invaluable information that I previously withheld from you, most coyly. By now you have advanced beyond the stage of neophyte in your studies. And by now you understand why I hesitated to reveal to you things that were precious, in the trite manner of gossip that is idly mouthed while sitting around a hearth. I deemed it necessary for you to visit the sacred sites with Uzziah before you were told certain things. And I deemed it necessary, as it has always been necessary through the ages, to reveal the mysteries in only in the subtlest of ways.

Why is this so? Why has this always been so? Why must the mysteries be revealed only in the subtlest of ways? Recall that the philosopher Demetrius once said, "Whatever is clear and manifest is as despised as are naked human beings." And the philosopher Macrobius once put it even better. He said, "Plain and naked exposition of herself is repugnant to Nature. She wishes her secrets to be revealed by myth. Thus the Mysteries themselves are hidden in the tunnels of figurative expression, so that not even to initiates may the nature of such realities present themselves naked. Such is the Mysterium."

Such is the Mysterium.

The *Second Book of Maccabees* mentions that Nehemiah's library, the central library of the Jewish people, was eventually lost to the ravages of time and human folly. It is known, to those who are truly in the know, that Jewish scripture, which is now often called the Torah or the *biblia*, was compiled from the little that remained of Nehemiah's library. This grand writing project was performed as one facet of the Maccabees' rededication of the Temple that occurred about a century before the arrival of the Romans, which is to say 264 years ago. A hint of the truth of that state of affairs is the fact that the chronology of the Jewish Torah or *biblia* is based on a Great Year that begins in *Genesis* and culminates in the year of the rededication of the Temple 264 years ago. What seems to be a vast corpus of holy literature, the Torah or *biblia,* is in reality only a tiny fragment of what once existed, a tiny fragment that offers only fleeting glimpses of a grand truth.

And part of that grand truth is the gripping fact that the myth-figure Jesus was originally based on a powerful myth-figure named Joshua who has existed for centuries. This is an essential ingredient of the core-of-truth that you have been searching for. "Jesus" is simply the Greek form of that name "Joshua." The holy personage known as Jesus was, in part, the holy personage known as Joshua who was revamped for a new era.

Ask Samaritans, and they will tell you that they have always believed that the Messiah would be named Joshua! That belief was a foreshadowing of the arrival of Jesus, and there have been numerous other such examples of foreshadowing. The proto-messiah Joshua is featured in the 600-year-old *Book of Zechariah*. In that book, a character named Joshua secures rule over all the earth and defeats Satan. Thus, *Zechariah* is the old source wherein this Joshua/Jesus savior-figure emerges most clearly. But there exist other such sources covered by the dusts of time.

Most texts have subordinated this proto-messiah Joshua to the greater prophet Moses. However, the *Book of Jude* has Joshua, rather than Moses (and rather than God for that matter) leading the Israelites out of Egypt. This particular "Joshua Messiah" wrought distinctive "Joshua miracles," such as parting the waters of the Jordan and making city walls fall down. And these miracles were emulated by relatively recent supposed prophets such as Judas of Galilee and Theudas the Magician. See Luke's *Acts* and Josephus' history for confirmation of what I'm saying here. Also, relatively recent would-be prophets adopted the Joshua name, or else the Jesus name, and some of those would-be prophets had some success in gathering followers.

Among them were Jesus ben Ananias, Jesus Justus, Jesus ben Sapphiah the bandit chief, Jesus Barabbas the insurrectionist, and Elymas bar Jesus the sorcerer. All of these men were would-be fulfillers of a mostly oral tradition that concerned a "Joshua Messiah" or a "Jesus Messiah" who was long predicted to arrive and redeem Israel.

Everyone is aware that the most famous prophet named Joshua, who has his own book in the Torah, is associated with the sun, mostly because one fine day he stopped the sun in its course. This prophet Joshua was buried on his own property at Timnath-heres, a place whose name intimates the sun. An image of the sun was placed on Joshua's grave. Now then, Jesus too bears many associations with the sun. His climactic moment was his resurrection on "the day of the sun," or "Sun Day." You may even find Jesus artistically represented as a sun that sits behind a crucifix. I need not go into in exhaustive detail here about Jesus' association with the sun. I believe that there is hardly a culture that does not equate the sun with the highest human essence. This is, of course, the crux of the nature of the Jesus, the mystery that you have sought. The crux of his nature is that he, Jesus, is the highest human essence.

Jesus, like all of the pharaohs and like so many other rulers worldwide, was the sun, the highest human essence.

There exists only one scriptural passage concerning Jesus' boyhood, and that passage subtly mentions the sun. At the age of 12, the lad went missing. His worried parents eventually found him conversing with the wise men of the Temple, who were astounded at his brilliance. Beyond the matter of the boy's brilliance, the point of the story was Jesus' *age*. His age was 12. When his parents found him, his comment was, "Did you not know that I would be in my Father's house?" This phrase "In the Father's house" was an old astrological phrase that meant "The sun at noon," and this phrase was the reason why the writer of the tale described Jesus as being 12 years of age. Additionally, of course you are aware that Jesus was a *"sun"* who had 12 apostles who were his "12 *signs of the zodiac*." And the 70 or 72 disciples mentioned by Luke represented the hoary tradition of 70 or 72 constellations that were non-zodiacal. Since Jesus was the *sun,* many have placed his birth at the time of the winter solstice, December, when the dying sun is eternally *born again.*

Innumerable traditions coalesced to construct the current myth of the man whom we now know as Jesus. Just one example is the way in which the Jesus whom we know from the gospels closely copied the miracles of the prophet Elisha, whose miracles included curing a leper, raising a child from the dead, and feeding the multitude with little bread. And it so happens that Elisha and Jesus have much more in common than just their miracles. The fact is, the names "Elisha" and "Jesus" mean exactly the same thing, namely "God's Salvation." There are those who wish to erase all evidence of Jesus' origins as a myth-man. Thus, you will find that there exist copies of Josephus' work in which the only large gap, the only place where much material has obviously been extracted, is the place where Josephus described Elisha's miracles. Antioch-style Christian fanatics extracted these Elisha miracles from Josephus because those miracles were almost identical to Jesus' miracles. These Elisha miracles were distasteful to the fanatics because they hinted at Jesus being mythical. Little pieces of evidence like this particular piece of "evidence-by-way-of-absence" in Josephus exist in abundance.

But snooping around for such trifles should be the least of your concerns by now. You have embarked on an adventure of boundless magnitude.

Though it is not often said, I believe it is valid to divide Judaism into halves. There is "Ezra Judaism," and there is "Enoch Judaism." I would claim further that there is now coming into existence things that I permit myself to call "Ezra Christianity" and "Enoch Christianity." Ezra and Nehemiah were the leaders of the Jews who returned to

Jerusalem from Babylonian exile. Nehemiah established a physically revived Jerusalem, while Ezra established a Jerusalem priesthood that aimed to monopolize all spirituality and keep the masses under their heel. That corrupt priesthood was nurtured first by Babylonian occupiers, then by Persian occupiers, and most recently by Greek and Roman occupiers. For that corrupt priesthood was always all-too-willing to sell out to the earthly powers-that-be. Ezra was real. All too real. He lives on, in the hearts of many humdrum, despicable men who will do anything to attain power.

Enoch, on the other hand, was a myth-man, and a great man. "Enoch" means "initiate." Enoch is the spirit of an ascent to God that owes nothing to middlemen or to priests. Enoch is a noble tradition. Enoch is the tradition of a human *coming directly to God*. Thus, Enoch is the patron of all Gnostics. And Enoch was a forerunner of the myth-man Jesus.

Jesus was not a man. *Jesus was man!* This was something that I tried to explain to you the first time we met. Jesus was not the Son of Man, as untalented translators would have it. When Jesus called himself Bar Nasha he meant *not* that he was the Son of Man, but that he was *Man*. At a certain point even the reprobate Pontius Pilate saw it, and said *"Ecce Homo,"* "Behold man!"

Oh, how fully is history repeating itself! Nowadays, within Christianity many are the falsifiers' attempts to squelch freedom and obliterate the tradition of the mystics. But Paul and Babylon and Rome will not have the final word. The *Book of Revelation* will have the final word! John, who is Enoch today, will have the final word! I know that to you the apocalypse work known as the *Book of Revelation* still seems nothing but a rant. But I also know that you will come to understand the work one day. Always remember that we told you that many Hebraic myth-men were actually *traditions*. Thus, there is a "John tradition," or a Johannine tradition. For your purposes, John the Baptist, and John the evangelist, and John the describer of apocalypse, will have the final word. "In the beginning was the Word," which means "In the beginning was John," since "John" means "God's Grace." And in the end there will also be "John"! That is why a "John" wrote the work that comes last, the *Book of Revelation.*

And of course there will always be Jesus. His parting words were, "I am with you always, to the end of time."

May the continuance of your quest in Egypt bear the precious fruit that is the Lord's. The Lord be with you.

This letter from Old Zadok, contained much that was stirring, but the last letter that Theophilus found among his letters was the most exciting of all. To Theophilus' great surprise Floralia had addressed a letter to him in Caesarea, but had, weeks later, arrived there herself. He read the letter.

Dearest Theophilus, we will meet up again in the holiest of lands! I am determined that it will be so! I'll send out spies to find you if necessary! When I was in Corinth recently, like a moonstruck girl I sought out your former slave Titus as my first step in trying to track you down. From all that I can ascertain you will be coming to Caesarea, so it is here in Caesarea that I will wait for you.

Curiously, our paths almost crossed already. I have come to this Holy Land on a spiritual quest like yours, something which, I laughingly recall now, I once told you I would never bother to do. I have my reasons, which I will reveal to you only in person. Our paths nearly crossed when I was far up north. I went to the northernmost site in what is considered the Holy Land. That site is Caesarea Philippi. There I enjoyed days at the most beautiful place in the Holy Land, the place in the Holy Land that is the most redolent of nature. It is a magnificent spring where the Jordan River begins, a spring that traditionally belongs to Pan. Of course you are aware that throughout the millennia before Roman occupation Caesarea Philippi was called Panias. This spring was in Caesarea Philippi. I arrived there in the hopes that it would be a healing spring. And one would like to think that exactly at this special spring Jesus first addressed Peter as The Rock, and decreed, "Upon this Rock I will build my Church," and then gave Peter the keys to heaven.

And now here I am here in the other Caesarea, Caesarea Maritima, waiting here with some remarkable things to tell you. Do you remember the incredible things that you and I discussed about Peter? Now I have so much more to tell you! I can scarcely believe how intricately our destinies are interconnected by the sinews of these mysterious matters! Please hasten here! Come to Ceasarea! Some weird 'spirit of Peter' ever unites you and me!

And now Floralia's "here" was exactly where he was!

In a matter of little more than an hour the delightful and the unexpected came to pass. Theophilus found Floralia!

# XVIII MITZRAIM... THE CALL TO EGYPT

With alacrity, Theophilus found out that he would be residing for a time in Caesarea in the most luxurious of surroundings. He found Floralia's rented villa, and was ushered into a vision of sea-breeze paradise. This was a villa where the delicious sea air wafted into large open rooms, through multiple colorful curtains and hangings.

"Yes, this place is absolutely exquisite," gushed Floralia as she showed Theophilus around her rented estate, where slaves were spraying scent all over the mural-filled walls and brightly-dyed drapery. "So much of Judea is nothing but a stone-farm! But one has to love the *coast*! How odd it is that the Jews developed the richest of spiritual traditions but had almost nothing to say about their coast! They couldn't care less about the sea. To them it's just a frightening place where one of the least admirable of the Jewish prophets got swallowed by a monstrous fish!"

"I'm not terribly fond of being out at sea myself," admitted Theophilus. "It's a frightening enough place even without any sea monsters. And yet I'm sure that monsters are out there, the sea being as incredibly vast as it is. If people started telling tales about a man named Jonah living for three days inside a whale, that's only to be expected. I've heard that since 'threes' are symbolic of the gestation of magic, Jonah's three days inside the whale are a parallel myth to Jesus' three days inside the tomb."

"Jonah sailed from Jaffa, unsuccessfully trying to get away from God's demands," recalled Floralia. "And that's almost the only mention of a port in the Jews' whole *biblia!* You know, Jaffa is even more beautiful than Caesarea. 'Jaffa' even means 'beauty'! But the tale about Jaffa that everyone knows concerns the notion of ugliness attacking beauty: the Greek tale about the enormous sea monster that rose up to attack lovely Andromeda as she lay tied to a rock."

Theophilus looked up at a sampling of gilded ceiling, the sort of action that would help jog his mind into remembering more about the tale under discussion. "Hmm. The name 'Andromeda' is quite a powerful one in Greek. It means 'human thought' or 'human destiny.' It seems to me that Andromeda's plight symbolized the plight of humankind in being tied to the material world, threatened by the monstrousness and beastliness of the material world, until arrives the savior. In this case the savior was Perseus. But people are invariably waiting for some savior or another. And now Jesus is the one that has come along, and the one that you and I like to discuss! And as you know, I've been devoting quite a lot of time and effort to the exploration!"

"It's enjoyable discussing these riddles with you,

Theophilus. I love puzzles! How all these things have been swirling in my head, now that they keep interconnecting so strangely and provocatively." Floralia paused and looked unexpectedly serious. "I keep getting the feeling that we're supposed to solve something, you and I. As though it's an assignment from the gods. And I'm running out of time. You remember how in Rome we kept getting drawn into the mystery of Peter, almost as if we were being drawn down into the underground center of the Vatican, where men are worshipping a Peter-rock called the Pater Patrum? And which is also called the Father, or the Papa? Well, I came to this country, this Holy Land, with absolutely no intention of getting involved with anything connected with Peter, and yet themes involving that character keeps hitting me in the face!"

"I'm very intrigued. Do go on."

"Well, I felt drawn to Caesarea Philippi, and once I was there I found it to be the most magical spot that I've found in this land. The spring where the Jordan River begins, the Pan place, is entirely enchanting. I found out that that was the very place where Jesus told the apostle Simon that he was now to be known as Cephas 'the Rock,' or Peter 'the Rock.' Then Jesus said that 'Upon this Rock I will build my Church,' and also that Peter would be given the keys to the kingdom of heaven. I tend to find myself being drawn to the most beautiful places, so after Caesarea Philippi I went to Jaffa. And what did I find there? Well! I found the whole story of Andromeda being tied to a rock and being the daughter of a King Cepheus whose name means 'rock'! That king was *Cepheus*. And Peter was *Cephas*.

Greeks told tales about *Cepheus* being active in Jaffa, and Christians told tales about *Cephas,* better known as Peter, being active in Jaffa. No coincidence this!"

Theophilus raised a finger. "Yes, yes, I'm familiar with that aspect of your discovery. The old tales about a King Cepheus of Jaffa surely influenced new tales about Peter Cephas being in Jaffa."

Just then a slave announced that dinner was about to be served. As Floralia had commanded, the dinner would be served on the roof to take advantage of the fine view and the pleasant sea breezes.

"This is becoming so very weird," sighed Floralia. "I hadn't planned it this way, but it just occurred to me how very weird this is going to get."

They reclined on their couches for a sumptuous meal on the sunny rooftop and Floralia explained.

"Observe how strange this gets, Theophilus. You know the story that I've been talking about that's in the *Book of Acts.* In Jaffa, Peter stayed at the house of a certain Simon the Tanner. Now observe the strangeness. I hadn't planned it like this, but this is how it has happened. On the roof of this house Peter experienced weird visions that were vitally determinative of the course that Christianity would take. Now then, when I stayed in Jaffa and rented a seaside house there, I was informed that I had happened to rent the house of Simon the Tanner, where Peter once lived and had his famous dream! I can't put much credence in such information, since I believe that Peter was legendary, after all. But, oh, what incredible dreams I had while staying in that house! And here comes the really strange part. Because likewise it was on the rooftop of this house in Jaffa that *Peter had visions of all of nature and all of its myriad creatures*! And he received the divine message that all of nature's creatures were now fit to eat! This message was a revolution in Jewish thinking! The end of the need for kosher rules! And here we are, you and I, banqueting on a similar seaside rooftop, largely on the bounteous seafood that is forbidden by Jewish law, banqueting on the 'myriad creatures' in a way that I hadn't planned and which I find exceedingly outlandish!"

Offered Theophilus, "And then came another point of the utmost significance. The first gentile convert to Christianity. Right here in Caesarea, a centurion named Cornelius was directed by an angel to ask Peter to come the short distance from Jaffa to preach to him and convert him.

Theophilus took up some more of the hmm-ing that this topic had instilled in him before. Then suddenly he felt odd, as if a taste of the divine inspiration that had been Peter's upon a rooftop was now his. He speculated as one inspired, surprising himself with the ease with which he solved the riddle silently to himself. I'm getting a grip on how this oriental mythmaking works. "Cornelius" is a name that has to do with the mythical object called The Horn of Plenty. In Jaffa Peter had most definitely just seen a vision of the Horn of Plenty. Then he got a call to come to Caesarea and convert the first non-Jew to Christianity. These two tales were obviously connected. Cornelius was, to be sure, a Horn of Plenty! He was the pioneer who demonstrated that the message of Christ *was for everyone!*

"I'm getting ever better at understanding these things. By 'these things,' I mean all of these invented stories about Jesus that were largely based on excerpts from the Torah. The Peter and Cornelius story echoes a story about Ezekiel. The heavens opened up for Ezekiel. And likewise the heavens opened up for Peter. Ezekiel was told to eat. And likewise Peter was told to eat. Ezekiel demurred with, 'By no means, Lord, I have never touched anything unclean.' And Peter likewise demurred with, 'By no means, Lord, I have never touched anything unclean.' The Peter-on-a-Jaffa-rooftop story begins as the story of a holy man beginning to have success in a world of gentiles, but the story proceeds to things much deeper than that."

"Do go on," requested Floralia.

"Of course it's all legend-talk. But it's very deep and significant legend-talk. The name 'Cornelius' points that fictional centurion squarely towards the old legendary Horn of Plenty, the Cornucopia. That's why Cornelius' house was described as a setting for visions of abundance! It all made perfect mythological sense! And part of the message of the tale is that *all of God's creation is good*! And the dexterous tale-spinner Luke described Cornelius as 'a commander of many,' hinting that he was a Father Nature figure. An example of another Father Nature figure was 'horned Pan,' who lurked behind the 'Simon-becomes-Peter' story that took place at Pan's very own place, Caesarea Philippi. Luke was skillful. He was always pressing his main point: that the Jesus story was so compelling that the Romans should now adopt the thought-world of the Jews. But at the same time he was touching on deep symbolism. Here's the remarkable thing: Peter and Cornelius were two versions of the same character, namely Father Nature! Father Nature! 'Peter the Rock' was the material world itself! No wonder that Peter's wife is often said to be named Perpetua, meaning 'eternity'! And Father Nature was *good*! He was extremely flawed in many ways, but he was nonetheless basically good! Father Nature was productive and worthy of reverence. But the crucial point was that Father Nature, be he the Roman version Cornelius or the Jewish version Peter, *was inferior in quality to Jesus,* and must now bow down to the superior spiritual power of Jesus!"

Floralia was not eating or drinking. She watched enraptured as Theophilus continued. To her, at this moment he looked different, looking like one who was in a state of *enthousiasmos*, a state of being 'imbued with a god.'

"Look at how much the two of them, Peter and Cornelius, are different presentations of the same entity: Father Nature. Remember how when you and I were in Rome we became convinced that Peter was the spirit of anthropocentric rule over nature, as represented all over the world by powerful 'peters,' which is to say phallic symbols or cairns. *Well, Cornelius too is the cairn! Just look at the name Cornelius!* Cornelius's identity as a cairn is so obvious that it hits us in the face! Peter and Cornelius are representative of the worldwide network of power-cairns that set up the world for rule by mankind! Dominion over all of God's myriad creatures!"

Theophilus was now too energized to remain reclined. He stood and looked out over the boundless ocean, confident that in his current state he could summon up even deeper visions.

"Do come back to our meal and tell me more!" implored Floralia. Her concern was not to lose the moment, as someone who was herself in a state approaching *enthousiasmos*.

Theophilus rejoined her and spoke on.

"I'm overcome with what I feel now about the importance of our rooftop banquet, Floralia. People think that the Cornelius episode in *Acts* instructs them that Jewish dietary laws are now unnecessary. Well that is so. But that's such an insignificant point compared to the deeper message! I just realized why Jesus' Last Supper was said to take place in an 'upper room.' Parallel to the fact that the Last Supper took place in an 'upper room,' Peter's revelation about God's myriad creatures took place on a *rooftop*! The 'upper room' is just a way of saying 'a higher state of consciousness.' What is a Last Supper, anyway? It is the Ultimate Sustenance! One needs no more sustenance after that ! The Last Supper is union with the Divine! And none of God's 'myriad creatures' is excluded from that union! All over the world there has existed an ancient formula: a ceremonial consumption of game animals in a hallowed way, with the request that the game animals come back to life as game animals again for the benefit of the participants. Now mankind is maturing. Now that *Eucharist* ceremony, that *giving-of-thanks* ceremony, which was performed since time immemorial for physical sustenance is destined to be re-enacted for *spiritual* sustenance!"

Floralia eyes were filling with tears. She voiced a continuation of what Theophilus was saying. "The upper room. The higher state of consciousness. Jesus made so many appearances to people after his resurrection. He appeared to Mary Magdalene first, then to the apostles and to many disciples. He appeared for no discernible reason to two undistinguished disciples on the road to Emmaus. He appeared in Bethany, and on a mountain in Galilee, and at the Sea of Galilee to the apostles while they were fishing, of all things. But the appearance that always touched me was the appearance *in an upper room.* I never understood why until now!"

Floralia now struggled to hold back sobs. Theophilus leaned forward to touch her hand. Then he clasped her hand gradually more firmly during the difficult utterance of the sentences that came next.

"It is the blessed tale of something that is the destiny of each one of us: resurrection from death. That's what this awesome Jesus tale is! I came to this Holy Land to come to understand that. It's clear to me now. You see, I've been ill, and I'm headed on that 'road to Emmaus,' or to heaven, or to whatever-in-Hades it is that awaits us after death. Please don't ask for details now. I'm sick-unto-death of discussions of my impending death, and discussions with physicians, and about physicians, and all their endless ministrations."

Said Theophilus, "I'm glad that it's a comfort to you that you came here to the Holy Land, and that we met as if by magic in a splendid upper room."

"Yes. Here in Caesarea. Here in the city of the Caesars. Here in the city of Roman power in the Holy Land. Here in the city's *best* upper room! You know, I've been finding out, as you have been finding out, about how Mark reworked old stories, old Midrash, into stories of Jesus that would fit contemporary needs. I've been thinking a lot lately about one of Mark's stories. He had Jesus go out into the desert, out into the bleakness, to find himself. There the devil offered Jesus three temptations. The first temptation was the offer to turn stones into bread to end his fast. The second temptation was dominion over all the world. And the third temptation was the suggestion to throw himself off the Temple's parapet and demonstrate that God will protect him. Thus were presented mankind's three great temptations: wealth, power and immortality. They're ever on offer, those three offers. They're on offer, but fraudulently, by Satan. But if you understand the upper room you see that they are also ever on offer, genuinely, *by God!"*

"So true." Theophilus pondered aloud. "Once we're 'in the upper room' so many things rush in at once and explain themselves. It's as though a mysterious enlightening light settles on one's head, as happened to the apostles in *Acts* on the occasion of the first Pentecost. That Pentecost is something that occurred in 'an upper room' according to some. The Christians invented Pentecost, the celebration of the fiftieth day after Christ's resurrection, to replace the Jews' Feast of Weeks, the celebration of the grain harvest which occurred seven weeks, which is to say 49 days, after Passover. One celebration of abundance replaced another! Pentecost replaced the Feast of Weeks! During Pentecost tongues of light settled on the heads of the apostles and they were inspired to speak in tongues foreign to them. And they found that they could speak with the multitudes of foreign pilgrims who had come to Jerusalem for the Feast of Weeks. This enhanced inter-ethnic interplay was supposed to be a *reversal* of the historical lack of understanding between nations that was initiated at the Tower of Babel. Now everyone could understand each other's babble! Now all of God's myriad creatures were one! Inspired by an influx of light in 'the upper room'!"

Floralia stood at a carved balustrade, seemingly appreciating the infinite abundance represented by the ocean, and breathed in deeply the strong sea wind.

"Do you see the near-end of the Forum of Caesarea over there? I've taken to standing here and contemplating that spot as I take in the mystery of the sea. Do you hear the waves, Theophilus? Their sound is subtle here, but infinitely lovely. Standing here I reminisce about many things. I reminisce about wonderful lovers. I reminisce about you. I reminisce about Cato. I reminisce about Josephus, whom I made love to right here in this wonderful seaside palace. Oh, how odd this all becomes once again! For it's so clear to me now that Josephus, and all the other Josephs too, are *Father Nature Figures*!"

"Of course," agreed Theophilus. "The Hebrew 'Joseph'

means 'he increases.' The Joseph of the Torah wore 'a coat of many colors,' and he was a 'spinner of dreams,' in other words a creator of the material world. The Joseph of the gospels, Jesus' stepfather, was likewise a 'spinner of dreams,' a creator of the material world, a carpenter some say, but really a *tekton* a creator. Since he was a spinner of dreams and a creator of the material world he was a mere *stepfather* of Jesus! The first Joseph brought the Israelites to Egypt, a country which stands for entrapment in the material world. And the second Joseph brought the baby Jesus to Egypt."

"Yes. You know, recently I was thinking about both Josephus and you, and a few things occurred to me that Josephus wrote about that would be of interest to you."

"I'd certainly love to hear that."

"Well, Josephus once mentioned that there was an old oracle stating that someone from the Jews' country would someday become the ruler of the world. Josephus knew where his daily bread came from, so in his public life he insisted that the Jews should have realized that this person was Vespasian, who conquered the Jews' country. But I certainly feel that nowadays this person sounds like… *Jesus!*"

"A fascinating 'first point' from Josephus," said Theophilus.

"And Josephus loved to talk about a concept called *devotio*. This involved a Roman sacrificing himself to neutralize the gods of an enemy people, and in some cases to save all people as well. There's certainly more than a little hint of Jesus there, in the concept of *devotio*."

"A fascinating 'second point' from Josephus," said Theophilus.

"And at a place called Theroa during the Jewish Revolt Josephus himself witnessed three of his own friends being crucified. He asked the general and future emperor Titus to spare them. Titus thereupon had the three men taken down from their crosses. And one of those men survived. Now see how this *tale of the three crucifixions* may have been the basis for the tale of Joseph of Arimathea, who received Jesus' body from the cross. Two of the crucified who were pardoned by Titus 'died,' and one 'lived.' But the subject here is Joseph of Arimathea. You see, Josephus' full name was 'Joseph bar Matthias.' I would think it possible that some author cleverly turned him into Joseph of Arimathea! This seems especially likely to me because there exists a *Gospel of Barnabas* which refers to Joseph of Arimathea by what seems to have been his original name: Joseph of Barimathea!"

"A fascinating 'third point' from Josephus," said Theophilus. "By the gods, that really is a good one! I seem to have found the origins of that elusive fictional rascal, Joseph of Arimathea!"

"I'm glad you like my lover Josephus's textual material, O lover from a later time in my life. I have one last point from that dear talented Josephus, for now. I've stayed in some of King Herod's glorious palaces, and, by the gods, in their heyday they were like visiting Olympus itself. The most majestic such palace of all was Masada, way up high in the clouds with the gods. Nowadays everybody knows of Masada as the place where the Jewish Revolt climaxed with a dramatic Roman siege of the last of the rebels, who in the end committed mass suicide rather than surrender. Well! Josephus confided to me that his narration of that story about Masada was one of his biggest fibs, ever! He told me that he made up that unforgettable story out of whole cloth! He said that the Romans wanted him to tell the story that way to encourage rebels of the future to seriously consider the charms and the glories of *suicide*! Very droll in a very macabre way! Josephus was so mischievous!"

"That's truly marvelous, Floralia! Not much to do with anything that I'm researching at present, but marvelous nonetheless! I would say that the real lesson there, in the Masada story, is to always keep in mind that writers are rarely telling the truth, but are *instead* generally striving to make a point, whatever the cost in making themselves downright liars!"

"We're Romans, aren't we? We love the glitter, the pomp, the noise, and, yes, the *lie*! That's why we took that Jewish scalawag Josephus to heart. He was all those things! How we loved him!"

Theophilus noticed that Floralia was staring off into the distance at a particular spot in the port facilities, and he asked about that. "What are you seeing over there, way over that way, so intently that it's burning your eyes?"

"I'm seeing something beastly. I've been told that sixty years ago an imported colossal statue of Caligula stood on that spot! That's quite something to picture in a country like Judea! Importing a statue like that was considered to be the most horrible possible abomination! And you can well imagine what it's like for me to picture that horrendous colossus and realize that it was an image of *my very own father!* My very own monster of a father! A colossal statue of my father in the most inappropriate land imaginable! Anathema! That statue was being readied for shipment to the Temple in Jerusalem, to stand in the Holy of Holies. Can you imagine the frightfulness of it? Can you imagine the dreams that that historical situation, in such close proximity, has given me? In the *Gospel of Matthew,* Jesus gives the longest sermon about the future that he would ever give. He describes signs indicating coming times of tribulation such as man has never seen before. He mentions one sign that was predicted by the prophet Daniel: a desecrating sacrilege will stand in the Holy Place. Quite a few people have told me, quite a few people have agreed, that the desecrating sacrilege that Jesus was woefully predicting and railing against was *this very statue*, the statue of *my father the Beast known as Caligula* that stood over there, ready at any moment to be dragged off to Jerusalem!"

"I'm afraid I don't really see why you're so distraught about all that. It's all in the dead past. Now there is no statue. Now there is no Caligula. For that matter, now there is not even a Jerusalem! But Jesus remains, and how we've come to love him!"

"I don't know, Theophilus. I don't really know why it all disturbs me so. I keep having horrible dreams about these matters. Dreams like Matthew probably had. Dreams like John who wrote the *Revelation* horror-presentation probably had. I don't know what to do about the grip that these things have on me. It's in my very blood, you know. My father was the Beast himself, the Beast of the Apocalypse. It has all come to matter much more to me now that my last days are near."

Offered Theophilus, "Would you like to accompany me to Egypt? No spiritual seeker's life should be lived without a visit to Egypt! Greeks and Romans, the arrogant conquerors of most of the world, disdain all other nationalities, with the only exception being that they've always remained in awe of Egypt. All indications are that the deepest answers lie waiting for me there, that the climax of my querying lies waiting for me there."

Floralia shook her head.

Then Theophilus shook his head. "Why is it that no one ever wants to go with me to Egypt?"

"Logically I should take you up on your offer. I should go to Egypt. But I'm going to be illogical right now. I've consulted augurs and astrologers and soothsayers and haruspices, and the results are more remarkable than anything else I've ever seen in my life. The results are completely remarkable because they are completely unanimous! I've been told that I should end my days on the isle of Lesbos! Lesbos, the wooded sacred isle of the greatest female poet, Sappho. I've never been there. But it appeals to me immensely. Do you know why?"

"I believe I do. Among all of my various mentors, and consultants, and experts, and chance encounters, you're the only one who ties me to the strange mystery of Peter. That night when we were together in Rome I felt the hidden subterranean Roman cairn of Peter pulling us, as though it were an actual world-conquering demon with untold power. But since we've chosen *not* to worship that particular 'peter,' or obey it, we remain outside its clutches. Just barely! Lesbos is for you, Floralia. The essence of Lesbos, sacred to all lesbians, is the opposite of the essence of Peter, the arch-materialist and arch-patriarch. You've fought the good fight, Floralia, as Paul would phrase it. You've rejected the Beast."

Floralia seemed to brighten at these last simple words. "Yes, Perhaps I have. But what is it, really? What is the Beast?"

"The Beast is in your blood, as you said, perhaps even more strongly than it is in most of us, but it's present in all of us. The Beast. The Beast is the beastly aspect of man. Writers have personified it as Caligula. The Beast. Writers have personified it as Nero. The Beast. And of course writers have personified it as Rome. 'All roads lead to Rome.' Rome conquers all. Rome enslaves all, and forces its slaves to participate in grim spectacles of combat. And where does this occur? In a horror-show *Colosseum* that was named for a *colossal* statue of Nero the Beast, and which was financed by treasure from the destroyed Temple of Jerusalem! And hidden underground in the most ill-omened outskirts of 'Rome-the-City-of-the-Beast,' the Vatican, is that object that so disturbs you and me: one of the most powerful of the world's Peter-cairns. It is the main worship-stone that serves the cause of tyranny. You were raised amidst all of that, and therefore cultivated a stronger desire than most have cultivated to escape all of that. I suppose that there do exist, hardly known, many isolated wooded isles that sing songs like

Sappho's songs, charming isles that exist outside the network of the harsh Peter-cairns and harsh Roman rule. Such a place is perfect for you. Rise, then, to heaven, while hearing Lesbos' gentle Sapphic song! Rise in Lesbos, where legend says that the severed head of Orpheus was sent, there eternally to sing on, and sing on, and sing on, in marvelous celestial harmony! Orpheus! Greek for 'the Light that Speaks'!"

At this point Theophilus thought he was done, but then found that he was not.

"Floralia, in my heart I understand your longing for Lesbos. You feel a longing for a return to the feminine, and I myself feel it too. I sense that such a return makes up a large part of the next step on my quest. In this quest of mine, this quest after Jesus, female characters haven't yet played a large part, but now I feel that that's about to change. Maybe that's part of the reason why I feel destined to go *alone* to Egypt! Everywhere I've been encountering textual hints and other hints that originally the role of women in the Jesus saga was enormous, and that most of that material was expunged by patriarchal sorts, in the tradition of Peter and Paul."

"*Kudos* to you indeed as you embark on that investigation!" exclaimed Floralia.

"Yes. Mary Magdalene was climactic, so very climactic. Jesus' various tomb stories were all confusing in the extreme, but they all centered on Mary Magdalene. In all four gospels Mary Magdalene arrived first at the tomb, but at four different times, and accompanied by different people, and encountering different people or non-human beings. And no one seems to be able to get straight what exactly she *did,* and *why!"*

"Straighten that out, by all means!"

"Someday, somehow, the miserably sad history of man has got to change. What a history! Multiple male tyrannies took over the world, and then all of those multiple male tyrannies were conquered by the *master-tyranny* called Rome! The Beast! The *Therion*! The Beast which has at its heart the spirit of Peter! Pater Patrum! Patriarchy.! We've got to do better! There's something better waiting to heal mankind with a long-missing feminine touch, something that still sits hidden behind a veil! A rectifying Goddess! A healing Goddess! Rome's antithesis! Rome's mystics know about this, this concept of 'turning Rome backwards.' So say the enlightened. They relish the uttering of the phrase, 'Not ROMA but AMOR!'"

Theophilus found himself immensely surprised that he had articulated this fluent sermon. He recalled how Paul was called upon to preach, and objected that he would not know what to say, but found that in the end the words just came to him. Theophilus realized that quite a number of times exactly that had happened to him, and it had just happened again.

Floralia nodded repeatedly. "It's all so true, what you've said. Beastly history has been enacted by beastly men. And history climaxes in Rome, the urban personification of the Beast. And the possibility of a worldwide comforting for all of these trials that were caused by beastly men comes from *women*. The faint voices of many women in many isolated spots! Spots like Lesbos! That having been said, and in the spirit of Lesbos, I propose that we invite in my two young ladies, whom I'm sure you remember. They will be dessert for our banquet!"

Theophilus well remembered Floralia's light-skinned and dark-skinned attendants, amusingly named North and South. The banquet in the upper room now proceeded with their company. Theophilus reflected: Had not Peter, the visionary of "the upper room," said it himself? *All* of God's myriad creations were to be enjoyed! Floralia opened the festivities by giggling and opening Theophilus' robe, to invite her ladies to join her in enjoying her favorite version of a firm "peter" stone. With the attentions of six hands, very stone-like indeed became Theophilus' *fascinum. Fascinum,* "the spellbinder," the most readily available symbol and instrument of the world's limitless potential for abundance and enjoyment. The feast developed naturally into a Sapphic feast, a celebration of fascination. All about the feast, foods were enlisted as ointments and playthings. Copious wine ingestion soon made all of the feast a blur. Toys were everywhere. Food and drink were everywhere. Naked limbs were everywhere. It was a feast of Cornelius, a cornucopia.

Said Theophilus, "Foreign folk think that they can calumniate us Romans by calling us too fond of banquets and orgies! Tsk, tsk! Jealous! Jealous!"

"The two lovely ladies are slaves, but they enjoy us, as we enjoy them. I can tell. They'll have a fine enough life," proclaimed

Floralia. "After I'm gone they'll be free, and they'll even be a rather wealthy. I've arranged for that. They'll lap up abundance! Much as they're lapping up fine comestibles, including *you*, right now!"

A little later, with some very Roman appetites exhausted, Theophilus once again found Floralia gazing towards the port facility where the statue of her father Caligula had once stood. But now there was an element of contentment in her look and in her voice."

"As I said a little while ago: we're Romans, aren't we? We love the glitter, the pomp, the noise, and, yes, *sex!"*

"Other cultures have their own ways. We're Romans. We unabashedly *feast!"*

Next, Theophilus searched for the right word to describe Floralia's facial expression as she looked out to sea. He found the word "wistful." As for her voice, it matched the gentle murmur of the sea, as she made a little speech that seemed to address Caesarea's glimmering sunset, and her own.

"We feast and we make love to celebrate God's world as he would have us celebrate it! All should be love, you know. *All should be love!* I lived and loved. I loved you. I loved Cato. I loved some of my husbands. I loved my children before they all died young. I loved those two sweet girls North and South that you see cuddling and making love over there, since apparently we've taught them to be true Romans! I never loved my father Caligula, as everyone should love their father, but he was a real challenge, too much of a challenge. He was the Beast after all! But most of all I loved

Josephus! Oh, how we made love, day and night, like god and goddess possessed, within these very walls of splendor! A Romanized Jew and a Judaized Roman, in love! What a spectacle life is! And now Josephus is with me here *only as these tears that you see,* these salty tears that are like a taste of the infinite ocean! Oh, how I loved him! Will I be with him? Will I be with him? Like two drops finding each other and merging in the immensity of the sea?"

Two lovers with tear-filled eyes and sleep filled eyes enjoyed a long embrace, then turned to fall down into a tranquil sleep, an easy thing to do with elaborately-stained cushions present everywhere.

How unbelievably quickly dawn arrived. The upper room had enabled its occupiers to taste of timelessness. Theophilus cast a glance at the sleeping trio who were headed for Lesbos, then out to sea towards his own land of irresistible beckoning. The land of irresistible beckoning was Egypt. Theophilus gazed out over the sea and felt inspired to repeat a line from *Matthew* that seemed pertinent, in reversal: "Out of Egypt I have called my son !"

A few days later the difficult final goodbyes to Floralia had been said, and Theophilus sat on the seashore, enjoying the sea breezes and the contemplation of the adventures he was about to have in fabled Egypt, down past Neptune's waves just out of sight.

Then a man tapped him on the shoulder and addressed to him a friendly greeting by name.

The man was tall and lean, and he was especially

recognizable by how neat he kept his beard and clothing.

Theophilus needed a few moments to come out of his reveries and recognize this man. Then he exclaimed, "By all the gods! It's Younger Andrew! Younger Andrew who taught me a Torah-torrent of knowledge, overlooking the Sea of Galilee, just hours before I entered the Holy Land!"

"Yes, it's me!" Younger Andrew sat down beside Theophilus. "As they're all too fond of saying in this sinful town: 'I'll wager!' I'll wager that you never expected to see me in Judea, after how adamantly I kept bawling that I'd never cross the Sea of Galilee and come to Judea! Well, in the end I decided to use part of the bag of coins that you gave me, way back then, to do exactly that! What better usage of coins could there be than that, anyway? As infidel as I am, I'm still a Jew after all, and this is the Holy Land, after all! And how I've enjoyed my look-see around Judea! Especially here in Caesarea! I'm getting to know a whole lot about a whole different world of fish of the sea, so different from the inland world of fish that I knew before!"

"Yes, it's a true cornucopia, you might say. And just like you, I've found my 'look-see' around the Holy Land to be very profitable," mentioned Theophilus.

"I know. Because I've run into various people who've told me what you've been up to in this land. And now it's 'off to Egypt' for you, so I understand.

"Yes, exactly. Hence all of this sitting on the beach and gazing fixedly out to sea that I'm doing. Goodness, how strange it is that when last we saw one another we were sitting and staring out over the Sea of Galilee, with me about to enter Judea! And now we're sitting and staring out over Rome's Great Sea, the Mare Nostrum, with me about to cross it to enter Egypt!"

Younger Andrew shrugged. "Yes, life is strange. Who can claim it isn't?

"Well then, why not come with me to Egypt?"

"Well, I'm a bit strange too, as you know. I don't feel a hankering to go to Egypt just now. But you never know. I do have a way of turning up unexpectedly, as you just experienced!"

"It's the land of magic, Egypt is. How odd it is. Why does nobody ever want to come with me to Egypt! Anything can happen in Egypt. And for my purposes, I have a feeling that it's in Egypt that I'll really get to the crux of the Jesus matter. You may have heard that the creation of the Jesus myth began with the *Gospel of Mark*. Well, Mark's tomb is in Egypt, and there's also said to be a *Secret Gospel of Mark* in Egypt. They say that the accepted gospels and other scriptures are *nothing* compared to the magnitude of the cosmic truths contained in the secret texts to be found in Egypt!"

Younger Andrew nodded. "So I've heard. And I've sometimes wondered about a statement in the *Book of Isaiah* about 'an altar to God at the heart of Egypt.' That phrase must refer to the pyramids. Some say that our Hebrew word for Egypt, Mitzraim, means 'the monuments,' and refers to the pyramids of Egypt."

"I've been reading everything that I could find about these matters while I've been here in Caesarea. Magic always seems to come back to the number *three*. The greater pyramids of Egypt are *three* in number. And the so-called Great Pyramid, the most majestic one of all, has *three* small pyramids standing before it, while inside that magnificent monument there are precisely *three* chambers. And inside one of those chambers there sits an empty tomb. So just who were those *three* women who found Jesus' tomb *empty* after he had risen after *three* days?"

Younger Andrew grimaced and looked skyward. "It looks as though you'll have quite some mysteries to investigate over there in Egypt. We Jews now have our man-god named Jesus who disappeared from a tomb even though it was sealed. The Egyptians seem to have always had such man-gods, disappearing from sealed tombs. And I can tell you something else, Theophilus. The Egyptians refer to their pyramids by the name Mer. And they also call their pyramids the Granaries of Joseph. Mer and Joseph. Be sure to investigate this matter when you're in Egypt. Mer and Joseph. Do you get it? *Mary and Joseph*!"

"Ah, younger Andrew, you have such a knack for understanding the deepest things. I certainly wish you'd come with me to Egypt to help me investigate this Jesus who was the mysterious son of Mary and the mysterious stepson of Joseph."

"Well, I do have a way of turning up later, unexpectedly, don't I?"

At this point the two men looked around all over the sky, which was a natural human impulse whenever thunder rumbled.

"This storm certainly came in awfully suddenly," observed

Theophilus. "When people used to be more superstitious they would have assumed that the gods were making commentary on what we had just said! Or what I was just *about* to say. I was about to say that I had thought that I was on the verge of discarding Jesus as someone mythical, but that now I'm looking forward to exploring the utterly wondrous *mysterium* of this god-man Jesus who was a mysterious son of Mary and stepson of Joseph!"

"Mary is Mother Earth, you know, Theophilus, and she's also the sea. She's what you Romans arrogantly call Mare Nostrum, 'Our Sea.' Now see how the sea is starting to get stirred up as we talk about her!"

The waves were indeed no longer as gentle as before. And now lightning flashed from one end of the sky to the other.

The men looked at each other.

"Are you thinking what I'm thinking," asked Theophilus.

Replied Younger Andrew, "Yes, I think that sometimes the gods supply us with the same thoughts. I'm thinking about... or, *we're* thinking about... We're thinking about the lines in which Matthew and Luke compared the coming of the Son of Man to the flashing of lightning from one end of the sky to another!"

Theophilus: "Yes, and here we are witnessing the flashing of lightning from one end of the sky to another! An omen! Exactly the same omen of lightning that you and I experienced looking out over my first view of the Holy Land at the Sea of Galilee! How stupendous!"

Younger Andrew: "Jesus is real after all, so it would seem.

And stupendous."

Theophilus threw some stones into the sea, throwing them northward. "Here in Caesarea I've been bidding farewell to that rapscallion Paul who has bedeviled me for so long. From here in Caesarea he headed off to Rome, to his death, wearing manacles." Theophilus threw some stones into the sea, throwing them southward. "And I head off to Egypt, wearing my usual bag of denarii tied to my belt, surely not to my death, not me, so young and vigorous. But to a new life!"

"I think I can read your mind again now."

"Yes. I've mentioned Paul. It all started with Paul. I thought him a crackpot. I criticized his opaque writings. I derided him. But I followed his trail through a dozen strange lands with strange people, over a thousand miles, all the same. There was something there in the legacy of Paul that I wanted, and wanted badly. And now it has arrived. Here's the thing now."

"Yes, I know, I know."

"Here's the thing now. The thing that changes everything. *Now I have the feeling that Paul really was seeing Jesus all along!*"

"Exactly so," said Younger Andrew. "I feel it. I see it."

Theophilus hesitated, then spoke again. "In all my travels, though I've heard much about how the earth can shake, I've never actually felt the earth shake. Yet now I feel that in Egypt, a land not known for shaking of the earth, there will be for me a sort of *seismos. For me the earth will shake!"*

Lightning flashed with exceeding brightness, so that the skyway to Egypt was crystal-clear and luminous, like a pathway for gods.


THERE WILL FOLLOW THE FINAL VOLUME OF THIS SERIES: *MYSTERIUM V EGYPT AND BEYOND*

# GLOSSARY

**Adonis**

A divinity who was Cosmic Man, and was perhaps to be equated with the similar-sounding Adonai, Adam, Atum, and even Atom. Adonis's shrine was in Bethlehem, at the grotto of his mother, the Virgin Myrrha.

**Agape**

Universal love.

**Anactoreum**

The "ascent backwards" of the cosmic waters of creation, which could be accomplished by major prophets such as Joshua and Jesus.

**Ark of the Covenant**

The most important object of veneration in the Old Testament. It was present in Solomon's Temple, but not in Herod's Temple of the first century, having disappeared.

**Bar Nasha**

What Jesus repeatedly called himself: Son of Man, seemingly meaning simply "Man." Pontius Pilate declared, *"Ecce homo!"* "There is man!"

**Ben Adam**

"Son of Adam," meaning a man, or a Son of Man.

**Bethesda**

The healing pool in Jerusalem where Jesus healed a man who had been paralyzed for 38 years. Perhaps the only site of Jesus' ministry that is still extant.

**Bethsaida**

Meaning "place of fishing" or "place of hunting," this name could refer to many small settlements in the Holy Land.

**Cana**

The site of Jesus' first miracle, the turning of water into wine at a wedding. This place may have been symbolic imagery for "Canaan," a land where the god Dionysus' rite of sacred marriage resembled the Jesus miracle in many respects.

**Cardo**

A Roman city's porticoed commercial main avenue.

**Colonia Agrippina**

The Roman-established German city on the Rhine that would become Cologne.

**Debir**

Oracle.

## Devotio
A Roman concept that may have influenced stories about Jesus. It involved a Roman sacrificing himself to neutralize the gods of an enemy, and perhaps to save all people as well.

## Eben Shetiyah
The world's foundation stone, said to lie beneath the Temple of Jerusalem.

## Elisha
Elijah's successor as a prophet. Many of Elisha's miracles foreshadowed the miracles of Jesus. The names Elisha and Jesus both meant "God's salvation."

## Enthousiasmos
A state of being "imbued with a god."

## Episkopos
The Greek word for "overseer" which later became the word "bishop."

## Fascinum
"The fascinator," the penis.

## Gehenna
Ancient Jerusalem's rubbish dump which was a model for Hell, because it was literally "the place where the fires are never extinguished."

## Hanan
Grace. "John" in Hebrew is "Yohanan," meaning "Yahweh's grace."

**Ha Olam Ha Ba**
Hebrew for "the world to come."

**Hekal**
The central sanctuary of the Temple of Jerusalem.

**Jaffa**
The seaside town associated with both the biblical Cephas-Peter and the Greek myth figure King Cepheus.

**Jesus Barabbas**
Jesus Barabbas was released while Jesus Christ was killed, in a reflection of the old Yom Kippur custom wherein one sacred "scapegoat" was released into the wilderness while another was slaughtered.

**Judaizer**
A Roman who took an interest in Judaism.

**Justus of Tiberias**
Along with Philo of Alexandria and Josephus, Justus of Tiberias was one of the three celebrated writers of Jesus' time and place who made no mention of Jesus in their writings.

**Kataluma**
An animal-filled cellar of the type where Jesus was supposed to have been born.

**Kittim**
To the ancient Jews: all of Judea's hated, conquering foreigners.

**Korban**
Sacrifice.

**Kotel**
Best known as the Western Wall or the Wailing Wall, it is the only remaining section of the Temple of Jerusalem.

**Limes**
The Roman Empire's line of defense against the wild northern Germanic tribes, consisting of the Rhine River, the Alps, the Danube River, and various fortifications.

**Magdala**
This Sea of Galilee fishing town, whose name meant "tower," was the purported home of Mary Magdalene.

**Midbar**
Desert.

**Midrash**
Jewish legends and commentary, based on stories from the Jewish Bible.

**Mikdash**
"The holy place." This was one term for the Temple of Jerusalem.

**Mishnah**
Jewish religious teachings, systematized by subject matter in a Greek manner.

## Mysterium

According to the philosopher Macrobius: "Plain and naked exposition of herself is repugnant to Nature. She wishes her secrets to be revealed by myth. Thus the Mysteries themselves are hidden in the tunnels of figurative expression, so that not even to initiates may the nature of such realities present themselves naked. Such is the Mysterium."

## Nahum

The prophet after whom was named Capernaum, the main town of Jesus' ministry. Nahum was the only Old Testament prophet who mentioned the word *evangelion*, the word that would come to refer to the gospels.

## Nazarenes

Age-old societies of Jewish holy men, who were also known as Nazarites, Noserim, Nosereans, Nasara, and Notzri, Some of these terms later became terms for Christians.

## Nomen Est Omen

"A name is an omen."

## Osiris

The Egyptian Lord of Death, whose name transmogrified from the original Ausar into El-Eazar, then Eleazer, and finally Lazarus.

## Pandocheion

The customary Greek word for "inn," which Luke noticeably did not use for the place where the Holy Family found accommodation in Bethlehem.

## Paradosis

The word which was used for Judas' betrayal, but which was properly a "giving over." Judas Iscariot represented that portion of the Jews that "gave over" its Jesus, which is to say "gave over its hopes for salvation," to the priests.

## Parthenos

In the Septuagint, *parthenos,* meaning "virgin," was the Greek mistranslation for the Hebrew word *alma*, meaning "young woman." Thus was Isaiah's "young woman" transformed into a virgin who was seen as a prediction of the existence of the Virgin Mary.

## Pelatha

Parables.

## Pharmakos

A healer, exorcist and charismatic person. Christian literature did not designate Jesus by this word, which was common in his time.

## Phimotheti kai ekselthe

"Be silent and be gone!" These words, uttered to a demoniac in Capernaum, were Jesus' first words associated with a miracle.

## Praetorium

A Roman governor's palace.

## Presbyter

The Greek word for "elder" which later became the word "priest."

## Prodromos

Forerunner. John the Baptist was called this, in relation to Jesus.

## Seamless Cloak

An ancient symbol of the pristine unity of existence, which, with high symbolism, oafish people ripped asunder, and gambled over, during the Crucifixion of Jesus.

## Sepphoris

Though the largest town in Galilee in Jesus' time, this town was never mentioned in the Bible. Sepphoris may have been the "city on a hill" mentioned by Jesus. This notably attractive city's name derived from *zipporah*, meaning "bird."

## Sicarii

The "dagger-men," the zealots who terrorized Judea with anti-Roman violence. The name "Judas Iscariot" was probably invented to associate Judas with them.

## Tehillim

"Songs of Praise." The Psalms.

## Tekton

A *tekton* was Jesus' occupation according to the gospels. A *tekton* was not an assembler of furniture and carts and the like, but a genuine builder, something like a mason, an occupation with many symbolic ramifications.

## Therion

The Beast. The *Book of Revelation* referred to the evil conqueror of the world during the End Time as "the Beast," not as "the Antichrist."

## TOPOS KRANIOU PARADEISOS GEGNON

"Paradise is born at the place of the skull." This inscription is to be found at Adam's Chapel at Golgotha in Jerusalem. "Golgotha" means "place of the skull."

## Via Maris

The Romans' updated version of the Euphrates-to-Nile international highway, mostly along the Judean coastline, which had existed since the most ancient times.

## Via Regia

The Royal Road constructed by the Romans, running north to south to the east of the Holy Land.

## Zechariah

This prophet of about 500 B.C. portrayed a savior figure named Joshua or Jesus, and prophesied that this figure would secure rule over all the world and defeat Satan

# RESOURCES

Atwill, Joseph, *Caesar's Messiah: The Roman Conspiracy to Invent Jesus,* CreateSpace, Charleston, SC, 2011

Brown, Raymond, *An Introduction to the Gospel of John,* Doubleday, New York, 2003

Callahan, Tim, *Secret Origins of the Bible,* Millennium Press, Altadena, CA, 2002

Carrier, Richard, *On the Historicity of Jesus: Why We Might Have Reason for Doubt,* Sheffield. Phoenix Press, Sheffield, UK, 2014

Crossan, John, and Reed, Jonathan, *Excavating Jesus: Beneath the Stones, Beneath the Texts,* HarperSanFrancisco, 2001

Doherty, Earl, *The Jesus Puzzle: Did Christianity Begin with a Mythical Christ?,* Canadian Humanist Publications, Ottawa, 1999

Ehrman, Bart, *How Jesus Became God: The Exaltation of a Jewish Preacher from Galilee,* HarperCollins, New York, 2014

Ehrman, Bart, *Jesus*: *Apocalyptic Prophet of the New Millennium,* Oxford University Press, Oxford, 1999

Ehrman, Bart, *Misquoting Jesus,* Harper, San Francisco, 2005

Freeman, Charles, *A New History of Early Christianity,* Yale University Press, New Haven and London, 2009

Freke and Gandy, *The Jesus Mysteries: Was the "Original Jesus" a Pagan God?,* Three Rivers Press, New York, 2001

Helms, Randel, *Gospel Fictions,* Prometheus Books, New York, 1988

Mack, Burton, *The Christian Myth: Origins Logic and Legacy,* The Continuum Int. Publishing Group, 2008

Martin, James, Beck, John, Hansen, David, *A Visual Guide to Gospel Events,* Baker Books, Grand Rapids, MI, 2010

Murdock, D.M., *Who Was Jesus?: Fingerprints of the Christ,* Stellar House Publishing, Seattle. 2007

Price, Robert, *The Christ Myth Theory and Its Problems,* American Atheist Press, Cranford, NJ, 2011

Salm, Rene, *The Myth of Nazareth: The Invented Town of Jesus,* American Atheist Press, Parsippany, NJ, 2008

Shinan, Avigdor and Zakovitch, Yair, *From Gods to God: How the Bible Debunked, Suppressed, or Changed Ancient Myths and Legends,* University of Nebraska Press, 2012

Smith, Morton, *Jesus the Magician,* Barnes and Noble Books, New York, 1978

Walker, Barbara, *The Woman's Encyclopedia of Myths and Secrets,* HarperSanFrancisco, 1983

Wells, G.A., *Who Was Jesus?,* Open Court Publishing, LaSalle, Il, 1989

Witherington, Ben, *New Testament History: A Narrative Account,* Baker Academic, Grand Rapids, MI, 2001

# DISCUSSION GUIDE

1   Can you describe the diet of ancient Judea and its significance, especially with regard to the symbolism of bread, grapes, and figs?

2   Like Jesus Christ himself, Uzziah was not quite a carpenter. What profession did these two men practice, and what was that profession's esoteric significance?

3   If you had to choose, would you prefer to live in ancient Capernaum, Sepphoris, Jericho, Bethlehem, or Caesarea? Why?

4   What was the nature of the lakeside town of Magdala? Why did it become apparent that Mary Magdalene was not from there?

5   What was the symbolism of Peter's denial of Jesus three times as the cock crowed three times?

6    How surprising was the reappearance, in Caesarea, of Andrew the Younger? What information did he convey to Theophilus?

7    What expectations does Theophilus have about the pyramids of Egypt as he prepares to depart for Egypt?

8    What did Hebrew, Homeric Greek, and Etruscan have in common?

9    What was the literal meaning of the place name Golgotha? What was the metaphorical meaning of this place?

10    What was the literal meaning of the place name Bethlehem? What was the metaphorical meaning of this place?

11    The three first-century historians who suspiciously failed to mention Jesus Christ were Josephus, Philo, and Justus of Tiberias. Who did Justus of Tiberias turn out to be, and what was the significance of his name and his pen name?

12    Can you reconstruct any of Uzziah's extremely detailed description of Jerusalem as it was in Jesus' time?

13    Who was Lilith, and how and why did she appear to Theophilus? How did she tie in with Jesus' brief mention of the Queen of Sheba?

14   Two characters, one very rich and one very poor, were placed by the gospels in Jericho. Who were they and what did they represent?

15   What was Arabia Felix and why was it called that? What were that land's signature products? What were Arabs known for in Jesus' time?

16   What can you recall about the city of Colonia Agrippina on the Rhine? What is that city called today?

17   What was your personal reaction to Floralia's surprise return to the story? What did she have to add to Theophilus's investigations, in her discussion of her lover Josephus, her father the Beast, and her own destiny?

18   How much Jewish life and presence remained in post-70 AD Judea? What was the Roman governmental presence like? What were the Romans doing in Armageddon, Jerusalem, and Caesarea?

19   What trace was there of the four gospel-writers in Judea? What trace of John the Baptist? Of Mary Magdalene? Of Paul?

20   The novel ventured opinions as to the true identities of Barabbas and Judas Iscariot. Who were they?

21  Compare and contrast the people of first century Judea with your contemporaries and peers.

22  Theophilus's introduction to Judea consisted of a conversation with a Roman officer in Capernaum. Who did this man turn out to be, and what information did he impart to Theophilus?

23  Jesus' activities in Capernaum were more important than his activities anywhere else except Jerusalem. Describe the town and Jesus' activities there.

24  "Gethsemane" meant "oil press." Why was that name appropriate for the episode involving Jesus in the Garden of Gethsemane?

25  Were you convinced by Floralia's claim that the fictional character Josephus of Arimathea was based on the historian Josephus?

26  What was the origin of the tale of Lazarus and his sisters Mary and Martha in Bethany?

27  What are your spiritual beliefs? How do they compare to the spiritual beliefs of early Christians as portrayed in this book?

# ABOUT THE AUTHOR

Mitchel Fidel has traveled to nearly all parts of the world, experiencing a full immersion in foreign languages and cultures. He was employed at the Multiversity for Personal Development in India, and his teaching experience has ranged from the Defense Department's National Cryptologic School to the Nizhoni School for Global Consciousness in Santa Fe. At one point, Mother Theresa asked him to work for her. With writing experience behind him that included Top Secret intelligence analysis for the National Security Agency and developmental work for two Hollywood internet firms, he undertook the Great Puzzle of first century A.D. spirituality, because so much information in that regard had come to light that it was practically begging to be put into the entertaining configuration of a novel.

Mitchel Fidel has been to all the locales that form the backdrop to the *Mysterium* series and has studied the relevant historical materials not for years but for decades, making him uniquely qualified to carry out such a project. His colorful lifetime travelogue is available on Facebook, and he welcomes discussion of the innately controversial material presented in his books. The *Mysterium* series that began with *Mysterium I Rome* continues with *Mysterium II Greece*, and *Mysterium III Asia,* and *Mysterium IV Judea,* and will continue with *Mysterium V Egypt and Beyond.*

Mitchel is a resident of Tampa, FL and is available for interviews, discussion groups, book signing events, and would be honored to speak with any local civic service group, religious organization, or business about travel, history, and the mysterium of Jesus.

# OTHER BOOKS BY MITCHEL FIDEL

 **Mysterium I Rome**
Kindle, paperback, hardcover, and audible

 **Mysterium II Greece**
Kindle, paperback, and hardcover

 **Mysterium III Asia**
Kindle, paperback, and hardcover

We are an exclusive publishing house. We specialize in uplifting, inspirational, and positive adult, juvenile and young adult, fiction and nonfiction, including poetry, native histories and spiritual paths, sermons, lectio divina, and pastoral and rabbinical resources in English, French, Spanish, Indigenous languages, and tri- and bilingual versions.

Our readers, once they finish one of our books, will be able to get up and face the world wiser, stronger, centered, and with the assurance that we are not alone: we are all a part of the Sheltering Tree on Earth.

If you as a writer feel that same calling, please refer to

**ShelteringTreeMedia.com**